SIXKILLER, U.S. MARSHAL

THE HOUR
OF DEATH

SIXKILLER, U.S. MARSHAL:
THE HOUR OF DEATH

William W. Johnstone

with J. A. Johnstone

PINNACLE BOOKS
Kensington Publishing Corp.
www.kensingtonbooks.com

PINNACLE BOOKS are published by

Kensington Publishing Corp.
119 West 40th Street
New York, NY 10018

PUBLISHER'S NOTE
Following the death of William W. Johnstone, the Johnstone family is working with a carefully selected writer to organize and complete Mr. Johnstone's outlines and many unfinished manuscripts to create additional novels in all of his series like The Last Gunfighter, Mountain Man, and Eagles, among others. This novel was inspired by Mr. Johnstone's superb storytelling.

All Kensington titles, imprints, and distributed lines are available at special quantity discounts for bulk purchases for sales promotions, premiums, fund-raising, educational, or institutional use. Special book excerpts or customized printings can also be created to fit specific needs. For details, write or phone the office of the Kensington sales manager: Kensington Publishing Corp., 119 West 40th Street, New York, NY 10018, attn: Sales Department; phone 1-800-221-2647.

PINNACLE BOOKS, the Pinnacle logo, and the WWJ steer head logo, are Reg. U.S. Pat. & TM Off.

ISBN-13: 978-0-7860-3947-0
ISBN-10: 0-7860-3947-7

First printing: July 2013

10 9 8 7 6 5 4 3 2

Printed in the United States of America

First electronic edition: August 2017

ISBN-13: 978-0-7860-3125-2
ISBN-10: 0-7860-3125-5

Chapter One

The hour of death had come. Twelve humans, men and women, had fallen into the killers' trap. Eleven would die, but one would live.

Because of that strange twist of fate, the Hour of Death would come again, more savage, violent, relentless.

Chapter Two

John Henry Sixkiller paid a courtesy call on the governor of New Mexico Territory, a good-bye visit that turned into hello to a dangerous new mission.

The Governor was working late at night in his office at the *Palacio del Gobernador* in Santa Fe. The building was three hundred years old, a massive structure of adobe and stone built by Indian slave labor toiling under the whips of the conquistadors to house the official administrators of Old Mexico when it was a colony of even older Spain.

Later generations of Indians had led a whole scale massacre of their colonial masters.

An assistant escorted Sixkiller inside the Governor's office and closed the door behind him.

Like most Westerners, he usually kept his hat on outdoors and indoors. But as a gesture of respect, he took it off and held it in both hands.

The governor sat behind a desk that seemed big as a freight wagon. The room's rich brown shadows were broken by a globe desk lamp and some smaller lamps set on side tables. With pen in hand, he was writing on a piece of paper. The metal-tipped quill pen made scratching sounds as it moved across the paper. A pile of papers some six inches high stood stacked at the right-hand corner of a green desk blotter.

Governor Lew Wallace was fiftyish, with a black beard and sharp eyes. He wore a smoking jacket over a white shirt and black tie. He had been a major general in the Union Army during the Civil War, not the winningest, but successful enough to keep moving upward through the hierarchy.

Wallace was a territorial governor, recently appointed by President Rutherford B. Hayes to curb the corruption and violence in which the vast region was steeped.

Big John Sixkiller had recently done his bit to clean up some of the mess. It had taken plenty of violence on his part to see the task through. That was his job. He was a lawman, a United States deputy marshal.

His usual bailiwick was the Oklahoma Territory. He hailed from Tahlequah in the Cherokee section of the territory reserved for the Five Civilized Nations, Southeastern Indian tribes who'd been forcibly removed from their home grounds and shipped west in the 1830s.

Sixkiller was half-Cherokee and half-White, a mountain of a man, a Titan standing six feet and four inches tall in his bare feet. His broad shoulders and straight torso were as wide across as a room door.

He had a massive leonine head with a hawk-like profile. He was beardless, the Cherokee way. As each facial hair had sprouted in adolescence, he'd plucked it out according to tribal tradition. His hair was cut short to collar length.

He had copper-colored skin, dark almond-shaped eyes and a wide thin-lipped mouth with the corners turned down. A long-barreled .45 Colt Peacemaker hung holstered on his right hip. Everything about him said *here is a man who could get the job done.*

He was a long way from home. He'd been sent to New Mexico where nobody knew him so he could take on an undercover job smashing a murderous outlaw gang.

Governor Lew Wallace put his pen down and rose, motioning to Sixkiller with a welcoming gesture that said *Advance, friend.*

Sixkiller crossed to him with long-legged strides that ate up the carpeted floor as Wallace came out from behind the desk, hand extended. They shook hands. Wallace was a good-sized man but his hand seemed to vanish when gripped by Sixkiller's oversized mitt.

"Welcome, Deputy. Good to see you," Wallace said. "You belong in politics. With a grip like that you could shake voters' hands morning, noon, and night without ever tiring."

"Reckon I'll stick to my line of country, Governor. The voters'll be better off that way, too."

"Sit down, make yourself comfortable." Wallace indicated a set of armchairs in front of his desk.

"Thanks." Sixkiller sank into an oversized armchair, leather-covered, deep-cushioned. He was grateful. Lots of times ordinary-sized furniture was too small for him.

"May I offer you a drink, Deputy?"

Sixkiller managed to accept without showing too much eagerness.

On a silver tray on the desk was a cut-glass crystal decanter filled with brandy. Wallace poured some into a glass and handed it to Sixkiller.

"Much obliged," the lawman said.

They clinked glasses and drank up.

"Sorry if it's a bit warm in here," Wallace said apologetically. "With some of the enemies I've made trying to suppress violence in the territory, I dare not leave the windows uncovered at night lest some sneaking assassin try to take a shot at me."

"Heat doesn't bother me."

"Lucky fellow."

Indicating the pile of papers on the desk, Sixkiller said, "Looks like you're working late tonight, Governor."

"I am, but not on official business. I don't want to give a false impression that I slave night and day strictly on territorial matters. This is something I've been working on for my own amusement. I'm writing a book." Wallace smiled sheepishly, as if confessing a secret vice. Warily, he steeled himself against jibes or mockery.

Sixkiller nodded, encouraging the other to continue. "Something about your wartime experiences?"

"Not a personal reminiscence, no. It's a work of fiction, a historical novel set in the days of the Roman Empire," Wallace said, warming to the subject.

"After all, if an English member of Parliament such as Lord Bulwer-Lytton could write *The Last Days of Pompeii,* I don't see why an American can't do something similar. I call it *Ben-Hur.* That's the name of the lead character, a Jew in Palestine during the days when our Lord walked the earth."

"Sounds inspirational," Sixkiller said. *Roman Empire?* It was all Greek to him. He wasn't much of a reader and on the rare occasion he cracked a book it was a dime novel with plenty of action.

Wallace refilled Sixkiller's glass and his own, then went behind his desk, lifting the lid of a handsome Moroccan leather-bound box. "Cigar?"

"Don't mind if I do," Sixkiller said.

Fortified with cigars and brandy, they sat smoking and drinking.

"I just stopped in to say so long. Time I was on my way home. My work here is done," Sixkiller said.

"Ably done, to be sure. There's not enough of that damned rascal gang left to hang."

"Well, that's how things work out sometimes, Governor. Those hombres weren't much minded to surrender, they wouldn't be taken alive—"

"You misunderstand me. That was a compliment, not a complaint. Those scoundrels needed killing."

"I didn't plan it that way. That's just how it works out some times." More often than not, when Sixkiller was on the case.

Governor Wallace got down to brass tacks. "I'm glad you stopped by. If you hadn't, I would have sent word requesting you to come in. Something's come up. Something important that's in your line.

"Your recent efforts have not gone unnoticed. The price of success, I'm afraid. It seems unfair, somehow, that your good work here puts you in line for another risky assignment. Though after seeing you in action, I'm convinced you're the man for the job.

"This isn't my idea, mind you. I'm just the middleman passing along a request. And it is a request. You're free to turn it down with no black marks against your record." Wallace rested his forearms against the desk's edge, leaning forward. "Frankly, I wouldn't blame you if you did turn it down. It's a dangerous mission, one that's already cost the lives of a half-dozen good men."

"You interest me, Governor." Sixkiller was stiff-faced as always, but his eyes were alight. Trouble was his meat.

"Ever been to Wyoming?" Wallace asked.

"No, sir," Sixkiller said.

"That's where the trouble is—in southeast Wyoming—in Ringgold in the Glint River Valley. Some damned fool of an Englishman seems to have gone missing there. Worse, he took a dozen or so of his people along with him. They're missing, too.

"Naturally it couldn't have been just any ordinary Englishman who disappeared with his entourage. Oh no. That would have been too easy," Wallace went on. "This one's a wealthy aristocrat from one of the leading families in England. Bletchley, Lord Dennis Bletchley. As if that weren't bad enough, he happens to be a close relative of Queen Victoria.

"She happens to be the Queen of England," Wallace added, in case U.S. Deputy Marshal John Sixkiller from Tahlequah, Oklahoma, had never heard of her.

Sixkiller had, though. The mission fathers

who'd educated him as a boy hadn't left him totally blank about people and places outside the United States. Hazy, yes, but not totally blank.

"Bletchley was touring the western United States on a combined business and pleasure trip," Wallace said. "Apparently he's a keen hunter who was eager to bag some of our native American wildlife for his trophy collection. He's also looking for business properties to invest in—timber, mining, that sort of thing. In Wyoming, cattle is the coming thing."

Sixkiller generally didn't crack too much, but he made some kind of sour face.

The governor found it necessary to respond. "An English lord getting into the cattle business on the Western frontier? It may not be as ridiculous as it sounds. It's no secret that the cattle business is booming in Wyoming. Look at Alex Swan, a foreigner who's become one of the biggest landholders and stockmen in Wyoming in recent years. He's already made millions of dollars." Wallace solemnly pronounced the phrase "millions of dollars" with the profound reverence for big money that American politicians so heartily express.

"The East has an insatiable appetite for Western beef, even that of the tough, stringy Texas longhorn. But the new trend in Wyoming is to mix blooded, pedigreed stock known for rich fat-marbled cuts of beef with the rugged hardy longhorn.

"Lord Bletchley wouldn't be directly involved with the operation. He'd have been a kind of absentee landlord with a hired foreman to manage the enterprise. Bletchley would have stayed back home in Old Blighty collecting his profits. By last report, he was quite interested in the prospects of the Glint River Valley northwest of Laramie.

"Bletchley was last seen in the town of Ringgold on the Glint. That may have been a fatal mistake, as you may or may not have heard," Wallace prompted.

Sixkiller allowed as to how Ringgold and its reputation was unknown to him.

Wallace was only too happy to enlighten him on that score. "Some funny business has been going on in Ringgold for some time now. Not that there's anything funny about robbery and murder. For the last year or so, but especially in the last few months, Ringgold has logged more than its share of killings—murders and so-called suicides and accidental deaths.

"Bletchley's isn't the only mysterious disappearance on the Glint, only the most recent. There have been other vanishings and violent deaths of wealthy men in the area—cattle buyers, bankers, big ranchers, and the like.

"Bletchley went to Ringgold two months ago, taking with him a dozen or so of his entourage—

friends, business advisors, even servants and a cook. They went into the hills north of town on a hunting trip and never returned. Vanished— swallowed up in the wilderness somewhere north of the valley. Search parties were unable to turn up a trace of them. Foul play is suspected, the worst is feared."

"Indians?" Sixkiller suggested halfheartedly, not really buying it himself. The days of the wild Plains Indians were pretty much done in the Central and Northern Rocky Mountain regions. Closer to Wallace's own New Mexico territory warlike Apaches under Victorio, Chato, and Geronimo were a real threat, but there was no similar threat from the northern tribes in the Laramie Mountains region.

Wallace agreed. "Four years ago, after Custer at the Little Big Horn maybe, but not now. The Sioux, Cheyenne, and Arapaho have all been neutralized. There was always the slim possibility that Bletchley might have been attacked by a renegade band of Arapaho or some far-ranging Ute, but recent events have ruled that out.

"Bletchley's family is wealthy with plenty of pull. Lawmen have gone up into the Glint to investigate, look for clues. They were killed, shot dead by person or persons unknown. The family hired detective agencies to do some digging—Pinkerton and the Continental. The investigators who couldn't turn up a lead went home empty-handed. The ones who thought they were on to something went home in coffins."

"So the savvy sleuths died and the dumb ones didn't," Sixkiller summarized.

"That's about the size of it. These murders of detectives is sure proof of criminal conspiracy. A robber gang killed and plundered Bletchley and his outfit. They'll kill again to preserve their secret.

"Ringgold is a problem without a solution. No authority is willing to take responsibility for cleaning up the mess. What passes for local law on the Glint is useless. The territorial governor is on the spot. The violence simply isn't enough out of hand to call in the army and besides, what could the troops do?

"But a manhunter might succeed where soldiers would fail. You're the best manhunter I know."

"Nice of you to say so, Governor."

"It would not be an overstatement to say that your country needs you."

That worried Sixkiller. The last time his country needed him, he wound up fighting in the Civil War, on both sides at different times.

"Bletchley's disappearance is in danger of becoming an international incident," Wallace said. "With the Queen of England taking a personal interest in Lord Dennis's fate, the affair reaches to the highest levels of our government. I can say this much to you in all confidentiality. The president is closely following the case and is anxious for a speedy resolution. I'd like to be able to report that we've got our best man—you—looking into the matter."

There was only one answer as Sixkiller saw it. "Can't say no to the president."

Wallace's smile showed real relief. "I'm glad to hear you say that. Your mission will be twofold. Find out what happened to Lord Bletchley and bring his killer or killers to justice."

"You've got some idea of how I go about my work, Governor," Sixkiller said guardedly. "It can get messy. Bodies tend to pile up. I wouldn't want to embarrass the White House."

"I can assure you that you'll have a free hand in this matter," Wallace said. "Do whatever it takes. Anything is better than the violent lawlessness running amok in Ringgold, Wyoming."

"In that case, I'm your huckleberry, Governor."

Wallace looked puzzled.

"That means it's a go," Sixkiller explained.

"Good man! I knew we could count on you," Wallace enthused.

"Of course, you'll have to clear it with my boss Judge Parker," Sixkiller said.

In the chain of command of federal marshals and magistrates, Sixkiller answered to Judge Isaac Parker, notorious throughout the frontier as The Hanging Judge. Parker was based in Fort Smith, Arkansas, but his jurisdiction also included sections of the Oklahoma territory—one of the most violent and lawless regions on the North American continent.

Sixkiller's bailiwick as U.S. deputy marshal covered the Indian Nations region of the territory, originally set up as a homeland/reservation for the Five Civilized tribes. One of those tribes were the Cherokee, Sixkiller's people. Or half his people, rather, for he was part-Indian and part-White.

Owing to the peculiar legal status of the Nations, fugitives from other states could not be easily extradited from there nor could outsider lawmen pursue fugitives into reservation lands, causing it to become a haven for some of the West's most vicious outlaws.

A quirk in the law prevented Indian tribal police from arresting, trying, and imprisoning non-Indians who committed a crime in the Nations. Judge Parker had gotten around that miscarriage of justice by appointing one John H. Sixkiller a deputy federal marshal under his jurisdiction.

Sixkiller was legally authorized to make arrests. Prisoners had to be taken to Fort Smith for incarceration and trial. Malefactors usually received short shrift and harsh penalties from the famous law-and-order judge.

Sixkiller was good at his job of man hunting, though generally he more often brought them in dead than alive, a policy with which Judge Parker could find no disagreement. The lawman's growing renown had become known to the higher-ups in the federal law enforcement system, who sent him on special assignments far outside his home grounds. Most recently he had served in New Mexico and now it seemed he was headed for Wyoming.

Sixkiller had no cause for complaint. He liked going to new places and meeting new people, even though he often wound up killing them in the name of the law.

Wallace assured Sixkiller there would be no problem squaring his temporary duty in Wyoming with Judge Parker. "After all, the judge works for the same boss as you, the president of the United States."

"Well, as long as Judge Parker's got no kick, I'm ready to pitch in and get to work," Sixkiller said.

"How soon can you hit the trail?" Wallace asked.

"Right now. My work here is done. Wyoming, here I come!"

"Not quite," Wallace said with a small smile. "The shortest distance between here and Ringgold is not necessarily a straight line." He leaned forward, intent. "Let me give you the rest of it."

Sixkiller did not take notes during Wallace's briefing. He was not much of one for keeping written records when he didn't absolutely have to, although he could read and write adequately well. The church fathers at the mission school had seen to that when he was growing up.

In his line of work, which frequently required him to go undercover with an assumed identity, anything written down had the potential danger of being able to unmask him to his enemies.

He committed the facts to memory.

"That's all I know about the case," Wallace said, summing up and bringing the interview to an end. "I'm satisfied the matter couldn't be in more capable hands."

Sixkiller drank the last of his drink, emptying his glass. It was good brandy. He and Wallace had made serious inroads on the liquid contents of the decanter.

The lawman rose, readying to depart. "Reckon I'll be on my way then, if that's all of it."

"The next man along the line—Vandaman, the federal agent in overall charge of the case— will fill you in on the rest." Wallace stood up behind his desk.

"It's been a pleasure working with you Governor, especially drinking your brandy and smoking your fine cigars," Sixkiller said.

They shook hands across the desk.

"No need to disturb yourself, Governor, I can find my way out. Maybe I can get a couple hours of shut-eye before catching the train early tomorrow morning."

"My only regret is that you can't extend your stay longer here in New Mexico," Wallace said, grim-faced. "I'd like to set you on Billy the Kid and the rest of those troublemakers who've been raising hell in Lincoln County—clean up on the whole kit and kaboodle of them!"

"Well . . . maybe next time Who knows? I might be passing this way again sooner than you think." Sixkiller crossed to the door.

"Good luck, and don't get killed!" Wallace called after him.

"I'll try not to, sir," Sixkiller said dryly.

He paused at the door gripping the door handle when a thought struck him. "Good luck with your book, Governor," he said over his shoulder.

"Thank you! I'll send you a copy when it's done! Whenever that is. At the rate I'm going, it might be several more years. At least it feels that way!"

"I'd surely appreciate it. Just send it to me care of the general post office in Tahlequah, Oklahoma."

"I'll make a note of it."

Sixkiller said good night and went out into the hall. The Palacio was largely deserted.

Office rooms were dark, doors were closed, long marble halls were dimly lit with scattered lamps. Few people were about—only sweepers, cleaning ladies, a couple guards.

Sixkiller's long, narrow, booted feet were surprisingly elegant for such a big man. He moved noiselessly along the bare marble floors. He went through the better-lit main hall and front lobby, nodding to the uniformed armed doorman. "Night."

Sixkiller exited into a broad square plaza, largely empty of all but a few scattered wanderers. Overhead, a black vault of star-dappled sky smeared with the city-light glow of Santa Fe.

He had a lot to think about during the walk back to his hotel, but not so much that he didn't keep his eyes and ears open and a ready hand near his gun, alert for trouble, though finding none. He couldn't help but chuckle at the thought of Governor Lew Wallace writing a book—and a novel at that! Of all the foolishness for a seemingly sensible hardheaded ex-military man and politician to devote himself to, that took the cake.

What was it the governor called his work in progress? *Ben-Hur?* Even if he finished the book and somehow managed to get it into print, it would most likely die a lonesome death by neglect, unsold and unnoticed by the world.

Shaking his head at the foolishness of the

mighty, Sixkiller made his way to the hotel, vowing to stick to his line of work. It was a lot easier and more profitable to bring in deadly WANTED outlaws than to chase the elusive phantoms of Fame and Glory.

Chapter Three

Sixkiller's trip from Santa Fe to Ringgold, Wyoming, took a detour by way of Salt Lake City, Utah. A thriving metropolis, it was brought forth out of the desert wasteland by the hard work and sacrifice of the community of the Mormons, the Church of the Latter Day Saints.

Thirty-six hours after boarding the north-west-bound train out of Santa Fe, Sixkiller found himself on a ridge with a posse readying for a pre-dawn raid on an outlaw hideout near the town of Rush Valley, one of a handful of would-be rivals to Salt Lake City as capital and predominant city in Utah Territory. The men were spread out among the rocks on a rise over-looking a stone cabin in a place called Red Ravine.

It was little more than hole in the rock walls, a cleft in red-orange-brown cliffs that was about an eighth of a mile deep. A box ravine, with one way in and no way out except by the original entrance, it lay in stony hills several miles outside of Nibiru. "A pretty poor excuse for a town," in the words of Malachi Keene, white-haired Mormon elder and leader of the posse.

When the transcontinental railroad was built in the late 1860s, Salt Lake City seemed like a natural depot for the line. But the Union Pacific was in a race with Central Pacific to lay the most track in the least amount of time in order to claim the most in government funds and bypassed Salt Lake City altogether, throwing its line north of the city.

A half dozen or so small towns along the line, one of them being Nibiru, tried to position themselves as the central city of the territory.

Ultimately and before too long, all the would-be usurpers fell by the wayside, unable to compete with the city in the desert by the Great Salt Lake. Undaunted, the citizenry of Salt Lake City held a massive fund-raising drive and got a spur rail line built connecting the city to the main trunk line.

Most of the challenger towns simply dried up and blew away. One or two managed to survive and hang on in a sickly kind of half-life. Prime among them was Nibiru, subsisting by becoming a nest of outlaws—rustlers, robbers, horse thieves, tinhorn gamblers, and whores.

Periodically, posses or vigilante bands cleaned

out the town, but the riffraff always came trickling back to start anew.

Federal agent Vandaman, Sixkiller's contact in the Bletchley Party Case, had trailed a lead to Nibiru. The bad men were holed up in Red Ravine.

The posse had set out after dark from a stable on the outskirts of Salt Lake City, taking a wide and circuitous path to bypass Nibiru unobserved. They'd ridden in single file, renowned lawman Malachi Keene at the point, and had reached the mouth of Red Ravine about an hour before dawn.

He addressed the men. "This should go without saying, but I've found out the hard way that the things you think should go without saying are usually better for being said. From here on, there'll be no smoking. The light of a match or glow of a lit cigarette can be seen a long way off in the dark. Burning tobacco can be smelled from a long way off. Mormons are forbidden the use of tobacco, but we're not all Mormons here so I want to make sure you all get the message. Our aim is to surprise our quarry, not be surprised by them."

Three posse members stayed behind to hold the horses. The others moved on ahead, light-footing it through the pre-dawn darkness. All had rifles and side guns.

The moon had already sunk behind a western scarp. Stars were hard bright pinholes of light in purple blackness. The Milky Way was a creamy, glowing blur in remote heights.

Sixkiller was happy in his way. It all spoke directly to him—the night, the stars, and the hunt. He moved along like a gliding shadow, never stepping on a twig or scuffing a stone, never rustling through dry, dead leaves or clinging, high weeds. A hulking shadow black against the purpling sky, starlight glimmered on the metal parts of his Winchester rifle.

Behind him was Vandaman, the man Governor Wallace had sent him to meet. Vandaman, too, was an outsider. It was impossible to tell from his face whether he was thirty or forty. He was medium-sized with short dark hair, dark eyes, and a mustache. He wore a brown suit, boots, and a side gun. Nothing about him made him stand out in a crowd, an asset in the detecting game.

A "government man" and a pretty high-up one, Vandaman had a treasury department badge that he kept out of sight in a thin leather cardholder except when he'd taken it out to identify himself to Sixkiller at the Salt Lake City train station.

Apart from the three stay-behind horse holders, there were ten men in the posse infiltrating the ravine.

Unlucky thirteen? wondered Sixkiller. *Or merely a baker's dozen?*

That remained to be seen.

During a pause, Malachi Keene passed along some information, low-voiced. "The ravine's the hideout for Towhead Jimson's outfit. Horse theft and cattle rustling is their game, mostly, but they'll set their hands to anything that turns a crooked dollar. Ever since Dean Richmond moved in, they've graduated to highway robbery, stagecoach holdups, and the like. Apparently Towhead don't like it much, but it's Dean who calls the shots now."

Malachi was one of Brigham Young's long-time, top law-enforcement agents. He was sixty, tall, spare, and straight-backed, hollow-cheeked and rawboned, with a full head of thick white hair and a bushy white mustache. Burning eyes were set back in deep sockets; cheekbones jutted like walnuts set beneath the skin.

He wore a black hat with rounded crown and round flat brim, black frock coat and pants, gray shirt with black ribbon tie knotted in a bow. A .44 was worn holstered low on his hip.

At various times he'd been a scout, Indian fighter, shotgun messenger for Wells Fargo, and before that for the Overland Stagecoach line. He'd also led a band that mercilessly harassed the invading U.S. Army infantry column to distraction during the U.S. government's abortive war on the Mormon colony in Utah several years before the Civil War. It was rumored he'd been one of the faithful's squad of elite Avenging Angels gunmen before graduating to become one of Brigham Young's personal bodyguards.

He circulated among the posse men in position on a rocky ridge overlooking a knoll with a small stone cabin, having a quiet word or two with them. They had nothing to do but wait for morning light. It was then, they'd make the strike.

Sixkiller and Vandaman sheltered in a hollow behind a big boulder. During a private moment, the federal agent said of Malachi, "That old gent has five wives, the youngest in her teens, and two of them currently pregnant. He's got enough grown sons to field his own posse except that he raised them to be professional men mostly—doctors, lawyers, bankers, businessmen. He discouraged them from going into the family business of shooting and getting shot at, all except Caleb, the black-bearded man on the dun horse.

"Caleb was too strong-willed to be denied. A good lawman and handy with a gun, he's a dependable, capable man. But not an Angel of Death like Malachi."

Presently, Malachi hunkered down beside Sixkiller and Vandaman. They talked in whispers of the Red Ravine bunch.

"Bart Skillern and Dean Richmond used to run the outfit, back in the day," Malachi began.

"Bart Skillern? Seems I've heard that name before," Sixkiller mused.

"You probably know him better by his nickname, the Utah Kid," Vandaman said, chuckling.

"That name I know." Sixkiller recognized it from any number of WANTED posters and circulars that had passed across his office desk in Tahlequah, though the Kid's base of operations was far west from Sixkiller's home ground of Oklahoma.

"Around here we call Skillern the *Wyoming* Kid," Malachi said, not without humor, though generally he was not a particularly humorous personality.

"I guess it's a case of whose ox is being gored, eh?" Vandaman asked.

"Skillern's what we call a gentile. That's non-Mormon to you. Dean Richmond's one of our own. Neither of them was ever any damned good," Malachi said. "Folks hereabouts were almighty glad to see the last of those two. Least we thought we'd seen the last of them.

"Dean came back about a month ago, returning to his old haunts and pards in Nibiru. He fell in with his old crowd and took it over from Towhead Jimson, who'd been running the bunch since Dean and Skillern first lit out for greener pastures. Towhead couldn't have been too happy about that. But not so unhappy that he was minded to go up against Dean, not face-to-face. A bullet in the back is more Towhead's style.

"He's been content to let things take their course. Dean's been making money for the boys. He's got big ideas. Since he came back a couple banks and stagecoaches have been robbed and mining payrolls have been snatched.

"More shootings, too. Guards have been wounded, hurt bad. One died from his injuries. That makes it murder," Malachi said grimly. "We ain't been able to prove it's the Red Ravine bunch because the outlaws always wore masks. None of the victims could make a proper identification. I've been itching to have a reason to move against them, but I didn't have one till now—thanks to Mr. Vandaman here."

Vandaman took up the tale. "That's where I come in—and you too, Sixkiller. Richmond and Skillern had been operating in the Glint River Valley for four months. Two months ago, Dean cleared out in an all-fired hurry and roamed around the Northern Range for a month before coming home to roost in Nibiru. Skillern stayed put in Ringgold."

"Those two have been pards since boyhood days. What could have made them split up?" wondered Malachi.

"Yes, why split up a successful partnership?" seconded Vandaman. "Especially when there was still plenty of money to be made selling their guns on the Glint."

Sixkiller knew what they were driving at, but decided to play devil's advocate. "Partnerships break up all the time. Gunmen are a restless breed. Their feet get itchy, and they like to wander. Or they fall out over some small thing—splitting the loot, a woman, the last drink in the bottle. They're a quarrelsome lot, too."

"Two red hots like Dean and Skillern fall out, it usually ends up with one or both going to Boot Hill," Malachi said.

"What, then?" Sixkiller asked.

"I figure Dean got spooked by something bigger than he wanted to tie into," Vandaman said.

"Like robbing and killing the Bletchley party?"

"It's starting to look that way," Vandaman said. "There's more. Dean brought back a souvenir of his Ringgold sojourn—a rifle, the likes of which has never been seen before in these parts and damned few places elsewhere."

"Tell me about this rifle," Sixkiller prompted.

"It's some piece of work, a heavy-caliber weapon made for big game hunting, the biggest of big game. It'll stop a charging elephant or rhinoceros dead in its tracks with one well-placed shot, by all accounts. It's a beautiful thing too, decorated with gold plates engraved with hunting scenes. It's one of a kind—literally." Vandaman paused, then delivered his tagline. "It was custom-made in London by a specialist gun maker exclusively for Lord Dennis Bletchley. There's not another one like it in the world.

"But Dean Richmond's not one to hide his light under a bushel. He couldn't resist the urge to show it off, make himself look like a big man. Turns out it's useful in holdups for potting stagecoach drivers and shotgun messengers. Leaves big holes in the bodies that could only be made by an elephant gun."

"That rifle's enough to put a rope around Dean's neck," Malachi said.

"We want to take Dean alive. He's got a lot of questions to answer," Sixkiller cautioned.

"That's a tall order. Dean's not one to give up without a fight. I don't want any of my men killed or hurt trying to take him alive," Malachi said as the sky was lightening in the east.

The three men turned their attention to the stone cabin. It had small square oil-papered windows, grimy yellow light glowing behind them. Horses milled about in a rail-fence corral to one side of the cabin.

A stir within the cabin caused shadows to flit across the window squares.

"Somebody's up. What do we do?" whispered Holtz, a posse man.

"Sit tight and do nothing till I give the signal. We want to catch as many as we can out in the open before making our move," Malachi said.

"Why don't we just rush them?" asked Judd, another of the posse.

"After you," Caleb Keene said sarcastically.

"I don't know," posse man Dillard mulled, thoughtful. "Maybe we should sneak up on them, take them while they're sleeping."

"One of them, at the least, is awake," Six-killer pointed out.

"Maybe he'll go back to sleep," a man named Brennan said.

"Dean and Towhead are tough men to catch napping," Malachi said.

"Get too close and those horses might spook and give us away," Caleb said.

Vandaman studied the scene. "Not much cover down there and a clear field of fire from the cabin. You wouldn't want to be caught out in the open when they start shooting."

"What if one of 'em tries to ride out?" asked Cort Randle.

Malachi shook his head. "Can't let that happen. That'll give away the game. Stop him cold. Dead."

The cabin's wooden front door creaked, swinging open. A man stood outlined in the doorframe. Shaggy-haired and bearded, he stepped outside, walking stiff-legged, staggering off to one side. He looked drunk.

A rifle hammer clicked into position as Judd drew a bead on the newcomer, the metallic click seemingly unheard by the man in the gun sights.

Caleb Keene went into motion quickly. Silently, he got behind Judd and placed a hand lightly on his shoulder so as not to startle him. "Ease off, Judd. Not yet. Pa will give the word."

Judd was an older, red-faced man with bushy eyebrows, a gray-flecked beard, and thick body.

Thick in the head, thought Sixkiller.

Judd slackened his finger off the trigger with obvious reluctance, but followed orders.

The drunken outlaw stood bracing himself with one hand against a tree. With the other he unbuttoned his trousers and urinated against the trunk. When his business was done he turned, buttoning up as he lurched back inside the cabin. He left the door wide open.

After a pause, somebody else inside reached out a hand and closed the door.

The posse resumed its wait. But waiting was hard on the nerves. Not on those of hardened manhunters as Sixkiller, Malachi, and son, who outwardly seemed to have no nerves. Vandaman, too, seemed to keep himself under iron control.

But the others? Sixkiller wondered how they would hold up.

It was a brisk morning and his hands were cold, fingers stiff. He couldn't have that and stuck his hands under his arms to keep them warm and supple for the work to come.

A quarter-hour passed, then another. Paling stars faded into the whitening sky. Light pulsed, shimmering in the east.

The grayish sky was slit with a razor line of pink color. A lone bird in a pine tree vented a few tentative chirps.

Movement once more sounded inside the cabin.

The lamp light went out, the windows becoming dull squares framing interior gloom.

After a while, the front door opened, revealing a different man from the drunkard. He was younger, with long, thin, dirty blond hair and a scraggly yellow beard. He was skinny, sharp-faced, pale, and sleepy-eyed.

He wore a faded red flannel shirt, jeans, and boots, and held something in his right hand, dangling down along his side.

"Bob Pingry. He's a bad 'un," Caleb rasped hoarsely. "Fast."

Pingry knuckled his eyes with his left hand, eyeing the coming day with little enthusiasm and less love. Apparently he saw nothing of the posse nor sensed the presence of it, judging by his sneeringly indifferent expression.

The object in his right hand was a gun belt complete with holstered gun. He started fastening it around his lean waist.

A shot exploded, shattering the stillness.

The bullet tore into the doorframe, spraying splinters into Pingry's startled face. Cursing, snarling, he jumped back indoors, throwing himself to one side out of sight and out of the line of fire.

One of the posse had gotten buck fever and jumped the gun, worst of all missing the target.

Caleb cursed the offender. "Damn it, Judd—"

"I thought he was reaching!" Judd protested.

"That's done it," Malachi said resignedly, matter-of-factly.

The posse waited a breathless delay of a few heartbeats—three or four—then oilskin window panes were torn down and rifle and six-gun barrels were thrust outside.

With a chorus of curses and shouts, the outlaws loosed a big blast of firepower at the ridge top, pumping out a fusillade.

Racketing noise crackled and spear-bladed muzzle flares were lancing lines of light. Bullets ripped into the rocks on the rise, gouging and cratering boulder faces, spewing rock shards and chips

Horses went wild in the corral, uprearing, pawing, whinnying as they ran around wildly in frantic circles. Some sideswiped the split-log fence, but it held.

Joining the jubilee of outlaw gunfire came a big booming blast with the bottom bass of a shotgun and the humming, hooting buzz of a high-velocity rifle. When it hit a rock, it ripped out a melon-sized crater.

A unique sound.

Sixkiller had never heard anything quite like it, yet realized immediately that it must be the exotic big-game rifle stolen by Dean Richmond . . . and undoubtedly being wielded by him.

On the extreme left flank of the posse as it lay just under the ridgeline facing the stone cabin, Sixkiller lay prone, face in the dirt. He wasn't going to stick up his head just yet to have it blown off by bad men's bullets. Not that he liked being shot at without returning fire.

He listened to the pattern of the shooting with peaks and lulls, the lulls occurring when guns ran out of bullets.

Timing it exactly during the next lull, he risked sticking a small part of his head around the protecting boulder to sneak a peek. He was just in time to see an outlaw thrust a long, black, denimed leg out of the window frame and double over to squeeze through the square hole of an open window on the left side of the cabin.

Sixkiller drew a bead on him with his rifle, squeezing the trigger. He tagged the escapee in mid-body. The impact threw the outlaw backward, causing him to fall out of the window and land in a heap on the ground below.

He was redheaded with a snakelike face, yellow eyes glaring. A line of blood trickled down the corner of his mouth. He had his gun in one hand, his free hand pressed to his middle, blood gushing through his fingers. Staggering to his knees, he swept his gun from side to side like a dowsing rod, as if trying to divine the location of the one who'd shot him.

Sixkiller didn't keep him guessing long. He squeezed off another shot from the Winchester, placing it dead center in the redhead's torso. That finished him.

Sixkiller had no need to take a second look and rolled to the right, clutching his rifle to him. He *knew* his bullet had gone home to deliver the death stroke. He lay on his back behind the bulk of the sheltering boulder just as the big-game rifle fired at him.

It had a sound like an express train highballing nonstop through a station as the high-velocity round ripped through the space his head had just quitted. Right on its heels a second shot came, smearing itself across the protecting boulder. The massive rock slab shuddered from the impact.

Sixkiller glanced sideways, making eye contact with Vandaman. "There's your elephant gun!"

Vandaman said nothing, just grinned tightly.

Someone in the cabin slammed the front door shut, drawing attention to the solid portal of thick oak reinforced with iron bands. Posse men fired at it with little or no effect. Sixkiller would have liked to take a shot at it with that elephant gun. That would have softened it up plenty,

Posse man Holtz toppled backward shot in the head, dead. Another—Judd—lay on his side kicking and writhing, bellowing in pain.

Malachi worked his six-gun, trading shots with Bob Pingry in the cabin, covering behind the stone wall, reaching around to shoot through one of the front windows.

He reached around too far in the open, exposing his gun hand.

Malachi winged him in the arm.

Pingry shouted, cursing, the gun dropping from his hand. He fell back, out of sight.

Posse men and outlaws continued to exchange shots, the racket of gunfire rising and falling, counterpointed by cries and groans of the wounded.

Rapid fire bursts settled down into vicious sniping.

From within the cabin came a hoarse bawling outcry, touched with a ragged edge of taunting mockery guaranteed to raise the ire of any serious-minded lawman. "That you, Malachi?"

"Yah! Who's that? Towhead?" Malachi shouted back.

"That's right! What for are you shooting at me?" queried Towhead Jimson.

"Come on out and I'll tell you."

"Haw! I reckon not, Malachi. Why don't you come on down here and tell me yourself?"

From behind a rock, Malachi popped up like a jack-in-the-box, triggering several rounds from his six-gun at the window to the left of the front door, where Towhead's voice seemed to emanate. He dropped out of sight a split second before a volley of rounds fired at him in quick succession, bursting from various gun ports and loopholes in the cabin.

Some of the posse men returned fire.

Brennan, on the far right flank, rose up from behind cover to take a few shots.

The elephant gun cannonaded, a round ripping through Brennan with a wet smacking sound, punching a hole right through him.

He lay on his back faceup, arms and legs sticking out, with a wound in his middle the size of a dinner plate.

Sixkiller and Caleb Keene fired at the spot where the shot had come from, but Dean had already taken cover.

A lull fell. Malachi shouted, "Still with us, Towhead?"

"To the finish!" came Towhead's reply. "Why you gunning for me, anyhow?"

"You shot up some of my posse."

"You shot at us first! We didn't know who you were. Thought you was dry gulchers or outlaws."

That got a nasty laugh from some of the

gunmen inside the stone cabin. Encouraged by their response, Towhead followed that one with another. "Ain't no jury'll say we did wrong, lawman! We was just defending ourselves!"

"Like you did at that stagecoach you held up last week at Rockrimmon?" Malachi returned.

"Don't know nothing about it. You got the wrong men."

"It won't work, Towhead. You and your gang signed your work at Rockrimmon! You can thank Dean for that."

"How so?"

"That big gun Dean's packing. The masks you wore hid your faces, but not the gun. All the stage passengers saw it. Too bad for you, Towhead. That gun's one of a kind. The only one in the world. It was made special for one of them British lords. There's not another like it. That gun's put a noose around all your necks, and you can thank Dean for that!"

The immediate silence was followed by an angry outburst of several voices in the cabin, each trying to outshout the other.

When they quieted down, Malachi threw some more fuel on the fire. Cupping a hand to his mouth to magnify his voice over the distance, he shouted, "Dean shot and killed the stagecoach guard. Why should the rest of you die for it?"

That triggered another outburst of angry arguing and recriminations.

"Sounds like tempers are running hot in there," Sixkiller said.

Malachi went back to work on the strained nerves of the desperadoes. "What's it to be, boys? You got a better chance with a jury than you do against our guns. None of you has to swing on a hang noose, except the one who pulled the trigger. You call the tune, but call it quick. Time's running out!"

"Maybe he's got something there, Towhead," said someone in the cabin.

"Quit crawfishing, Dunc," Towhead replied.

"Dunc. That's Jimmy Duncan," Caleb noted in an aside. "Always did have a yellow streak."

"Time's up. What do you say, boys?" Malachi asked.

"We like our chances here!" a new voice called.

"Dean Richmond," Caleb said, making the identification.

Malachi laughed. "You speaking for the bunch now, Dean? What about you, Towhead? And the rest of you?"

"What Dean's saying makes sense to me," Towhead said, though with no great surge of enthusiasm.

"Not me!" Jimmy Duncan burst in. "Why should I die for what Dean did? Wait! No, don't—*please!*"

There were sounds of a brief savage struggle,

a blow being struck, a pained outcry—then silence.

Jimmy Duncan's voice was heard no more.

Malachi looked downcast. "Thought I had a chance of making them see sense, but no such luck. They're more scared of Dean than they are of me or the noose. Reckon we'll have to do it the hard way."

"They've got a pretty strong hand. Bullets can't shoot through those stone walls," Caleb said glumly.

Sixkiller cleared his throat to get their attention. "Seems to me those stone walls work two ways for those owlhoots in the cabin—for them and against them."

A stir of interest flickered through the posse men.

"You see the way bullets bounce off these rocks when they hit," he went on. "One of those ricochets could tear your head off if it hits you the wrong way. Now what do you think will happen if we pour a whole hell of a lot of hot rounds through the windows into the cabin? The lead'll bounce off stone walls and tear up anything in its way."

Sixkiller finished by spelling it out for them. "When lead bullets get bent out of shape against solid stone, they'll play pure hell on any flesh and blood that's in their way . . . I'm talking about those outlaws."

"Mister, I'd say you know how to flush out a passel of bad hombres," Malachi said, smiling.

"I'd like it if we could take Dean Richmond alive, but some folk just won't listen to reason," Sixkiller said.

The posse was down three members. Brennan and Holtz were dead and Judd was wounded, out of action.

Malachi spoke to the others. "Well men, let's get to it. Pour your fire into them windows and make it hot. And be careful not to get yourself shot."

The posse men got into position, laying prone in a loose line just below the cover of the ridgetop, rifle barrels sticking out from between gaps in the rampart of boulders.

Malachi called downhill to the stone cabin. "This is your last chance to give up. Throw down your guns and come out one at a time with your hands up—"

The reply from the outlaws came as a blistering volley that did no harm whatsoever to the posse men, safe behind their stone bulwarks.

But being enclosed on all four sides by upright stone walls was not the same as being behind a bulwark.

Malachi thundered, "Let 'em have it!" and the posse opened fire.

Twin trails of lead targeted the cabin's two front windows, streaming through the square-cut openings.

Dum-dum bullets—so deadly because they fragmented into irregular scraps of lead, inflicting particularly nasty wounds—pinged off the walls, shrieking shrilly on their secondary tangents. The barrage sent them screeching on a three-dimensional web that ran riot through the stone cabin's interior and woe to the man who got in their way.

Malachi made a chopping gesture with one hand. "Cease fire!"

The posse men's volley became ragged, falling off.

No shots were fired from within the stone cabin.

"Any of you still with us down there?" Malachi called from behind the safety of a tilted rock slab.

"No thanks to you, lawman!" cried Towhead Jimson. "We're coming out so don't get trigger-happy."

"We won't . . . but no tricks!"

"Hell no. We're plumb out of tricks!"

The front door opened wide, an empty oblong of blackness with no one enclosed in its frame. Then a figure swung into view from one side of the doorway and propelled through it into the open. As if he were flying, his booted feet barely touched floor and ground.

"That's Jimmy Duncan!" Caleb said.

"He's got his guns!" cried Dillard.

Duncan lurched forward, head down, stumbling on rubbery legs, trying to keep from falling. His face was badly bruised, swollen. A nasty cut on his scalp bloodied his hair; blood tracks streaked his face. His eyes were wide in a face of fear.

He waved his arms wildly as if trying to throw his guns away, but they remained attached to the ends of his arms as if fastened there. "Don't shoot!" he shrieked.

A handgun began firing from one of the front windows shooting at the posse . . . or at least in their general direction.

"It's a double cross!" Cort Randle shouted, shouldering his rifle.

Caleb and Dillard did the same. All three opened fire, bullets tearing into Jimmy Duncan, cutting him down. He spun from the impact of slugs tearing into him from several directions, then fell crashing to the ground.

Outlaws in the stone cabin blasted away at the posse.

In the middle of the chaos and confusion, Bob Pingry dove headfirst out a window in the right-side wall. He leaped to his feet and took off running, gun in hand as he angled toward a clump of trees, rocks, and brush. Fear and adrenaline combined to give him speed in spite of the flesh wound in his arm from Malachi's earlier bullet.

Posse men began potting at Pingry, bullets whipping around him. He snapped off a couple shots while on the run, venting noise and muzzle flares, hitting nothing.

Sixkiller knew from hard experience that when everybody is looking at something on the right it's often wise policy to see what's happening on the left. He kept a wide focus while holding his fire when Pingry made his break.

Why shoot when other posse men were targeting Pingry?

Ignoring the distraction, Sixkiller was the first to notice a disturbance on the roof of the stone cabin. On the far side of the slanted rooftop, a hatch opened and a rifle barrel was thrust through the hatchway, protruding over the edge of the roofline.

He realized that a sniper under the angled rooftop was setting up Malachi for a kill and pointed his rifle in that direction. He could have shot the sniper's rifle, but preferred to shoot the man, waiting until the sniper stuck his head, shoulders, and upper body out through the hatchway, pointing his rifle at an oblivious Malachi Keene.

Sixkiller fired first, tagging the sniper with several quick shots.

The top of the sniper's head above the eyebrows flew off. The rifle fell from its wielder's dead hands, skittering down the front side of the roof and onto the ground as the sniper dropped out of sight through the hatchway, falling back into the cabin.

There was a thud as of something heavy slamming into the dirt floor.

Sixkiller remained mindful of his own admonition about the perils of misdirection, maintaining wide-angle vigilance over the battle scene.

A figure broke into view from behind the cabin. Rifle in hand, he raced for the corral. Receiver, lever, and side plates on the rifle glinted like molten gold in the first rays of the rising sun shafting into Red Ravine. It could only be Lord Bletchley's fabled big-game rifle and the man fleeing with it, Dean Richmond.

Either there was a back door to the cabin—unlikely, since the others would also have made use of it—or Richmond had exited earlier via the roof hatch, managing to not show himself by sliding down the far side of the roof, dropping to the ground, and hiding behind the cabin until he could make a break to the corral, grab a horse, and escape.

He ran fast—but not faster than the bullet from Sixkiller's rifle. It tagged the outlaw, knocking him to one side and sending him stumbling off on a tangent.

The shot caught the attention of the posse men. They turned their weapons on Dean and opened fire. He did a crazy whirling dance as slugs hammered into him, body twitching and jerking as it fell into the dust.

Dean sprawled facedown, motionless, one hand clutching the gold-plated rifle in a death grip.

The shooting stopped.

Towhead Jimson emerged from the stone cabin with his hands up, covered by the gun in Malachi's hand.

In the Mississippi River country, a towhead is a partly submerged isle breaking the surface of the water with weeds and reeds dangling down on all sides. That described Towhead Jimson.

He sported a poor man's haircut, one performed by an amateur barber putting a bowl over the top of the person's head and cutting all the hair hanging down below the rim. A boyish haircut that contrasted uneasily with an old, sharp-featured wrinkled face.

Malachi made Towhead turn around and show his back to make sure the outlaw didn't have a gun tucked in the waistband behind his back. He came up clean.

"Watch him, son. He's tricky," Malachi cautioned Caleb.

"If he moves wrong, I'll put a bullet in him," Caleb said.

"Nothing fatal. He's got to talk. Shoot him in the knee if you have to."

"It'll be a pleasure."

Malachi motioned to Dillard and Randle.

"Go around to the back of the cabin and make sure none of them are hiding back there."

They went. "All clear!" came the cry from behind the cabin.

Malachi went into the stone cabin to check on the outlaws there. They were all dead. "Better that way," he said to himself as he went back outside.

Sixkiller and Vandaman examined Jimmy Duncan's dead body. Rawhide thongs wrapped his hands, binding the fists tightly around a revolver so they were unable to open and release their grip on the guns. which were empty, of course.

"He was a decoy, nothing more," Sixkiller said. "They used him as a diversion to draw fire while they made their play."

"Poor sod," Vandaman said, curiously unmoved. "He wanted to run with the big dogs and they had him for breakfast."

"His epitaph," Sixkiller said.

They went to Dean Richmond to pry the gold-plated rifle from his cold dead hands. His hands were cold, but not dead, and neither was he. A flicker of life still clung to his bullet-ridden body. They rolled him onto his back, faceup.

Posse men gathered around to marvel that the outlaw still lived after taking so many bullets and spilling so much blood. Finally, his own blood had spilled instead of that of others.

Some of the men were up for hanging him on general principles, but it was agreed that the effort of standing him upright to fit a noose around his neck would kill him on the spot so they let him be.

"Anybody got a smoke?" Dean whispered.

Cort Randle snorted with indignation. "Smoke! You'll be burning in Hell soon enough!"

Vandaman lit up a cheroot, holding it to Dean's quivering lips so he could inhale.

"Phaugh! These skinny cigars taste like horse turds," Dean rasped, making a face. "What is that, a piece of a hangman's rope?"

"You ought to know. And by the way, you're welcome," Vandaman said sarcastically, upper lip curling in a sneer.

"Oh well. Reckon it'll have to do. Got any whiskey?"

"Not a drop."

"Just my luck. But you ain't no Mormon."

"No," Vandaman said.

"Knew it. Mormons ain't allowed tobacco . . . or whiskey, neither. I was raised in the faith, but I . . . drifted." Dean grimaced in pain.

Vandaman held the cheroot to Dean's mouth, occasionally flicking off ash from the burning tip. He had to. The outlaw couldn't move his arms. A bullet had paralyzed him below the neck.

Vandaman put the question to the outlaw.

"What happened to Bletchley, Dean? Lord Bletchley, the owner of the golden rifle."

"I'm the owner of the golden rifle." Dean sneered. "As for the Englishman, what do you think happened to him?"

"I think you killed him," Vandaman said.

"We all killed him."

"We?"

"Me and Bart and Lonnie and all the rest of the bunch. We killed them all together—the Englishman and his butler, maids, whores . . . there was a lot of them, dozen or so. We . . . lined them up against the wall of the cave and opened up on them, shot them to bits. That was something. I seen more people killed . . . down in Mexico during one of their revolutions, but that's the most I ever killed at one sitting." Dean smiled reminiscently, a faraway look in his eyes. "That sure was something . . . Good times . . ."

"Why'd you do it? Why'd you kill them?" Vandaman asked.

Dean was fading fast, but he still managed to summon up enough contempt to sneer as if Vandaman had asked the dumbest question imaginable. "Had to kill them. We robbed them and then there was the women, what we done to them. We'd have hanged for that sure if they were alive to set the law on our trail."

"Where are they? The bodies?"

"The cave. Funny . . . the Englishman was

looking for a gold mine and he thought this was it when we took him down in the mine. But he found out different quick enough. They all did. They're all dead. Every one of them . . . everyone but one."

Sixkiller and Vandaman were electrified by the dying man's revelation. They exchanged quick glances. Both were careful not to display any emotion, for fear of shattering the mood or stopping Dean from talking.

"I'd have thought you'd have made a clean sweep out of it," Vandaman said. "What's the point of killing the others if there's one left alive to identify you? Did one escape?"

"Hell no. It was the Kid."

"Kid? What kid, Dean? There were no children with the Bletchley party."

"The Utah Kid. Man you really are green. The Utah Kid. Bart Skillern. My pard, my amigo . . . until the woman came along. That was the end of it. The handwriting on the wall. I should have killed her right off before she got between us but then that . . . would have ruined the whole scheme to skin the Englishman. I held my hand and now I'm dying and she's probably . . . still alive and kicking."

"She must've been some kind of woman to get between two good pards like you and the Kid, Dean."

"She was just a high-class whore with high-falutin airs, as far as I was concerned, but the Kid couldn't see her for what she was the Englishman's whore, that's all. You'd have thought she was some kind of royalty the way she carried herself. Even had a name like a princess. La Valletta. La Valletta, can you beat that? The Englishman called her The Maltese. Damned if I know why. Some kind of pet name for her or something.

"The Kid thought she was something out of a storybook . . . a fairy-tale princess. She was good-looking, I'll give her that. Like a circus queen, all curly, golden hair and spangles and a body on her that wouldn't quit. But you could find hundreds like her in St. Louis or New Orleans. Just don't try to tell the Kid that. He'd shoot your guts out for even looking at her crosswise.

"He wasn't thinking straight because of her. She got in his blood and he had to have her. Let the rest of the world go to rot and ruin.

"I told him he was loco to let her keep on living. She *knew* . . . everything. She wasn't at the mine for the killings because he had already hidden her in a safe place. Safe for her, but not for the rest of us.

"That's what ended my partnership with the Kid. We'd been pards since we were kids. We grew up here. I was Mormon and he wasn't, but we always had one thing in common. We couldn't wait to get out of here and raise hell. We sure raised it since.

"I knew it was only a matter of time before it came down to a choice for him between her and me. Hell, he already made that choice the night he let her live while we killed all the rest of them. Alive, she was death at the end of a rope for us all.

"So I cleared out. The only thing I took with me was the Englishman's rifle. I'd wanted that piece from the moment I first laid eyes on it. The hole it could blow through a buffalo at distances make a Big .50 look like a popgun. I guess you could say that that rifle was to me what La Valletta is to the Kid.

"And what's that? Death. The rifle killed me sure as the woman's going to kill the Kid—"

"What mine, Dean? Where's the mine?" Vandaman pressed. "Where's the Bletchley party buried?"

"Figure it out for yourself, lawman. I talked . . . to get a smoke—no damn good . . . nohow. But then . . . neither am I." Dean chuckled and it started him coughing. He coughed up blood.

"The cigar's done . . . and so am I. I'm done talking. I'm . . ."

The old Mormon hunkered down beside Dean Richmond. "It's me, Dean. Malachi."

"I know. Things 're . . . fading in and out on me . . . but I'd know you . . . from a long way off, old man."

"Listen up, Dean. You were raised in the

faith like you said. You done a lot of bad things, but there's still time for you to repent and seek forgiveness from your Maker."

"Too late. There's no . . . forgiveness for me. I'm Hell bound." Dean started coughing, blood spewing down his chin and neck. He made a noise like he had something caught in his throat and he was trying to clear it. He froze, stiffened, and went inert, unmoving.

His eyes were open, unblinking. Staring. But whatever he was looking at was not to be seen by anyone on This Side.

For Dean Richmond, it was the Hour of Death.

"He just plain stopped," Caleb said.

"Yup. About twenty years too late. He spoke true at the last, though. He's Hell bound for sure." Malachi closed Dean's eyes with his fingertips. He rose, groaning, but only because age was leaving him stiff-jointed and his legs ached from squatting down beside the dying man.

He turned, facing Sixkiller and Vandaman. "You fellows get what you want?"

"Most of it," Vandaman said. "Not all, but— enough."

"Reckon that La Vallette gal is still alive?" Sixkiller asked.

Vandaman shrugged. "Maybe yes, maybe no. Bart Skillern is a creature of whims. One day it pleases him to keep the woman alive, the next he might put a bullet in her head without thinking twice. I just don't know."

"From the way Dean was talking, Skillern wants her bad."

"He did two months ago. A lot could have happened since then. I wanted to ask where Skillern was keeping the girl, but I didn't dare. Dean hated her so much that if he thought there was a chance of her being saved he'd start lying or else just stop talking," Vandaman said.

Sixkiller nodded. "That's how I figured it, too." He looked around. "We're done here. Reckon I know where my next stop is now."

"Ringgold?"

"That's right."

Chapter Four

Two men lurked at the top of a ridge on an early Wyoming morning. They were bush-whackers, killers.

Freedy was stocky, grizzled, hard-faced. He was holding a rifle.

Hooper was younger, not yet out of his teens. He'd gotten his growth, but his face still showed traces of baby fat. With a thatch of yellow hair and a ready smile, he seemed like a pleasant-enough youth, except for his eyes. They were the eyes of a rattlesnake, bright, alert, and pitiless.

Twin guns were worn low on his hips, tied-down. His hands hovered at his sides, ever-ready, never straying far from his gun butts.

Their horses were tethered in a clump of trees at the base of the rise. It was generally felt to be an unnatural condition for a Western man, going about on foot instead of astride a horse. But this time it came with the job—the job of murder.

The ridge ran east-west, cut by a trail that went north-south. The duo were perched just below the crest on the left-hand side of the trail, facing south.

Watching. Waiting.

The far side of the ridge sloped gently down to a flat, the edge of a shallow, saucer-shaped basin that stretched east, south, and west as far as the eye could see. The ridge was its northern boundary.

Shot through with rock spurs and boulders, the depression was riven by cuts. No plants grew, no trees or brush, not even the toughest cactus.

The trail dipped down the far side of the slope to the flat, stretching south across the basin, running straight as a string. Lighter in color than the rest of the scenery, it was the only way to distinguish it from its surroundings.

Strong, gusty winds, with a hint of chill even in the heat of a late summer day, blew predominantly from the north, powdering the ridge with alkali dust. Freedy and Hooper had their hats jammed down tight on their heads to keep them from blowing away when the irregular winds gusted strong.

Freedy lay belly-down, the barrel of his rifle protruding over the ridgeline. He was careful to keep the muzzle clear of the ground and dirt-free. The rifle was his stock-in-trade.

Hooper hunkered down beside him.

Freedy's eyes were narrowed, dark glittering slits in a wide, flat face seamed like old saddle leather. His gaze was restless, searching, peering south along the trail into the distances of the basin.

The Wyoming wind was changeable. One minute it blew strong and gusty, whipping up dust and chaff; the next, it died down to near stillness.

A dusty haze hung over the basin, a permanent pall. It thickened and lessened according to the winds, but even in a rare flat calm it never went away.

Hooper rose, straightening up. He was a long, lanky youngster. "See him?"

"Nope. If I saw him, I'd shoot him and we'd be done with it." Freedy was gruff, short-tempered, and sometimes hard to get along with. But he was useful.

He was a veteran bad man, wise in the ways of the owlhoot trail with criminal connections throughout the West. He knew the fences of stolen goods, the forgers, madams and tinhorns, the crooked lawmen and the ones who couldn't be bought, the proprietors of hideouts and refuges for fugitives.

That's why Hooper had partnered up with

him. There was a lot an up-and-coming young gunman could learn from a man like Freedy.

Hooper went to the top of the ridge, peering south.

"Quit skylining," Freedy said, irritated.

"What for? You said you don't see him. And I don't see nothing."

"That don't mean he can't see you. Maybe his eyes are better."

"Than yours, maybe."

For some reason that tickled Freedy, renowned in the trade for his keen eyesight. He grunted, a corner of his wide, flat mouth quirking upward in what might have passed for a smile in a more good-humored fellow. "Yeah. That's why I'm working the rifle."

"You're the better rifleman, no doubt about that." Hooper patted the sides of his holstered guns. "The ploughshares is my specialty."

"Yeah, and don't you love to use 'em!"

"I like to work up close, see the look on the other fellow's face when I'm burning him down. There's no fun in this long-distance stuff."

"I ain't in this business for fun, Hoop."

"Don't I know it! For you, it's just a cold-blooded business proposition."

"That's right. And business is good."

Hooper snorted, shaking his head in disbelief. "Man! I hope I never get that old!"

Freedy grinned. "Keep on the way you're

going and that's one thing you ain't never gonna have to worry about."

The sun was a yellow smear above the eastern horizon. Half-moons of sweat banded the underarms of Hooper's shirt. He swore. "Getting hot already."

"Um," Freedy said, nodding. His face shone with sweat. He pushed his hat back on his head, wiping the sweat on the inside of a shirtsleeve.

A canteen hung by a strap down from Hooper's neck. He unscrewed the cap and drank deep. "Ahh . . ."

Freedy curled up into a sitting position, resting the rifle across the tops of his crossed legs and reaching up. "Lemme have some of that, I got me a cotton mouth."

Hooper unslung the canteen, passing it to the other, the cap making tiny jingling noises where a thin chain linked it to the spout.

Freedy took a swallow, then spat it out, making a face.

"Hey, don't waste it!"

"Whiskey!" Freedy exclaimed.

"Sure, what'd you expect?"

"Water. What else, you danged fool!"

"You put what you want in your canteen and I'll put what I want in mine," Hooper said, almost fussily. "Give it back if you don't want it." He took the canteen from Freedy.

"A damn-fool kid trick," Freedy said, shaking his head. "You ought to have more sense than that. You won't think it's so funny on the ride back to Ringgold. You get thirsty, don't go asking for any of my water."

"Just so happens I filled my other canteen with water," Hooper retorted, his tone saying *So there!* "I ain't as green as you think."

"Lord, I hope not," Freedy said feelingly. He stood up and started downhill, rifle in hand.

"Where you going?"

"To get my canteen like I shoulda done in the first place."

Hooper did not volunteer to get it for him and Freedy did not ask. He went downhill, his back stiff with indignation.

Hooper's sides quaked with silent laughter. He was careful to show no outward sign of mirth at the other's discomfort. Freedy was a bad man to get down on someone. Hooper could beat him on the draw, no question. But Freedy was a rifleman and could stand off at a distance and pick him off. He was a dead shot with a rifle. For his part, he could use Hooper's quick and deadly guns.

The partnership suited the younger man for now. When—not if, but when—it should prove advantageous to him to dissolve it, he'd do so at close range with blazing guns. Hooper was ever on the alert for the main chance—his.

Freedy went to the clump of trees where the horses were tied. He got his canteen from the saddle, took a long drink, and carried it with him, trudging back uphill.

Hooper stood at the crest, facing south. Planted atop the ridgetop, hands on hips, his posture suggested he was master of all he surveyed.

It burned Freedy that the kid was skylining again, but he let it pass. More, he went against his professional instincts and stood beside him. There was a reason for it. The standing man had the better view.

"Nothing," Hooper said in answer to the other's unspoken query. "Not a sign of him. Maybe we missed him."

Freedy shook his head. "We cleared out of town way ahead of him, while he was still breakfasting."

"Maybe he ain't coming this way."

"He is."

Both men's skins were burned brown by long exposure to the outdoor life, but Hooper's face flushed redder under the rising heat. He was sullen, pouty.

That was the youngster in him showing, thought Freedy.

"What makes you so sure he's a-coming this way?" Hooper demanded.

"This is the way to Ringgold," Freedy said matter-of-factly.

"Maybe he ain't going to Ringgold," Hooper said, knowing better, but argumentative, anyway.

"He wouldn't have been poking around asking about Bart Skillern, if he wasn't going to Ringgold," Freedy said. "Besides, where else could he go? Ain't nothing around these parts but Ringgold and Rock Spring, and Rock Spring's a flyspeck, a one-horse whistle-stop town—if you can even call it a town.

"He might be delayed for any number of reasons, but he'll be along this way, sooner or later."

"Well, I almighty hope it's soon. I'm getting tired of waiting!"

"We're getting paid for it, Hoop. Mighty well-paid, if you ask me. Hundred dollars for each of us to kill a stranger, a nobody."

"I'm worth it."

"I ain't arguing. My point is we're on to a good thing here, so why kick about it?"

"I want to collect the other half of my money and cut loose in Ringgold for some high living," Hooper said.

"We'll be there before sundown."

"Who is this stranger, anyway?"

"Nobody," Freedy said definitively. "Calls himself Quinto. I never seed him before. Never heard of him. If he was somebody, I'd know who he was. I don't know him from Adam so it stands to reason he ain't nothing, nothing a-tall."

"You know 'em all, Freed," Hooper said a bit admiringly.

"Damned straight," Freedy agreed.

"Big though, ain't he? Almost as big as Bull Raymond. He looks like some kind of Injin."

"Who, Bull?"

"No, the stranger."

"A breed, I'd say. He's got some white blood in him, looks like," Freedy said. "Big or small, it don't matter to me. He'll go down the same as anybody else once my bullet's in him. I don't need to know nothin' about the mark 'ceptin the money's good and the man is dead." Freedy took a small tobacco patch out of the breast pocket of his flannel shirt. He creased a cigarette paper into a V, shook tobacco into it, and rolled it up.

Hooper had ideas. "I figure this Quinto's some kind of lawman or bounty killer, like the others were."

"Most likely. He signed his own death warrant when he come looking for the Utah Kid," Freedy pronounced. "Bart's got standing orders to kill anyone who comes looking for him. Not that he couldn't do it himself, fast as he is. But he can't be bothered. He's too busy keeping the money coming in. He's a coming man, Bart Skillern is.

"He's got spotters planted in Ringgold and all through the valley, posted to keep an eye out for manhunters looking for his scalp.

Even got a man in Rock Spring to check out anybody that gets off the train. Nobody ever caught the Utah Kid napping. He sleeps with one eye open."

"I would too, if I had a fancy gal like that Val keeping my bed warm." Hooper leered.

Freedy was not amused. "That's one way to talk yourself into an early grave. Bart'll shoot the eyes out of any man he catches looking at his woman the wrong way."

"I'm just saying that's probably why Bart's willing to spend good money to get killings done he could do himself. He don't want to leave that gal alone too long. Hell, I wouldn't neither."

"That's killing talk, Hoop."

"I'm just thinking out loud. No harm in that."

"I reckon not, long as it's between just you and me—out here in the open, with no one to spy on us and go running, telling tales out of school where they can get back to the Kid. But it's a bad habit to get into," Freedy said. "Get in your cups and drunk some night in Ringgold and you might let something slip. Next thing you know, Bart comes a-looking for you.

"And don't think some of our so-called *friends* in the valley wouldn't go running to drop a word in his ear."

"The Kid's fast, no doubt about it, but I ain't

a-feared of him," Hooper said, thrusting his chin out aggressively.

Freedy laughed humorlessly. "The hell of it, Hoop, is that I know you believe it."

"I surely do," Hooper declared with the fervor of a true believer taking an oath on the Bible. "I say I'm as fast as any man on the Glint—faster! And I aim to prove it any time I'm called out. Maybe I will prove it, before we're done in Ringgold. See if I don't!"

"I wish you luck. You'll need it."

"Skill beats luck."

"The Utah Kid's got both."

All the while they'd been talking, Freedy's attention had never wandered from the basin below, constantly scanning the southern landscape. He started subtly, but perceptibly. He stiffened, eyes narrowing, body quivering like a hunting dog on point.

"What is it, Freed?"

"Thought I saw something." Freedy's gaze fastened on a point in the background, at the limits of vision where objects swam in and out of focus.

The gray-yellow wastes of the basin reflected a lot of light and glare. Strands and veils of dust swirled in the hazy air, swaying this way and that. Somewhere south along the trail, at the edge of visibility, Freedy saw—something. . . .

Sweat stung his eyes. He blinked, looked

again. Whatever he had seen was gone. He kept looking, but that antlike blur did not reappear.

Hooper said doubtfully, "I don't see nothing."

"It's gone now, whatever it was," Freedy said.

"Sure you saw something? Just because I ain't much of a hand with a rifle don't mean my eyes don't work and I didn't see a thing."

"Maybe not," Freedy said, unconvinced. "Let's get down below the ridgetop. We shouldn't be skylining."

"What the hell? If you can't see him, he can't see you."

"That ain't how it always works out, Hoop." Freedy moved down below the crest until only his head showed above it. Hooper followed.

Freedy was not wrong. He had seen something.

In the southern part of the basin, a lone rider paused on the trail, looking north. Rider and horse seemed to be the only living creatures in the basin, not counting the hawks and buzzards soaring on the thermals high overhead the wilderness bursting with majestic scenery. The alkali basin with its harsh mineralized dirt was a wasteland.

The roan horse was the color of dried blood. A massive animal, it was part quarter horse crossbred with a strain of Arapaho pony. The result was a steed built along the massive lines of a charger or war horse with much of the endurance and surefootedness of a mountain Indian pony.

A splendid specimen, big-boned and sturdy, with a rider to match, an outsized individual even in the larger than life expansiveness of the West.

An ordinary-sized horse's back would have been deeply bent bowed by the heft of the man in the saddle, but the roan was undaunted by its weighty burden. A big man on a big horse, both were sweaty and dust-covered.

The rider looked north again. He could barely make out the ridge, a flat two-dimensional shape curtaining the rim of the northern horizon. It was enough. He'd seen what he wanted to see—or rather, what he expected to see. His hand rested on the Colt Peacemaker holstered on his hip.

Sixkiller had come to Wyoming.

Chapter Five

After rousting the Red Ravine gang, Sixkiller had taken a train from Salt Lake City to Laramie, where federal agent Vandaman had set up a temporary operating base. It was the nearest big town to Ringgold. Sixkiller had bought the roan horse in Laramie and rather than taking the train, had ridden it to Rock Spring, arriving two days before. It was a good way to get to know the horse and for the horse to know him. His own prized horse Ironheart was back in the Nations, being tended by a friend.

West of Laramie, Rock Spring wasn't even a small town, more like a hamlet. A handful of one-story, wooden frame buildings and shacks had been thrown up around the resource which gave it its name and its reason for existence—a small but reliable source of water that trickled from a spring in a crack in the ground rock.

The most prominent structure in town was the massive water tank rising beside the tracks of the Union Pacific railroad line, which stretched east-west across southern Wyoming. In the vast dusty plains and alkali deserts, water for the boilers of its steam-driven locomotives was not easy to come by. Rock Spring was literally a "tank town."

It was also the jumping-off place to Ringgold in the lush Glint River Valley. That's all Rock Spring would ever be, a way station en route to somewhere else, Sixkiller had decided.

There was a saloon, a trading post, a café with some rooms to rent that provided lodging for travelers, and a ragtag assortment of other shacks and huts of dubious provenance.

An hour and more had passed since Freedy thought he saw something.

It seemed an eternity to Hooper. He was not one for waiting. The impatience of youth mixed with the arrogance of one who is used to taking what he wants when he wants it, the young gunman was getting antsy waiting for the marked man to show.

"I should have gunned down the big lout in Rock Spring yesterday," he declared, his voice thick, the words slurred. Hooper had drunk deeply of the whiskey canteen.

Freedy shook his head. "Bart said no more killings in Rock Spring for a while."

"Yeah, well, he don't have to sit here in the hot sun all day waiting for some slow-footed breed to show up," Hooper said.

"The job gets done the way the Kid wants."

"It would've been so easy," Hooper went on. "I'd've put a couple slugs in that red man and we'd've been long back in Ringgold, with cold beer and hot women. Hell, there ain't even no law in Rock Spring to kick about the kill!"

"Maybe that's how Bart likes it and wants to keep it that way," Freedy said.

Hooper took another long pull of whiskey from the canteen.

"Go easy on that stuff, Hoop."

Hooper made a face. "I ain't drunk."

"Who said you was? But the whizz and the hot sun don't mix so good."

"I'm as fast drunk as sober, Freed."

"Nobody said you ain't. Anyhow it ain't gonna matter. The mark's gonna be stretched out in the dust long before them guns of yours can make a difference. Soon's I get a bead on him, I'm gonna pot him with this rifle."

"Do me a favor. Give him one in the belly so he's a long time dying," Hooper said feelingly. "Make him suffer for making us wait here for him."

"I don't go for the fancy stuff," Freedy said noncommittally.

"Don't give me that." Hooper scoffed. "I've seen what you can do with a rifle. You can tag a man anywhere you want without half trying."

Freedy chuckled dryly. "Thought you was in a hurry. Now you want to stretch it out. Can't have it both ways. Which is it?"

"Put a bullet in his guts and I'll finish him off. That'll give me another kill," Hooper said. "You know what my goal is."

"I should. You talk about it enough."

Hooper went on, oblivious. "I want a man dead for each year I've been alive. Eighteen years—eighteen men. I'm more than halfway there. Twelve down, only six more to go."

"And when you reach eighteen, then what?" Freedy asked.

"Oh, I'll keep on doing like I been doing. Only once I got that tally under my belt I can relax some."

"Not you, Hoop. You ain't the type. You ain't easygoing like me."

Hooper snorted. "Easygoing? Is that what you call yourself?"

Freedy let it pass. He never stopped studying the landscape.

Hooper joined him peering down into the basin. "Still nothing! Ain't he never gonna show? Why don't you use them binoculars you got in your saddle bags?"

"I told you," Freedy began, in patient long-suffering tones. "Can't risk sunlight glaring off the lenses. Our man could see it for miles off. If he's even a little bit trail-savvy he'd know someone was up here laying for him. Whoever he is, he's no greenhorn. One look at him and you can see that."

"That's what I'd like—a look at him! Ain't he ever gonna show?" Hooper complained again.

In an instant, his query was answered in the affirmative. A new voice rang out from behind and below the two killers. "You up there! Drop your guns and turn around slow!"

Freedy and Hooper stiffened. They rose slowly, standing up with their backs to the newcomer. Freedy held his rifle in both hands so that it stretched horizontally across the tops of his thighs. Hooper, empty-handed, stood with hands poised over his guns.

The stranger, Freedy told himself with bulging eyes, his mouth hanging open. He was awe-struck, stupefied. He never heard the stranger coming. He hadn't thought anyone could sneak up on *him*!

He cut a sidewise glance at Hooper. Eyes glittering, nostrils flaring the youngster smiled with his lips closed. He trembled a little, but not with fear. It was the excitement of a horse at the starting gate right before the bell goes off to signal the start of a race.

In that moment, Freedy knew exactly what was going to happen and what he had to do when it did, if he wanted to live. And he wanted to live more than anything. The two of them were under a gun, covered. But there was a chance for one of them—*him*—if he played his cards right. A slim chance, sure, but better than none.

Besides, what choice did he have?

Click.

There it was, the unmistakable sound of a gun being cocked, hammer clicking into place.

"I ain't funning," the stranger said. "Drop 'em or I drop you!"

Freedy turned his head, looking back over his shoulder. He wanted a look at the man who, for the moment at least, had gotten the better of him. What he saw gave him another jolt.

The stranger was a man of stone!

Dust mixed with sweat, formed a kind of thin paste on his exposed flesh, making him look like he was made of crumbling stone.

An illusion, of course, but that's how it looked to Freedy in that terrible instant. The stranger, Quinto as he called himself, stood at the bottom of the ridge, holding a gun pointed up at Freedy and Hooper.

There was no mistaking the hulking outlines of the big breed, now neither red nor white man. He was covered from head to toe in powdery gray-yellow dust, like something not made of flesh and blood, but rather something from the mineral kingdom, looking like a crumbling, ancient statue come to life.

A weird effect! It was the basin's alkali dust that covered Sixkiller—for the stranger Quint was none other than he. Stony dust covered all of him but his hands—his hands and the Colt in his fist. Its long barrel gleamed blue-black, spotless and unwavering.

"Hey, you!" Hooper shouted, his voice ringing clear, fine, and strong. He wasn't yellow. There was no fear in the youngster.

Freedy knew that. He also knew what Hooper was going to do and what he, as the one with the most experience, must do to take advantage of such knowledge.

"Gonna shoot us in the back?" Hooper's voice held a mocking quality, like a schoolboy sassing back his elders.

Sixkiller said, "If that's how you want it—"

Hooper drew wicked fast. With lightning speed, his hands were a blur of motion snaking the twin guns out of their holsters. At the same time, he spun to his left, playing it cute. Instead of turning all the way around to face his man, he tried to sneak a shot under his left arm with the gun in his right hand. He was so quick that he almost made it . . . he got a shot off.

It followed less than an eye blink after the second of two shots spitting from Sixkiller's gun, both shots tagging Hooper in the back, knocking him down.

Freedy had known all along that Hooper was going to make a play—never any doubt about it. A damn-fool kid stunt, drawing against an already drawn gun, but that hadn't stopped Hoop. It distracted the stranger for a split-second, a delay of less than a heartbeat, but maybe enough time to make a difference.

Freedy wasn't one for trick shots. He whirled around, swinging the rifle with him, sweeping the muzzle in line with the stranger's torso— and a thunderbolt hammered him—no, two. Double sledgehammer blows hammered his chest, pounding him down.

Sky and earth spun in a dizzying vortex, then Freedy lay on his back looking up at the hazy blue sky. Blackness boiled, seething at the edge of his vision. His eyes still worked, but not much else. He tried to sit up, but nothing happened.

He couldn't feel his hands—or much of anything else—as he reached out to find his rifle. The smell of grass was sweet in his nostrils.

Freedy heaved for breath, making a ghastly bubbling sound, like fat sputtering on a fire. It was the sound of a sucking chest wound from one of the bullets that had torn through his lungs.

He couldn't breathe! Sparks of panic flew upward against the great suffocating weight of nothingness pressing down on him.

A figure loomed, blotting out a big swatch of sky. The stranger, looming titanic and treetop tall, looked down at Freedy from a remote height. He was a mountain of a man with rocklike solidity.

Freedy's lips formed a single word. "Who . . . ?"

The stranger understood. "John Henry Six-killer."

Sixkiller! Freedy's eyes widened. He knew the name and had heard tell of the man, a big Cherokee lawman from the Nations in Oklahoma Territory. But that was a long way off and Freedy would never have figured him to operate so far from his home grounds.

That explained a lot, including why Freedy lay on his back with two slugs in his chest, dying. His heart lurched like a machine throwing a wheel. The darkness edging his vision arrowed inward, racing to the centers of his eyes. Total blackness filled his sight.

And then he was dead.

Chapter Six

Sixkiller reloaded his gun. The Colt was clean and so were his hands. No dirt or grit to foul its workings. He'd made sure of that before making his move on Freedy and Hooper. His life depended on his gun being in perfect working order.

He must look a sight, he thought, covered as he was with yellow-gray alkali dust from head to boot toe. Powdery specks flecked off him with every move . . . and when he was standing still, too.

He holstered his gun.

Down on one knee, he turned out Freedy's pockets, looking for clues that would lead him to Bart Skillern, the Utah Kid. It was too much to hope that Skillern would come in person, but Sixkiller couldn't help but feel a twinge of disappointment. Coming face to face with Bart

Skillern was an encounter he anticipated with relish.

He found a thin fold of small denomination greenbacks and some loose change. The only object of interest was a fifty-dollar gold piece, shiny and new. Sixkiller gripped it in blunt, square-tipped fingers, holding it up to the light. *Blood money?* Maybe so. Payment in part or full for killing him. He hoped it was in part. He liked the idea of being worth a hundred dollars dead more than being worth fifty dollars dead.

Back in Oklahoma and throughout the border states and Texas, there were more than a few men and some women, too, who would have paid a whole lot more than one hundred dollars to see John H. Sixkiller dead.

But Bart Skillern didn't know Sixkiller was on his trail—or did he?

If he did, and he'd only posted a price of a hundred dollars per man to would-be killers, it was kind of insulting. Sixkiller vowed that the Utah Kid would set his value a lot higher than that before he was done.

He pocketed the cash and the gold piece and patted Freedy down, squeezing the folds of cloth of his garments to make sure nothing was hidden in a secret pocket or hiding place. He wrestled off the killer's boots and searched them to determine that nothing was hidden inside. Freedy's corpse yielded nothing more.

Rolling Hooper's corpse on its back, he repeated the process—patient, painstaking, and methodical. Sixkiller made the shiny new fifty-dollar gold piece and the small amount of money his own. Neither gunman had further use for it.

"All in the line of duty," Sixkiller said to himself. He was liable to run up some expenses working in the field. He had to eat, and had a big appetite. Hard to get along on a U.S. deputy marshal's pay.

The pocket litter and the personal items the two had been carrying, he let slip through his fingers to the ground. Whoever found them was welcome to them, or the wind could carry them away.

Careful not to skyline, he stood, thinking of the two men he'd killed. He had no trouble recognizing them, though he did not know their names. They'd come into town the day after he'd arrived in Rock Spring, trying to get a line on him without betraying their interest—impossible in a place as small as Rock Spring.

He'd spent a day and night circulating around, drinking and buying drinks, roping the locals into conversations which inevitably included inquiries about the Utah Kid. Nobody had known anything useful, of course. He wondered which of his newfound acquaintances had given him up. Not that it really mattered.

The older man had tried to avoid tipping

their hand, but the youngster hadn't been bothered. He'd eyed Sixkiller like he was measuring him for a coffin.

They were gunmen, hired killers, a type Sixkiller knew well. He'd seen hundreds in his day. Their faces didn't match any of those on the countless WANTED posters and circulars that had gone through his hands in his office back in Tahlequah. But then he was a long way from there.

The old man and his partner had made their play and died trying. They could stay there until Doomsday as far as Sixkiller was concerned. In other circumstances he might have taken them into town and turned them over to the local law, claiming whatever reward there was, but for his present purposes, he didn't want to be tied to their killing.

He turned away and scanned the landscape in all directions for other humans. Seeing none, he thought, *Mighty lonely country.*

Taking one last look at the corpses before collecting his horse at the bottom of the rise, he said harshly, "A couple varmints aiming to dry-gulch me. Damned if I'm gonna go to the trouble of burying you. The buzzards can have you for all I care. It ain't nothing to me."

Chapter Seven

Sixkiller halted at the top of a rise facing north. The wind blew stiffly at times, but with far less dust than in the Powder Basin. Breezes were rich with the scent of sweet grasses and rich dark loam. A rampart of the Black Hills was visible in the distant northeast.

Below, lay Ringgold in the heart of the Glint River Valley. The landscape presented a broad and pleasing prospect of gently rolling hills and vast meadows spread out under strong, slanting rays of the late afternoon sunlight. The blocky mass of the town threw a long shadow eastward.

Sixkiller reviewed some of the history of the area that Vandaman had given him.

North of the valley lay a wide, gentle slope climbing to the base of the Lonesome Hills. It topped out on the level plateau of Sagebrush Flats, a kind of shelf, fronting apronlike at the foot of the hills.

Lead mines in the area had long been a mainstay of the town's economic activity.

Originally a trading post for fur trappers back in the heyday of the mountain men, Ringgold first came into being as a boomtown borne from a gold strike on Yellow Creek, a feeder stream of the Glint River. The initial gold strike was fast and furious, fortunes made and won literally overnight. Later, it served as a jumping-off place into the Yellow Creek gold diggings. But like so many other such finds, the riches of Yellow Creek gold had proved short-lived. The vein of precious metal was substantial, but not inexhaustible.

When the lode played out, the boom went bust. Bitter survivors sardonically renamed Yellow Creek to Fool's Gold Creek. The miners went elsewhere, trailed by their legions of camp followers—merchants, traders, tinhorns, whores, and such—leaving Ringgold almost as much of a flyspeck town as it had been before the boom.

Almost, but not quite.

Yellow Creek, Fools Gold Creek, call it what you will, took its source in streams running down from the mountains. Prospectors were hopeful creatures, romantic and filled with illusions as young girls. Hope sprung eternal in their hardened hearts. Perhaps higher up was the mother lode, source of the gold that had trickled its way down the creek to lay up in deposits in the Glint River Valley.

Prospectors and geologists surveyed the hundred foothills rising from Lonesome Hills in search of that precious yellow gold. They found none, but did not come up empty-handed. The foothills were rich with deposits of another ore, one less glamorous, less valuable than gold, but not without worth to a growing national economy. *Plumbum*—Latin for lead. By any name, a valuable mineral vital to Manifest Destiny and the spread of Empire. Lead for making bullets, shot, and shells. The deposits were found at a critical time, right on the eve of the Civil War.

Mining resumed on a grand scale in the Lonesome Hills, requiring millions in capital from Eastern investors and mining syndicates. They supplied the massive industrial base for hard rock mining to dig networks of shafts and tunnels. They provided rock crushers to pulverize the ore and separators to draw the pure elemental lead from rock.

The nature of the terrain made it impractical and too costly to run a railroad spur through steep and jagged foothills to reach the mines. Traffic was handled by fleets of freight wagons running the ore down to the depot at Rock Spring for transshipment nationwide.

The premier operation was the Western Territories Mining Company. On the western side of the flat, hidden by a limb of one of the Lonesome Hills, was Mine Shaft Number Seven. It showed every sign of being a rich deposit of lead and indeed it was. In its first few months it yielded lead-bearing ore that assayed of a high purity.

The tunnels were dug deeper—only to break through a rock wall behind which lay an underground spring.

Mine Shaft Seven flooded. A number of miners working the lethal rock face lost their lives in the sudden surprise flooding that submerged the lower levels, but most made it to safety.

The mining company made heroic efforts to plug the leak, seal it off, but to no avail. The volume of flood water made it impossible. The mine was so drowned there was no way to salvage it, and Mine Shaft Seven was abandoned. All that remained to mark it was a fresh torrent of water that streamed from the tunnel mouth to spill down the northwest slope of the rise.

Up on Sagebrush Flats near the tunnels in the northeast side of the hills were the main diggings, safe from the danger of flooding. Lead mining furnished steady dependable returns year after year. No fabulous fortunes were made boom-style, but it was good, dependable, steady money for the mining company and steady work for several hundred miners who had built a shantytown on the flat and who did their business and bought their provisions in Ringgold.

In recent years, the Glint River Valley had begun to experience a cattle boom. The cattle-raising lands were well west of the mine areas, avoiding the risk of lead-contaminated waters that otherwise might have proved detrimental, if not fatal, to the growing cattle empires in the northwest part of the valley. The miners were eating well on prime beef at rock bottom prices thanks to the availability of stock from Glint River Valley ranches.

As he scanned the hills and the valley, Big John Sixkiller mused on The Western Territories Mining Company's current big headache—robbers. Road agents in general and Bart Skillern in particular. It was said in grim jest that the freight haulers and shotgun messengers responsible for getting payroll funds to the WTMC camp saw more of Skillern than anyone, except for his gang.

The Utah Kid threw a wide loop when it came to frontier crime. As the cattle ranches prospered, he divided his energies between stagecoach robberies and cattle rustling, with a nice sideline in horse theft.

Sixkiller knew a little about mining and a lot about cattle and cattle raising. He eyed the land that Skillern regularly plundered and found it good, sizing it up as prime grazing ground for livestock. It was a land blue-veined by the Glint River and its feeder streams and tributaries, marbled like a side of richly fatted, succulent beef—the kind being raised on the Glint in contrast to tough stringy longhorns.

He moved his gaze to Ringgold, nestled in a bend of the river. Buildings with the bright yellow newness of raw pine and other lumber brought down from the wooded foothills populated the town.

Wagon trails and dirt roads arrowed into Ringgold, one from the northeast mines on Sagebrush Flats and beyond them the Black Hills, another from the northwest and the rich cattle country along the main stem of the Glint. A southeast road angled from Laramie and the south road headed up from Rock Spring. A number of lesser trails wound their way to the town.

Sixkiller's first impression was one of liveliness. Lush green meadows bordered the town. Swarms of people threaded the street grid.

Ringgold! A tough town, by all accounts.

Sixkiller had faced tough towns before and tamed them.

Ringgold! He rode down to meet it.

The *Banner* was Ringgold's weekly newspaper. Its *only* newspaper. The office was located on the northern side of Liberty Street, set down near the edge of town in a row of shabby, marginal enterprises—a laundry, a seedy boarding-house, a pawnshop, and a couple rowdy dives and saloons.

The stand-alone, one-story, wooden-frame building was a single room with a waist-high, dark-wood balustrade dividing it in half. The front half held the administrative office area where publisher-editor Cassandra Horgan—Cass to her friends—had her work space. It was furnished with secondhand furniture, dingy and shabby. A rolltop desk backed with pigeon-hole shelving held an ink well, steel-quill pens, scissors, paste pots, and suchlike paraphernalia.

Thirty years old, she was a full-bodied red-head with green eyes and a heart-shaped face. She looked a little tired around the eyes, but was strong, vital, and lovely.

She wore a lightweight, pale green-and-white-checked gingham dress, with the sleeves rolled up to the elbows. Her hands and forearms were ink-stained and smudged and the hair piled up high on her head seemed in imminent danger of becoming disarranged. On her feet were black leather ankle boots that laced up the front.

Edmond Bigelow, a printer and editorial assistant, sat at a second desk, even more battered and less fancy. It had been said that he put the *tramp* in *tramp printer* and he would have been the first to agree. He was fortyish, a hard forty that looked more like fifty. He was grizzled and thick-bodied with a red bulbous nose, small narrow eyes nested in a mass of wrinkles, and a bristly beard which failed to hide the many gin blossoms on his weathered face. He wore a brown jacket with yellow spiderweb pattern, an orange-and-silver checkered vest, no tie, and rust-colored pants.

The massive printing press, bristling with levers, hand cranks, rollers, and metal wheels sat in the rear, midpoint of the long east wall. More than one visitor had observed that it looked like some kind of medieval torture machine. Bigelow maintained that's exactly what it was.

Near the press were racks with shallow metal trays and pans filled with blocks of type, rollers for applying ink, scrapers, flatteners, paper cutters, and more. Massive rolls of newsprint paper and rows of ink-filled carboys lined the back wall.

Reeve Westbrook, the *Banner*'s feature writer, columnist, reviewer and jack-of-all-reportorial trades made up the third member of the staff. He was slim and straight, with a sharp-featured, birdlike face. He had wispy fair hair, a thin mustache and reedy chin whiskers. He wore a maroon velvet jacket and tan pants over elegant mahogany-colored custom-tailored boots.

Members of the Fourth Estate, all three were at work, putting out the next edition of the *Banner*.

Bigelow was going over pages of handwritten

notes, musing aloud. "A brawl at the Lucky Star saloon that left seven miners laid up with fractured skulls and broken bones . . . two soiled doves fighting it out with a razor in the street in broad daylight . . . six shootings two of them fatal, five stabbings none fatal . . . man dragged by runaway horse, he's expected to live—the man that is. The horse had to be shot to save him—"

"I call that a waste of a damned good horse," Westbrook said.

"Depends on the man," Cass said. "Who was it?"

"Damned if I know," Bigelow said, shrugging.

"You're supposed to know. You're a *newspaperman.*" Cass said the last word like it meant something, which to her, it did.

"Around here I'm a glorified typesetter," Bigelow said cheerfully enough. He nodded at Westbrook. "Ask Golden Boy here. He's Johnny-on-the-spot when it comes to local doings."

"Powell. Bud Powell," Westbrook said.

Cass frowned. "Who?"

"Bud Powell. He's the one who was dragged by the horse," Westbrook explained.

"What'd I tell you? He knows," Bigelow said.

"If you got off that oversized rump of yours and got around town to see what's going on, you might break a few stories yourself," Cass said.

"I resent that, madam. Whenever something

happens in the saloons, I'm right on top of it." Bigelow put down the pages of notes he'd been examining. "If things keep on as quiet as they've been, we'll have to go to a bi-weekly edition or maybe even a monthly."

"I shouldn't worry," Westbrook said. "Come Friday night when the cowboys are in town, there'll be more than enough killings to fill the front page and then some."

"That's for next week's issue, but what about this week? If things don't pick up by tomorrow we'll have to run Parson Brown's sermon on the front page," Bigelow said.

"This town could use it," Cass said sharply.

"Possibly, but it's not the kind of thing that sells newspapers," Westbrook said.

"What we need is a six-gun free-for-all in some bucket of blood dive like the Paradise Club, one that leaves a half-dozen corpses when the smoke clears," Bigelow said. "Or even a cave-in at the lead mines with some miners trapped underground."

"You two sound like a pair of ghouls," Cass snapped.

"This is the right town for it," Bigelow said.

"Though maybe not this week," Westbrook added.

"I need some fresh air." Cass rose and stretched.

It was something to see. Uncoiling like a big cat, her high firm breasts thrust against the bodice of her dress. She tossed her head, shaking coppery ringlets, and ran fingers through her hair, pushing it off her face and back on top of her head.

Out through the open doorway of the front entrance and onto the boardwalk she went. The air was fresh compared to that inside the office, notwithstanding the omnipresent smell of horse manure on the street.

The sun was lowering in the west, but the sunlight was warm and sensuous. From nearby came the sharp, brassy sound of a blacksmith hammering on an anvil.

A rider came into view riding west along the street. *Nothing unusual in that,* Cass thought. Nothing so unusual in the type of rider, either.

Whatever you called the breed—saddle tramp, gunman, drifter, long rider—the town and the valley were full of them, with more arriving every day. They threatened to soon outnumber the decent law-abiding citizens whose lives and property they so casually endangered.

The newcomer was apparently doing just that, arriving, judging by his trail dust and bedraggled condition. Ringgold was a small town and if Cass had seen this one before she'd have remembered. He was not one easily forgotten.

The stranger was a big man even in a time and a place where the man-plant tended to grow to outsize proportions. A big head crowned that big body. He had a wide face, clean-shaven and copper-red, an eagle-beak nose, long slit-like pale eyes and lots of chin and jaw.

Topping that head was a high-crowned, round-topped, dun-colored hat with a broad, stiff brim and a foot-long eagle feather stuck in the hatband. He wore a buckskin vest over a rust-colored flannel shirt with sleeves rolled up past the elbows and dark gray denims over cowboy boots. A six-gun was holstered low on his right hip.

A man who'd done some hard traveling on a dusty road, he walked the horse slowly and deliberately down the middle of the street. *Clip-clop.* The roan's hooves struck the hard-packed dirt of the street, a metronome beat like the ticking of a clock or the beating of a heart.

"Whew! That's a big one," Westbrook said. "Is it a man or a shaved bear?"

Cass gave a slight start, unaware that the feature writer had come out to stand beside her on the front walkway.

"Just what Ringgold doesn't need, another gun-toting saddle tramp" Cass tsk-tsked. "As if the town isn't overfull of them as it is."

"It's like shipping cattle to Texas or ice to the North Pole," Westbrook agreed.

Looking straight ahead, the stranger drew abreast of the *Banner* office. He stopped and turned his head to the side, casting his pale-eyed gaze at Cass and Westbrook. Especially at Cass.

His wide jack-o'-lantern mouth turned up at the corners in what might have been a friendly smile.

Cass's face twisted in an expression of mingled scorn and contempt. "Humph!"

Westbrook, more politic perhaps, raised a hand in a half wave.

Sixkiller's close-mouthed smile widened at the sign of the redhead's disdain. He rode on. Cass stood with hands on hips watching him go.

"A fine figure of a woman," Sixkiller said only to himself. When his horse had walked on several lengths, he looked back over his shoulder.

Cass harrumphed with a toss of her head to underline her derision and turned away.

"Why so hostile, Cass?" Westbrook asked.

"What do you expect me to do, lay out the Welcome mat?" she fired back.

"The *Banner* can't afford to scare off any potential customers."

"That one? What makes you think he can read?"

"Appearances can be deceiving. For all we know, he might be a perfectly decent fellow."

"I thought a reporter is supposed to know something about people," Cass said, red color in her cheeks.

"I'm interested in facts. What people do,

that's what counts," Westbrook said. "Still . . . an interesting fellow, don't you think?"

"He's a troublemaker. One look at him is all you need to know that."

"He certainly seems built for it. I daresay if that fellow set out to raise Cain he'd make quite a splash. Maybe he'll make some news. We could use some."

Bigelow stepped outside, firing up a cigar butt. He looked at the dwindling form of Sixkiller riding down the street. "What was that all about?"

"Nothing. Just another piece of trash come to town," Cass said.

"No ordinary piece of trash, I'd say. He's huge. As big as Bull Raymond," Westbrook said.

"That'd make him a pretty big ol' boy," Bigelow said.

Westbrook reached into a hip pocket, pulled out a silver flask, and took a drink from it.

"Where'd that come from?" Bigelow asked. "You've been holding out on me, you son of a gun."

"That's the only way to make it last with you around," Westbrook said.

Bigelow stopped chewing on the cigar butt in the corner of his mouth long enough to smack his lips meaningfully several times. "How's about sparing a snort for a colleague?"

Westbrook handed him the flask. Bigelow

took it, a slight tremor in his hands. He paused only long enough to wipe the spout of the flask on the edge of his sleeve.

"How do you like that? *He* wipes it clean after I drink from it," Westbrook said in mock outrage.

Bigelow drank deep.

Westbrook reached to wrestle it away from him, finally succeeding but not without a struggle. "There's some left, no thanks to you."

Bigelow shuddered, a red flush overshadowing his face. "Ah—that's good stuff!"

"Brandy. Better than that rotgut you drink," Westbrook retorted.

"That's all I can afford on my salary," Bigelow said.

"The way you drink you'd soon run dry even if you had Vanderbilt's millions," Cass said.

Westbrook screwed the flask's cap closed.

"Aw, not another little taste?" Bigelow said, wheedling.

"I need it myself. I can't do my job without a drink," Westbrook said.

"But you're not working now," Bigelow pointed out.

"I'm going to be. I'm about to ply the journalist's art." Westbrook pocketed the flask.

"That gleam in your eye indicates you're cooking up something." Cass arched an interrogative eyebrow. "Where are you going?"

"That stranger looks interesting. Could be a story there. I've got a hunch. Call it my nose for news."

"Get on the wrong side of that big tramp and you're liable to get your nose bloodied . . . and maybe a pair of black eyes and a broken jaw, as well!"

"Sounds like a front page story," Westbrook said.

Cass made a face and started into the office, pausing long enough to tell cigar-puffing Bigelow, "If you insist on smoking that piece of rope, you can smoke it outside!"

Sixkiller rode along the street, chuckling to himself. "That redhead is a whole lot of woman! Worth coming to Ringgold for, remains to be seen."

He'd seen several livery stables from the rise. He didn't care for the first one he came to. Didn't like the way the place was kept, dirty and sloppy.

"You deserve better, hoss," he told the roan, riding on.

A boy of about twelve was sweeping the sidewalk in front of a barber shop. He was skinny, sharp-faced, and intelligent-looking. Sixkiller asked him where he could find a good, clean livery stable.

"Noble's at the west end of Liberty Street," the boy said, giving him directions.

"What's your name, son?" Sixkiller asked.

"Eli."

"I'm Quinto. Thanks!" He tossed a coin to the youngster.

"Thanks, mister," Eli said, plucking the coin out of the air and making it disappear into his pocket. He made quick furtive glances to see if anybody had observed him receiving the money. Nobody had. He waved so-long and ducked inside the barber shop, out of sight.

The entire sequence told Sixkiller something important about Ringgold. A fellow had to look sharp to keep hold of his money.

"The only kind of town they send me to. And I wouldn't have it any other way."

That wasn't really true. He'd like to visit some nice, quiet, peaceful burg to serve a writ or warrant or collect some back taxes for which he'd get a percentage of the take. But it just wasn't in the cards. He sighed.

The bold, full-bodied redhead evoked a different kind of sigh from him, one tinged with hard-breathing, hot-blooded lust, and longing.

He rode west on Liberty Street. Along the way, he saw a couple of ragged boys throwing rocks at a mangy yellow dog. A stone hit its hindquarters and the dog yelped, scooting under a porch and out of reach of his tormentors.

A drunk sprawled in a shadowed alley slumped against a wall, sleeping it off. At least, he looked drunk, but he could have been dead.

Sixkiller didn't give enough of a damn to check. "Ain't nothing to me."

A pair of fancy women painted up like a carousel's wooden horse exited the front door of a cheap rooming house. They had hourglass figures, but it looked like some of the sand was leaking out. Both wore satin dresses, one scarlet, the other bottle green. They walked along the boardwalk arm in arm, with bold looks and flashing eyes, casting long appraising looks at Sixkiller.

He touched the brim of his hat politely. That set off a round of rude, shrill, raucous laughter and shrieks. One of the women called something after him as he rode on. He couldn't quite make out what she said, but he got the general idea.

Ahead, noise—loud voices, rinky-dink piano playing, the clink and rattle of glasses, shouts and shrieks—billowed like a puff of smoke or a haze hanging over the end of the street. Its source was a rowdy saloon. NED HICKORY'S PARADISE CLUB proclaimed a red and gold painted marquee sign board swinging in the wind, hinges squeaking.

Sixkiller drew nigh as a bouncer built like a circus strongman and garbed like a barkeep, with a striped shirt, sleeve garters and a white bib-front apron emerged through the batwing doors. He was giving a customer the classic bum's rush, with one hand on his collar and the other hand on the seat of his pants. He propelled the ex-patron headfirst out of the bar and across the plank sidewalk.

The hapless man flew through the air in an arching curve, landing in the middle of the street right in front of the roan. Sixkiller reined to a halt.

The bouncer waited to see if the drunk still had fight in him, then made a hands-washing gesture—good riddance to bad rubbish—as the patron struggled to hands and knees and crawled across the street in the opposite direction.

Stiffening some when he made eye contact with Sixkiller, the bouncer's face hardened in sullen lines, one big man sizing up another.

Sixkiller touched heels to the horse's flanks, moving on. He had a feeling he'd be dropping by the Paradise Club before too long.

Noble's livery stable was at the edge of town. It looked and smelled clean enough. So did the proprietor, a compact, sandy-haired man with a long seamed face and alert eyes. He minded his own business, asking no questions beyond what he needed to know regarding the upkeep of the horse.

Sixkiller made arrangements to have the

roan put up at the stable, paying a week in advance. "What's a good place to stay?"

"Laramie," Noble said.

"Ha-ha. I meant in town."

"Afton's where cattle buyers and the gentry stay. Drummers and such roost at the Culhane. The Atlas is pretty decent I hear, but I never stayed at none of them places myself."

Drummers, salesmen, and their ilk irritated Sixkiller with their incessant chattering. Besides, they were transients unlikely to have much of an inside on what made Ringgold tick. "Where's the Atlas?"

Noble gave him directions. Sixkiller said thanks and moved on. He took his rifle and saddlebags with him, tossing the bags over a shoulder and carrying the rifle in his left hand, keeping his right hand, his gun hand, free.

He walked back the way he'd come, along the north side of Liberty Street. The route would take him past the newspaper office. He wouldn't mind getting another look at the redhead.

Sixkiller passed the Paradise Club entrance quickly, not wanting to be hit by any more ejected customers. A strong fume of whiskey reek and haze of tobacco smoke wafted out the door, stinging his eyes. The drunk who'd been thrown into the street was gone, nowhere in sight. The two fancy women were gone, too. They'd be back on the street soon enough, he reckoned. The drunk too, probably.

It was not the kind of place he liked to turn his back on, either.

A couple more blocks took him to the *Banner* office. Reeve Westbrook stood leaning against a wall, smoking a long thin cigar. He looked pleasantly amused, but not so much that somebody might take offense and decide to wipe the smile off his face.

Sixkiller paused, looking through the window, but there was no sign of the redhead.

"You're out of luck, friend. She's not here," Westbrook said.

"Oh? Too bad. Who is she?"

"Mrs. Horgan, publisher and managing editor of the Ringgold *Banner*, our town newspaper."

"Married, eh?"

"Widowed. But don't get your hopes set on her. She's spoken for by Colonel Tim Donovan, owner of the B Square B ranch. Biggest in the valley."

"That's nice to know," said Sixkiller.

"Did you have some business with her? I only ask because perhaps I can be of some assistance in her absence."

"Business? Not yet. I just got into town. Once I get settled in maybe I could take a look at some of your back issues, get a feel for Ringgold and the valley."

"Come by anytime, I'll show you around," Westbrook offered.

"Much obliged. I like to know about a place before I start prospecting."

"A prospector? Hope you haven't come a long way for nothing."

"How do you know I've come a long way?"

"You look it, if you don't mind my saying so. You and your horse. I saw you ride in earlier. I'm a reporter, a kind of professional snoop you might say. Keeping my eyes and ears open is all in a day's work for me."

Me too, thought Sixkiller.

"Asking questions is part of my game, too. Being in the news business I'm always on the lookout for whatever's fresh and new. I'm Reeve Westbrook, at your service."

"Quinto's my handle."

"Is that your first name or your last?"

"Both. Just plain Quinto."

"Welcome to Ringgold."

"Thanks."

Westbrook pulled the silver flask from a hip pocket, having refilled it since sharing a drink with Bigelow. He took a long pull, then offered some to Sixkiller. "Brandy, if you're of a mind to."

"Don't mind if I do." Sixkiller drank. "That's good, cuts the dust." He handed back the flask. "What did you mean when you said I might have come a long way for nothing?"

"Ringgold was the site of a big gold strike, but that was some time ago. The vein played out and the crash damn near finished the town. The lead mines kept us from going under and the cattle boom brought us back. The Glint River Valley is top grazing land and the railroad allows ranchers to ship their livestock to market. Cattle is the true wealth of Ringgold."

"If gold's been found in these parts before, it can happen again," Sixkiller said, putting on a front of stubbornness, stubborn as only a gold seeker can be.

"I don't want to discourage you. Maybe you'll be the lucky one. Let's drink to it. Success and good fortune!" Westbrook passed the flask and they each had another drink, emptying it.

"The well has run dry," he said ruefully.

"Let me get settled in and I'll buy you a drink," Sixkiller offered.

"Most hospitable of you. Where are you staying?'

"I heard the Atlas is pretty good."

"It's acceptable enough. Heading there now? I'll be glad to show you the way. I've got to refill anyway so I'll just nip into the Jackpot, our most fashionable watering hole. The drinks aren't watered down, the girls are clean and good-looking, and the games of chance are straight, which means you have a chance however slim." Westbrook grinned.

"Like prospecting, eh?" Sixkiller said with a sly smile.

"You said it, not me."

They set off east on Liberty.

"Where do you hail from, Quinto?"

"I've been doing some prospecting in the Bitter Creek area. Slim pickings, so I thought I'd try my luck hereabouts. If the Lonesome Hills don't pan out, I'll keep on heading north to the Black Hills. They're proven gold-rich and might still yield a strike. But first I'll give the Glint River Valley a try."

"I wish you luck," Westbrook said. "What's new in Bitter Creek? Always on the lookout for news. Gunfights, floods, droughts, it's all grist for my mill."

"News? Not much happens in Bitter Creek. Every now and then some renegade Arapahos or bandits jump a prospector, but you're more likely to get killed by another prospector who figures you made a strike. I saw no color, no flash of that yellow gold so I decided to pack up stakes and try my luck here."

"Well, who knows? Ringgold may pan out for you yet."

"Never can tell."

They came to the Atlas Hotel, a modest two-story, wooden-frame building with a veranda bordering three sides of the building. The structure was white-painted with green trim on moldings, doors, window frames, and cornices.

They went inside.

Sixkiller looked around. The place was clean without making a fetish out of it, though a tad rundown at the edges. He crowded the front desk, filling the clerk's field of vision with his big frame.

The desk clerk flinched. He was balding, with his remaining hair cropped close to the scalp. He had bushy eyebrows and a neat mustache. He flinched as Sixkiller crowded the front desk, his big form filling the clerk's field of vision with his physically imposing presence. "Ah . . . yes, sir?" the clerk said.

"A room, please," Sixkiller said.

The clerk fiddled with the register, opening it while muttering to himself, running his finger down a column of names. He seemed distinctly unhappy. "We're awfully full right now, very busy."

Westbrook put himself forward, smoothly interceding. "Mr. Quinto is a friend of mine and the *Banner*'s, Bert. I'm sure you can find some accommodations for him."

Bert looked relieved to see a friendly face and was reassured that someone he knew and respected vouched for the big stranger. "Oh! Didn't see you standing there, Reeve. When you put it that way, the Atlas is always ready to extend its hospitality to any friend of yours, of course—"

"Something in front, looking down on the street," Sixkiller interrupted.

"Sure you don't want a room in the back of the house? It's a lot quieter," Bert said.

"I like to watch the comings and goings."

"Very well sir, how long will you be staying with us?"

Sixkiller paid a week in advance. "Got a place I can stow my rifle? I'm used to it. I'd hate to have to replace it if it got stolen."

"The Atlas is not a haunt of sneak thieves," Bert said stiffly, giving him the key for room 203.

"Sure, but crime never sleeps. Theft happens in the best hotels."

"We've got a storeroom here behind the desk. It's locked. Only the manager, that's me, and the night clerk have the keys." Bert reached under the counter and retrieved a tag with numbers on two halves. He tore it in two, fixing one half to the rifle and handing the other half to Sixkiller. "Here's your check. Just present this to me or the night clerk to retrieve your rifle. We also have a safe if you have any valuables or funds to secure."

"Just the rifle. The rest I'll look after myself," Sixkiller said.

Bert used a key to unlock the storeroom door and went inside with the rifle. The space was an overgrown windowless closet, long and narrow with storage shelves lining both walls. Sitting against the rear wall was a short, square, combination safe, black and rough as a cast-iron skillet, squatting on four stubby legs. He put the rifle on a shelf and came out, locking the door.

"Much obliged," Sixkiller said, hefting his saddlebags. "I can find my way, thanks."

Like most stopping places in the West, there were no bellhops at the Atlas, the prevailing attitude being that the guests could carry their own damned bags.

"I'll stow my gear in my room and be right down, then we'll go get that drink," Sixkiller told Westbrook.

"Or ten. I'll pass the time shooting the breeze with Bert here."

Sixkiller climbed the stairs to the second floor. He unlocked the door to room 203 and went in, entering a small modest room with a stuffy musty smell. He could tell in a glance that the narrow bed with the square-shaped wooden bedstead would be too short to fit him unless he slept curled up on his side all night. It was a problem he ran into a lot. He knew he'd wind up putting the mattress on the floor and sleeping there.

He opened the windows partway to air out the room. He had a couple clean shirts and pairs of socks in his saddlebags, also a shaving kit and some personal items, but he could put them away later. They'd keep. He could use a bath, but his attitude was *What's the rush?*

He had a quart bottle of red whiskey in one

of the saddlebags. Thirsty, he took a couple long pulls from it.

He looked around the room. It was wide-open to any thief or prowler who really wanted to get in. He reckoned the Atlas probably didn't harbor too many sneak thieves. Prowlers and snoops wanting to get a line on him by searching his belongings, that was a different story.

Well, let them look. His gear was clean of any telltales to betray his real identity and the purpose of his mission. Let them prowl. Nothing they could use to get a handle on him, on who he really was.

He went out, locking the door behind him. He crossed the landing, went downstairs.

Westbrook stood leaning across the front desk, an elbow on the counter, as he chatted with Bert. He saw Sixkiller enter the lobby. "All squared away? Let's go. See you, Bert."

Sixkiller and Westbrook went out. The sun was low in the west.

"Where to?" Sixkiller asked.

"The Jackpot Saloon is across the street. That's the one I was telling you about before," Westbrook said.

"It's a go."

They walked west on Market into the strong bright rays of the setting sun. Entering the open square of the intersection, they were hit by a gust of north wind sweeping grit and street dirt with it. Sixkiller put a hand—not his gun hand—on his tall-crowned hat to keep it from being blown off.

"You're going to need a shorter hat. This one's like a sail in a stiff wind," Westbrook said.

"I like this one," Sixkiller said with characteristic stubbornness.

"Suit yourself."

"I usually do."

The Jackpot Saloon was a big impressive place, a two-story structure fronting south with its long walls on the north and south. It was painted tan with dark brown trim and had dark green window shades. Twin bow windows with fancy gridded square panes flanked the arched front entrance. The hitching posts were already fully lined with horses, running the full length of the long front wall.

"Doing a land-office business," Sixkiller said, "and it's early yet."

"Mason Rourke's place. He's a high-stakes gambler who's run gambling houses in Colorado Springs, Denver, and Silver City. A good hand with a gun who's killed his man—plenty of them. Mase setting up on a big scale like this is a real vote of confidence in Ringgold."

Westbrook pronounced *Mase* so that it sounded like *mace*, the kind of war club you use to knock somebody's brains out, thought Sixkiller.

They went inside. There was a long bar with a brass foot rail, tables and chairs, a dance floor, a modest stage, and a jumbo gambling area with wheels, keno, faro, and poker tables. The place was fairly well filled, but not yet roaring.

The saloon girls were outfitted in black lace and purple satin dresses that showed plenty of flesh. A group of them immediately fastened their eagle eyes on Sixkiller and Westbrook, but most circulated and mingled among the crowd, making the rounds of "sociable" drinkers to encourage them to be more sociable and drink more.

"High-toned place. No sawdust on the floor," Sixkiller said, looking around.

"That's Mase Rourke for you. He lives it high, wide, and handsome," Westbrook said. "The Jackpot is an oasis of civilization in the desert wastes of Wyoming Territory."

"You should put that in your paper."

"I did."

The two men sat down at a table.

Several saloon girls started toward them, a tall long-legged brunette elbowing her sisters aside to come swooping down on the table. "Reeve Westbrook, my favorite scribbler! You're in early tonight," the brunette said.

"Brenda, darling," Westbrook said.

Brenda was in her mid-twenties with long, raven's-wing black hair pinned up at the top of her head. She was attractive, but hard. She'd been around. Her features were perhaps a tad too sharp, the eyes too narrow and calculating. Small hard lines bracketed a ripe, red-painted mouth. But she was slender, supple, high-breasted, and long-legged. A red satin ribbon with cameo brooch was worn as a choker around her long, swanlike neck.

Brenda looked Sixkiller over, her eyes widening with real or affected astonishment. "Lord, he's a big one! Who's your oversized friend, Reeve?"

"Brenda, meet Quinto. Quinto, meet Brenda," Westbrook said, taking care of the introductions.

"Glad to know you, Brenda," Sixkiller said with real enthusiasm.

"You'll be even gladder when you get to know me better," Brenda said, winking saucily. "What'll you have, gents? Name your poison!"

"A bottle of redeye and two glasses," Westbrook said.

"That'll do for me, but what'll you have to drink?" Sixkiller said, not entirely joking.

"Make that two bottles and two glasses," Westbrook said, laughing . . . but meaning it, too.

"Why bother with glasses when you can drink it straight from the bottle?" Brenda asked.

"A single word my dear, and one not often heard in Ringgold. *Class*," Westbrook replied.

Brenda flounced away to fill the order.

"A spicy morsel, Brenda. Tasty, but a trifle on the tough side," Westbrook said breezily.

"Saloon gal's got a hard life. Got to make her

way in the world," Sixkiller said. "If she's too soft, she won't last long."

"It could be worse," Westbrook said, waving aside the other's observation. "The girls here are *saloon* girls, not prostitutes. They don't have to sleep with the customers. They just have to hustle them into drinking more and spending all their money."

"Not sleep with the customers? I'm not sure I like that," Sixkiller joked.

"No, they don't have to sleep with the clientele . . . unless they want to. If they do, Rourke makes it easy for them. Rooms are available upstairs and he splits the profits with them."

"Sounds fair."

"If it's a sure thing you're looking for, Quinto, then it's the Paradise Club you want. The girls there are all out-and-out whores. Of course, it's also a pretty sure thing you'll catch a disease from them."

"I'm not that hard up for female companionship, amigo." Sixkiller slapped a ten-dollar coin down on the table. "When it comes to whiskey, though, I'm buying. This ought to cover us for a while."

"No, no. You're my guest," Westbrook demurred, not very forcefully.

Sixkiller stood by his offer in a gruff but friendly way.

"Well . . . since you insist," Westbrook conceded. "Thanks. I appreciate it. It's not easy to get along on a newspaperman's salary. The *Banner* doesn't even pay enough for me to drink myself to death."

"When the ten dollars runs out, you can buy the next round," Sixkiller said.

"The next round! I like that," Westbrook said, laughing. "I have a feeling we're going to get along fine, Quinto."

"Hell, ain't that what we've been doing?"

Brenda returned, carrying a tray on which was set two bottles of whiskey and two glass tumblers. She set them out on the table. "What, no water for a chaser?" she teased.

"Water?! Too dangerous! You never know what's in that stuff," Sixkiller said, mock-shuddering.

Brenda scooped up the gold coin.

"Keep the change," Sixkiller said, playing it big.

"Thanks, sport!" Brenda leaned in. "I'll give you fair warning, big man. Don't underestimate Reeve here. He may be a skinny galoot who looks like a stiff gust of wind would blow him away, but he can really soak up the hooch. I'm not joking. If you're not careful, he'll drink you under the table."

"In the unlikely event that happens, you'll know where to find me," Sixkiller said. "Come on down and join me."

"Careful. I might take you up on that offer."

"Quit pestifying, Brenda, and let us get down to some serious drinking," Westbrook said.

Brenda stuck her tongue out at him and went away.

The bottles were uncorked, each man filling his glass from his own bottle.

"Here's how," Westbrook said, raising his glass.

Sixkiller saluted. "Mud in your eye."

The first glasses were drained in a gulp. Sixkiller's shudder was not so mocking. Glasses were quickly refilled and quaffed, a pleasant warmth blossoming in the pit of Sixkiller's belly, spreading out to send white heat racing through his veins.

"You must know something about Ringgold, being a reporter and all," Sixkiller began.

"I like to think so," Westbrook said.

"Who's the top man? I mean, who runs the town?"

"Curious question coming from a man like you, who says he's just passing through, Quinto."

"I'll be in town for a few days and up in the hills for a few months, longer if I strike pay dirt. I always like to know who runs the show. It generally saves trouble all around."

"The mayor is Dawes Ivey. He fronts for the Western Territories lead mines so he's got plenty of pull. A big man in town, but not the only one. There's Mase Rourke, always a factor to consider, and on the lower end there's

Hickory Ned Hampton with his Paradise Club—the bucket of blood joint and outlaw roost." Westbrook drank some more and looked thoughtful, as if pondering the matter. "Cattle ranchers are the rising powers. Colonel Tim Donovan's the biggest of the big ranchers with his B Square B spread. A war hero and straight as an arrow.

"Harl Endicott's another coming man on the Glint. He heads the Highline outfit. The local wits call it 'the Highbinder,' but none dare say it to his face or to any of his riders. They're a bad bunch, more gun hands than ranch hands. Endicott's been crowding Colonel Tim pretty hard lately. A range war could break out any day between the two.

"And there's one more power that has to be taken into account on the Glint. That's Bart Skillern, the Utah Kid. The valley's thick with robbers and killers, but the Kid's gang is the wildest and woolliest of all. He's made life hell for the mine owners and big ranchers alike . . . although the inside is that Endicott's Highline ranch has been curiously free from Skillern's depredations. Make of that what you will, but you didn't hear it from me."

"Whew! Sounds like I'll be safer rock hunting in the hills than anywhere's else." Sixkiller paused, mulling over the players Westbrook had identified.

"Of course, a prospector's got to walk soft

with eyes open. There's always plenty of rannies looking to dry-gulch him for his outfit and horse, especially out in the brush where there's no law and no witnesses."

"That's right," Westbrook agreed. "Why, not long ago a whole party of gold hunters disappeared up in the hills. Vanished without a trace.

They were headed by Dennis Bletchley, a titled English lord no less. I interviewed him when he first came to town. He was looking to get in on the cattle boom, but then he got bitten by the gold bug, some Lost Gold Mine razzle-dazzle."

"I do believe I've heard tell of some such story," Sixkiller said, too casually. "That's the Frenchman Woods-runner's Lost Gold Mine, no?"

Westbrook burst out laughing. "Oh no! Don't tell me you've fallen for that old chestnut, Quinto!"

"I've heard the legend, sure. What prospector hasn't?"

"Then you should know that hoary old myth's long been exploded. Men have been hunting for that mine for a hundred years without finding a trace of it."

"That don't mean it ain't there, only that it ain't been found. Must be something to it to set all those folks searching for all those years."

"That's what they said about the Fountain

of Youth, El Dorado, and the Seven Cities of Gold, too."

"Hell, Westbrook, that Lord Somebody you was talking about must've thought there was something to it or he wouldn't have been after it."

"Sure, and look what happened to him," Westbrook said.

"What did happen to him?" Sixkiller asked.

"Who knows?" Westbrook shrugged. "Search parties were unable to turn up any sign of Bletchley and his party, over a dozen souls in all. Dead, of course, but nobody knows who, how, or where."

"Somebody knows—the killers."

Westbrook nodded. "It was quite a sensation for a while. Sold a whole lot of extras of the *Banner*. Lord Dennis was twice crazy. He was an aristocrat and a foreigner. In the end, he came a long way to die."

"But I can take care of myself," Sixkiller said dryly.

"If you think you can find the Lost Gold Mine, you need a keeper," Westbrook scoffed.

They drank some more. While they'd been talking, the room had gotten noisier and noisier, forcing them to talk progressively louder to be overheard. Like the buzzing of a fly that keeps circling closer and closer to a man's head, the clamor nudged its way into Sixkiller's awareness. He looked up for the source of the disturbance.

He did not have to look far.

Seated at a nearby table was a clutch of hard-looking cowboys, a half-dozen or more. They sized up as a pretty rough bunch, shifty-eyed, whiskey-guzzling, cigar-smoking rowdies with their gun belts worn low. At the epicenter of the racket was a big man and big noisemaker, "a real stampeder" in the argot of the West. He was a head taller than his fellows, themselves large-sized.

He wore a black leather vest studded with silver conchas and black leather batwing chaps. His head was seemingly almost as wide as it was long. Bushy black eyebrows met in the center of his forehead, forming a uni-brow. Blue-black beard stubble bristled on his granite chin and jutting jaw.

The big fellow was hitting the whiskey hard, starting to get well-oiled. He showed all the signs of a man setting out on a mighty big tear. Everything about him was outsized. When he talked, he bellowed. When he laughed, he roared, drowning out his raucous fellow booze hounds.

Sixkiller frowned, a reaction not unnoticed by Westbrook.

He smiled slyly. "That's Bull Raymond, one of our leading local personalities. You've heard the expression, Bull of the Woods? That's our

Bull, the champion scrapper and fist fighter in the valley.

"Nobody's ever whipped him in a bare-knuckle brawl and most of those who've tried have never been the same since. He can shoot, too. He's killed five men of the valley in gun-fights and they were all fair duels."

"Loud son of a gun," Sixkiller said.

Chapter Eight

Bull Raymond got drunker and louder by the minute.

"Looks like Mase is keeping a weather eye on Bull." Westbrook indicated a silver-haired man with a thin, iron-gray mustache standing off to one side conferring with a couple burly Jackpot staffers. The man wore a gray suit and a gun belt.

The ever-more frequent glances Rourke cast in Bull's direction were cold-eyed and disapproving. His sidemen were grim-faced and apprehensive.

"Bull's off his bailiwick," Westbrook went on. "The Paradise Club is his usual haunt. He must have come into some money. He used to be a top hand for Donovan's B Square B ranch until Colonel Tim fired him for drunkenness and brawling. It's been pretty slim pickings for Bull ever since, although it's an open secret that he's taken to rustling. He's said to wield a mean running iron, and is not afraid to poach on any of the big ranchers, but he's got a special grudge against Colonel Tim."

Bull suddenly pushed back his chair and stood up.

"Here he goes," Westbrook said.

Bull whipped off his sombrero-style hat and whirled it in circles over his head while venting an ear-splitting cowboy yell. "I'm a ripsnorting, fire-breathing, earth-stomping, maverick longhorn!" He launched into his big brag.

"He must be from Texas," Sixkiller said sourly.

"Yes, but how did you know?" Westbrook asked.

"Of all the loud braggarts in the world, Texans are the loudest." Sixkiller, a native son of Oklahoma, harbored a natural-born antipathy for the neighboring Lone Star State and its denizens.

Bull's cronies urged him on. "You go, Bull! Damned right, Bull!" came the cries.

"I rope twisters, wrassle grizzly bears, and use prairie fires to light my see-gars!" Bull declared. "I'm a lover, a fighter, a wild horse rider! Strong men cry when they see me coming and pretty women cry when they see me leaving!"

Sixkiller rose. He tilted the bottle to his lips, draining the last few mouthfuls of whiskey. He set the empty down on the table and wiped his mouth with the back of his hand. He took off his hat, handing it to Westbrook. "Take care of this. I don't want to get it dented."

Westbrook gaped, openmouthed, eyes bulging. "What are you going to do?!"

"I hate Texas loudmouths."

"Wait a minute you're not going to—"

Sixkiller walked away, angling toward Bull's table.

"I guess he is at that," Westbrook said, bemused.

Bull had been going on uninterrupted, not even pausing for breath, and was still going strong. "I can out-fight, out-shoot, out-ride, and out-talk any hombre west of the Mississippi . . . or east of it, for that matter! Ain't a man in the territory with the guts to lock horns and butt heads with me! I use the lightning for a lasso and the storm for a bronc. I come to town to hoot and honk!"

Sixkiller shouldered his way through the cluster of Bull's cronies and was none too gentle about it. They were hard-headed, horny-handed hombres not used to being pushed around, but when they got a good look at Sixkiller they decided not to push back.

"Bull will handle it," one muttered under his breath.

A path opened for Sixkiller at the end of which stood Bull Raymond.

Bull caught sight of the newcomer closing on him and seemed more surprised than anything else. "Something you want, stranger?" he demanded.

"Yeah," Sixkiller said. "Shut the hell up." It was simply a flat-voiced declaration that was a command, not a request. No yelling, no shouting, Sixkiller's remark was underlined by a short stiff right-handed jab that cracked a fist against the blunt point of Bull's chin.

Bull's head snapped back. His mighty frame was rocked, but not to the extent that he was forced to take a step back. He threw an allover shudder like a wet dog shaking off water.

Silence fell over the saloon, then scattered gasps could be heard.

A trickle of blood ran down Bull's chin from a split lower lip. His eyes lit up with genuine delight. "Mister, you showed up just in time. I was starting to get bored."

"A man can't drink in peace with all that bellowing of yours," Sixkiller said.

"No? What do you aim to do about it?"

"I just did it."

"If that's the best you can do, you're in trouble, hoss."

"That? My hand was itching. That was my way of scratching it."

"I know you?" Bull asked, puzzled.

"Nope." Sixkiller shook his head.

"And you don't know me, because if you did you'd have rode a thousand miles to get shucked of me. Man, you must be a stranger. None of these rannies in town have got the guts to buck Bull Raymond. You got guts—no brains, but guts—I'll give you that. Who are you? I mean, what's your name? We'll need something to carve on the marker of your grave on Boot Hill."

"The name's Quinto."

"You some kind of Injun? You look it," Bull said. "You should've laid off the firewater, Chief, it'll be the death of you."

"There you go, jawing again. You gonna fight or talk me to death?" Sixkiller asked.

"Just satisfying my natural curiosity. I hate to break a man's back without even knowing his name."

Sixkiller sighed. "Let's get to it before you get to running your mouth again. Anything's better than that. It makes my ears hurt."

"Don't you worry about that. I'm gonna rip 'em both off. Then I'm gonna tear out your spine and whip you into little pieces with it." Bull started forward.

A fair-minded onlooker stepped between the two. "Best shuck off those gun belts, men. Let's keep it a friendly fight."

"That suits me fine. Nothing I like better than taking a man apart with my bare hands."

Bull unbuckled his gun belt, handing it to one of his cronies.

Sixkiller took off his gun belt, never taking his eyes off Bull.

Worried, Westbrook moved into the inner circle. "I hope you know what you're doing."

"You're not getting out of buying the next round that easily," Sixkiller told him.

The crowd was excited. A fight was real entertainment, though with Bull Raymond as one of the participants it was not likely to last long, and neither was the mystery challenger. There were few sources of excitement in Ringgold and fewer that came for free.

More people were gathering to see the fight than had been present before Sixkiller first socked Bull. Word had spread fast.

Before the two could begin butting heads, Rourke pushed his way to the fore, bolstered by a handful of sidemen. He was careful not to get between the two combatants. His silver hair lay across his scalp neat and orderly, like a seamless metal skullcap. Not a hair was out of place. His cold green eyes were the color of the sea on a sunless day. "Hold it!" he barked. "If you want to fight that's your business, but you're not going to do it in the Jackpot—"

Bull put his head down, charging. Sixkiller rushed to meet him.

And the fight was on.

The crowd roared its delight as the two collided with a meaty thud. Sixkiller got his left shoulder under Bull's reaching arms, driving it into the other's midsection. It was like slamming into a tree trunk.

Bull's brawny arms churned massive uppercuts toward Sixkiller's middle. Sixkiller blocked them with his forearms held close to his body, absorbing the blows and fending them off. He couldn't move his arms without opening himself to rib-crushing blows from Bull's rocklike fists.

Sixkiller sidestepped, hooking a wicked left to Bull's jaw. The two broke apart for an instant, a man's length between them. Bull seemed unhurt by the blow.

Sixkiller's left fist hurt, and he realized he could ruin his hands hammering away uselessly at Bull's hard head without making a dent in it.

They mixed it up some more, trading punches. Bull threw wild haymakers that would have torn Sixkiller's head off his neck if they'd connected. He managed a glancing blow to the side of Sixkiller's head, which felt like the kick of a mule. Sixkiller saw stars.

A couple inches shorter than Sixkiller's six feet four inches, Bull was wider, thicker in the shoulders and upper body. He seemed to have no neck, his shoulder muscles starting right below the ears, so that his head was perched atop a pyramid of muscle. He outweighed Sixkiller by forty to fifty pounds, none of it fat. He was fast-moving, surprisingly quick.

He grinned, showing a massive set of choppers that would have done a horse proud. He was having fun.

The battlers circled each other, looking for an opening. Bull shuffled forward, lashing out with a looping roundhouse right.

Sixkiller bobbed his head out of the way, saving his skull from a sure cave in, the breeze of the punch fanning his face.

Bull followed up with a powerhouse left. He was a big puncher, putting all he had into each swing.

Sixkiller stopped Bull's advance with a series of short snappy jabs to the head, stinging Bull, but nothing more. He struck around the eyes, trying to open up a cut to obstruct the braggart's vision. One punch connected with Bull's nose, squashing it flat, blood spurting. But that was nothing new. The nose showed signs of having been broken any number of times.

Sixkiller backed into a table, rocking it. Bull rushed, driving into him. They locked up again, grappling, struggling for holds. Bull's superior weight forced Sixkiller back, upsetting the table and chairs. Bottles and tumblers flew, sounding the jingle of breaking glass.

Sixkiller fired a flurry of pile-drivers into Bull's middle trying to soften him up, a ploy which proved an exercise in futility as the man encircled him in a bear hug, pinning his arms to his sides.

Bull locked the fingers of both hands together, interlacing them for a tighter grip. He squeezed, pouring it on. Tremendous viselike pressure was exerted on Sixkiller whose ribs would have cracked if not for the cushioning of his arms.

Bull lifted Sixkiller so that his feet left the floor.

Danger! Bull could slam him into something hard . . . to break his back against it.

But Bull whisked him across the floor in a dizzying rush.

Sixkiller head butted Bull, striking with the hard, horny, upper ridge of his forehead along the hairline where the bone structure was thick. Sixkiller was an accomplished "nutter" in street fighting parlance.

The head butt squashed Bull's already tormented nose. Bull roared, staggered by blinding pain. The crushing force of his grip slackened.

Sixkiller got his thumbs under Bull's rib cage and dug in hard. His pinioned arms lacked freedom to deliver the crippling strike at full force, but it still hurt.

Bull's interlocked hands faltered and Sixkiller broke free. He grabbed Bull's arm by the wrist and swung him around like a kid's game of crack the whip. But this was no game. It was real—a deadly matter of life and death.

Sixkiller swung Bull in a circle and suddenly let go. Like the last man in line in crack the whip, Bull went flying. He pitched forward, bent almost double, tree-trunk legs churning.

Unable to keep up with the impetus of his flying feet, Bull was propelled into a human wall of frenzied spectators ringing the combat. He cannonballed into them, scattering them like bowling pins.

Bad luck for them, but good luck for him, they halted his momentum. Instead of crashing headfirst into a wall of wood, stone, and plaster, cushiony flesh and blood absorbed the impact.

Shouts and shrieks sang out from the tangle of arms and legs, of struggling squalling bodies. On top of the pile, Bull rolled clear, bounding to his feet.

Sixkiller was glad of the opportunity to suck wind, grabbing a few heaving breaths, each one sending fresh aches and pains through bruised ribs.

He'd wanted to get Bull mad because angry fighters were losing fighters. Well, he had succeeded all right. Bull was mad clear through.

Wild-eyed, with squashed nostrils bubbling blood whenever he forgot to breathe through his mouth, Bull's lungs worked like bellows, his massive chest heaving.

Sixkiller started for him, Bull coming to meet him.

Shots were fired!

Rourke was pretty damned mad himself, venting a stream of fiery oaths. He fired several more shots into the ceiling to get the fighters' attention. Gunfire competed with the uproar of shouting spectators whooping it up, yelling and hollering with each punch and counterpunch.

Rourke shouted, "Take it outside, damn you!"

They took it outside, all right.

Locked up, Sixkiller wrestled Bull around, propelling him toward one of the bay windows bracketing the front entrance. Bull held tight to his opponent.

Gawkers pressed up close to the window saw the duo coming at them and scattered for the sidelines just in time.

Sixkiller was moving at a pretty good clip when Bull's broad back hit the window made of small squares of glass, impacting it like a battering ram. When the two massive bodies hit the window head-on something had to give.

A *whoomping* sound as of a muffled explosion was followed by a cascading torrent of glass shards and broken wooden ribs bursting outward.

Sixkiller tucked his head down, snuggling chin to chest to protect against getting his throat cut by broken glass. He squeezed his eyes shut for protection, if only for an instant.

Each clutching the other with a death grip the two combatants went through the broken window to fall crashing to the wooden plank sidewalk fronting the saloon. They grappled, rolling around on the boardwalk atop broken glass and busted wood, tearing at each other. Bull clawed at Sixkiller's face, Sixkiller punched Bull in the head and ribs. First one was on top, then the other.

Commotion erupted from the horses lining the hitching rail, spooked by the sudden melee. They fought to break free, uprearing, sidling, straining against their tethered reins. Some reins snapped, and the horses ran wild and free.

Sixkiller and Bull rolled off the edge of the boardwalk into the street, hitting the ground with a *whoof*. Lucky to avoid being trampled as they rolled clear of the remaining horses, they kept at it, rolling and tumbling, hammering at each other.

Patrons and owner of the Jackpot poured out to watch the rest of the fight. It also attracted passersby. They came running, shouting, "Fight! Fight!" Excited mongrel dogs ran along, barking and nipping at the flashing legs of excited runners.

Sixkiller and Bull somehow managed to stand on their knees. The Oklahoman hurled a one-two combination that knocked Bull back down to the ground, then struggled to his feet in a crouch. Bull heaved himself upright. Both men were dead beat. Nothing took it out of men like mixing it up in all-out knockdown fight.

"Might as well make hay when the sun shines," Rourke told himself, true to his gambler's vocation. He and his sidemen started taking bets on the fight.

Ordinarily the odds would have highly favored Bull, but the fight had pretty much evened up, though the hometown boy was still the favorite on points. The Jackpot gamblers handled lots of action, the sporting element thrilled by the novelty of something fresh and unexpected to bet on. Lots of money was clenched in excited fists as the wagering went on.

Citizens made small side bets among themselves.

The fighters closed once more. Bull played it tricky, holding back and feigning weakness to lure in his opponent, then lashing out with a brutal kick aimed at Sixkiller's knee.

Sixkiller stalled, laying back at the last second and the kick missed, leaving Bull off balance. Plowing into him, Sixkiller straightened Bull up with some stiff left jabs to the chin, getting him into position. He thrust in with a fierce knuckle punch to the solar plexus of the other. That blow told.

Bull paled under his deep tan, mouth widening into a sucking O shape. He looked green around the gills.

Giving Bull not a moment's—not a second's—

respite, Sixkiller crowded him with a flurry of hard rights and lefts to the breadbasket.

The formerly rock-hard midsection had been well softened up. Bull backpedaled, purely on the defensive. His guard failing, he let through more punches than he parried.

Sixkiller steered Bull toward a street-side watering trough and moved in for the kill. His right shoulder dipping, he launched a sizzling right hand, putting much of his weight behind it. Walnut-sized knuckles cracked home against the point of Bull's jaw.

Whiplash! Bull's head snapped back from the blow, the rest of him following. Arms windmilling, he toppled backward into the horse trough, raising a waterspout.

He tried to rise, but couldn't. Draped across the trough at right angles, body in a V-shape with his hindquarters submerged in the tank, he just lay there.

Sixkiller sank to his knees, head held high. He closed his eyes, unsure how much time passed—a heartbeat or a minute.

When he opened his eyes he was looking into the twin bores of a double-barreled shotgun pointed down at his head. It was in the hands of a man with a badge.

The big brawl was officially over.

The law had arrived.

Chapter Nine

"I'm of no mind to mix it up with you two," Marshal Braddock said. "Cut up and I'll cut loose with this scattergun. You think this is a bluff, call it."

Braddock and two deputies had Sixkiller and Bull covered. They had a clear field of fire if they had to open up and start blasting.

A mighty yellow-bellied way of breaking up a fistfight, Sixkiller thought, but he kept his opinions to himself. Braddock struck him as a hard man with a mean mouth.

"I'd just as soon shoot as not," Braddock went on. "Life's hard enough in Ringgold without a couple damned troublemakers trying to bust up the town."

He was playing to the crowd, but that came with the job of town marshal, Sixkiller thought. He kept his mouth shut on that score, too, saying only, "I'll go quietly, Marshal."

"Damned right you will."

Sixkiller meant it. Scrapping with Bull had taken a hell of a lot out of him and his capacity for raising more hell was pretty much nil. He was glad of the rest.

Not to mention that looking down those shotgun double barrels put a man in a more reasonable frame of mind.

Apparently Bull felt the same way, for he went along without kicking or complaint.

Sixkiller rose, forcing himself to his feet. It was a hardship to get there and another to stay upright. He noted a tendency to veer off-center from the strictly vertical plumb line.

None of the lawmen offered to lend a hand.

Well, why should they?

Bull labored to haul himself out of the horse trough, rank streams of water that smelled none too good running off him. But then, Bull hadn't been over-fragrant to start with.

Titters and smirks from the crowd were instantly stifled when the amused ones came under the glare of Bull's wicked red eyes. He rubbed his face with open hands, trying to restore feeling in it. "Lucky for you the law showed up when it did. Saved you from a beating," Bull said to Sixkiller.

Sixkiller laughed at him. It hurt when he laughed, it hurt when he didn't. He was hurting all over, but damned if he'd let on and show weak.

"Shut up, the both of you. I'm in no mood for any nonsense," Braddock said.

He and the two deputies readied to march Sixkiller and Bull off to jail. It was not much of a march on the part of the arrestees. They shambled and stumbled along like a pair of drunken bears walking upright on their hind legs.

No spectators laughed at the sight. They knew better.

Mase Rourke watched the brawlers go, his cold eyes looking down his long straight nose at them. He stood with fists on hips, his attitude seeming to say, *Hanging's too good for them.*

Sixkiller couldn't blame the gambler. After all, it was his place that had gotten busted up. The money his henchmen were collecting from the many side bets they'd taken seemed unable to ease his pain.

An argument was starting.

"Come on, pay up. Your man lost," a Rourke staffer said.

"Says who?" the bettor demanded.

"You bet on Bull. He lost."

"That's your story. They didn't fight to a finish. The marshal broke it up first, so there ain't no winner or loser."

"The stranger whupped Bull *before* Braddock showed up."

"Bull had plenty of fight left in him. He'd've climbed out of that horse tank and given that other fellow what-for—"

"Quit chiseling. Anybody could see Bull had had it!"

Similar heated disputes sparked through the sporting crowd. The issue was sure to be a bone of contention.

The law and its prisoners left the scene behind, the entire group proceeding down the middle of the street. Wagons, riders, and pedestrians made way for them.

Sixkiller was feeling mighty shaky, a mass of aches and pains. His head hurt, each step he took making it hurt worse. Still, there was nothing for it but to keep picking his feet up and putting them down. It stirred up distant memories of when he had been on the raggedy-ass end of some of the forced marches he'd taken as a soldier in the army during the late war.

The jail was only a couple blocks away, but it seemed a lot longer.

The jailhouse was a square-built, one-story, stone-walled structure. Once inside, Braddock and the deputies kept their guns trained on Sixkiller and Bull while compelling the two to turn out their pockets to be relieved of their possessions.

Bull yielded a clasp knife with bone handles and a six-inch blade.

Sixkiller turned over his poke, a rawhide

pouch that held some gold coins and a wad of greenbacks. Braddock seemed mighty interested in Sixkiller's belongings.

Let him look, the Oklahoman thought. There was nothing on him to give away his true identity or his mission in Ringgold. No badges, warrants, papers, documents, train ticket stubs, baggage claims—nothing. He was too sure a hand in the sleuthing game to make a rookie mistake like that.

A slim, envelope-sized, leather case containing his U.S. deputy marshal's badge and a few important papers was stashed in a secret pouch hidden within his saddle stowed at Noble's livery stable.

The dodge had its drawbacks. His credentials often smelled of horse sweat, an embarrassing situation when he had to identify himself to some high mucky-muck in the law enforcement line. But that was better than a bullet in the head for being found out as an undercover investigator by the wrong parties.

Sixkiller was glad he'd hidden the gold coins he'd taken from Harper and Freedy in the secret saddle compartment instead of carrying them around with them. There weren't too many of those shiny, newly-minted, fifty-dollar gold pieces floating around and he didn't want to be linked with anything connected to the dead ambushers.

He also didn't know if Braddock was honest

or not, and even if he was there wcrc his two deputies to be concerned about. One local lawman might be honest, maybe even two, but three out of three honest lawmen in a town like Ringgold?

Uh-uh. Nope, the odds were against it.

He guessed Deputy Chet Wheeler was about thirty years old. Of medium height, he was well built, with a shaggy sheepdog mop of golden hair. Deputy Kev Porrock looked to be in his early twenties. Tall, skinny, sharp-faced, he was a bit dull-eyed.

Sixkiller took inventory of his injuries. His face and head were numb from catching too many of Bull's punches. One was too many and he'd stopped more than that with his head. A big cut had opened up over one cheekbone, bleeding steadily. Bruised ribs ached but luckily—and it was luck as much as fighting skill—nothing was broken.

"Why don't you let him go?" Sixkiller queried, indicating Bull. His voice sounded funny, and he had trouble forming the words with his smashed mouth. "Bull didn't do nothing. I started it by punching him in the face."

"Hah! You call that a punch?" Bull taunted.

"Takes two to tangle," Braddock said. "Bull didn't have to fight."

"What was I supposed to do?" Bull demanded incredulously. "File a complaint?!"

"Technically, uh, yeah," Wheeler said.

"When somebody slugs me—and that don't happen too damned often—I slug back," Bull said.

"When somebody brawls within town limits, I arrest him," Braddock said.

Sixkiller looked around the office front of the jail. One wall was papered with WANTED posters and flyers. Prominently displayed was a reward poster of Bart Skillern, the Utah Kid—Wanted for Murder, Bank Robbery, Highway Robbery, Horse Theft, Rustling, Rape, and Passing Counterfeit Money.

No mention of the Bletchley party or the Kid's possible role in the disappearance of same, Sixkiller noted.

Wheeler put Bull's holstered gun into a tall, side drawer in the marshal's desk. He said, "Bet you'd like to get your hands on this shooting iron, eh Bull?"

"I'd like to get my hands on your neck," Bull growled.

"Threatening an officer of the law. That's a crime, ain't it?" Porrock said.

"He's already got enough charges to hold him," Braddock said matter-of-factly.

"What's all the fuss about a friendly little fight?" Bull asked.

"Shut up, Bull." This from Porrock.

"You're pretty tough behind that gun, ain't you, Marshal?" Sixkiller remarked.

"That's right," Braddock said, smiling thinly.

"You'd think I robbed a bank or something!"

"You busted up the Jackpot pretty good," Wheeler said, amused.

"The Highline bunch hoorah Ringgold and shoot up the town every Friday and Saturday night and you don't crack down on them," Bull countered.

"They didn't bust up Mase Rourke's place," Wheeler said.

"Or maybe you're scared of Endicott," Bull pressed.

"You're talking yourself into a broken jaw, Bull," Braddock said, starting to get sore.

"Who's gonna break it? You? That's a laugh." Bull indicated Sixkiller. "If *he* couldn't do it, you sure ain't gonna."

"I wasn't half trying," Sixkiller said, pouring oil on the fire.

"Both of you keep your traps shut," Braddock said briskly, businesslike, not rising to the bait. "A man gets mighty hungry in a jail cell if nobody feeds him. If you want to eat regular, quit flapping your gums."

Bull fell silent, giving Braddock a dirty look. He forked out a wad of greenbacks, plunking them down on the desk. The size of the wad raised eyebrows among the lawmen.

"Count it, Chet," Braddock said.

Wheeler was careful to keep out of the reach of Bull's gorilla-like arms as he scooped up the money and counted it. "One hundred and sixty-four dollars, Dick."

"Pretty good money for someone who hasn't done an honest day's work since he got fired off the B Square spread," Braddock commented.

"I saved my wages," Bull said, on the defensive.

"You drank up your wages on a two-day drunk right after Colonel Tim fired you," Porrock said.

"He didn't fire me. I quit."

That got a laugh from the three town lawmen.

"You seen it. They're stealing my money," Bull complained to Sixkiller.

"Nobody howls louder than a thief who gets robbed," Porrock smirked.

"I won it in a poker game!" Bull howled.

"Who with?" Braddock returned.

"I don't remember. I was too drunk."

"That I could almost believe—the part about being drunk that is, not the rest of your story."

"You got to prove it first."

"I'm holding the cash for safekeeping," Braddock said. "If it turns out not to be stolen or the product of unlawful activity, you'll get it back. More likely, it'll be credited toward paying off your fine and damages, which are liable to be considerable. Put it in an envelope, Chet."

Wheeler put the money in a brown paper envelope, writing Bull's name and the amount on the outside of it.

"You gonna give me a receipt for that ?" Bull sneered.

"You're just going to have to trust us, Bull," Wheeler said.

"Step back Bull, against the wall," Braddock said.

Bull complied.

The marshal focused his attention on Sixkiller as if seeing him for the first time. "I don't know you. Who are you?"

"The name's Quinto," Sixkiller said.

"Quinto what?"

"Just Quinto."

"Probably an alias," Porrock said importantly, with the air of one imparting some great revealed truth.

"No," Braddock said with dripping sarcasm.

Porrock's face reddened.

"You must be new in town," Braddock said,

"Just got here," Sixkiller confirmed.

"Didn't take you long to get into trouble."

"I'm a fast worker."

"Yeah? We don't like fast workers in Ringgold," the marshal said. "Why no gun?"

"Didn't think I'd need one. This seemed like such a peaceful town," Sixkiller said.

"Brother, you *must* be new in Ringgold!" Bull cracked, guffawing.

"What're you doing here, Quinto?"

"I'm a prospector, Marshal. Reckoned I'd work the Hills for that yellow gold."

"Nobody's struck gold there since the vein tapped out years ago!" Wheeler laughed.

"Hell, you're even dumber than Bull here, Chief!" Porrock snickered.

"You talk funny. You don't sound like you come from around here, Quinto. Where do you hail from?"

"Oklahoma Territory, Marshal."

Bull snorted, slapping his knees. "Oklahoma?! That figures!"

"You're a long way from home, Quinto," Braddock said.

"You should've stayed there," Porrock said.

"I go where the gold is," Sixkiller said.

"Nobody but a danged idjit would go gold hunting in the Hills."

"That ain't what I heard, Deputy."

"Yeah? What did you hear?"

"Everybody knows there was a gold hunting party in the Hills this summer," Sixkiller said.

"That's dangerous country," Braddock weighed in. "Lots of outlaws and renegade Indians up there." He studied Sixkiller. "You look like you got redskin blood in you, but I don't reckon the Arapahos will extend you any professional courtesy on that score."

"Maybe they'll only scalp you halfway," Porrock said. "The white half. Haw haw haw!"

"That's what you'd say if you didn't want anybody to find the gold," Sixkiller said.

"Why you danged fool!"

"Let it go, Kev. Some folks are just too damned dumb to listen to good advice," Wheeler said.

"You came to the wrong place, Quinto—for hunting gold and making trouble," Braddock said. "We don't like outsiders coming into our town to start trouble."

"Then what're you picking on me for?" Bull demanded. "I'm no outsider!"

"You, we just plain don't like, so shut up," Braddock said. He returned his attention to Sixkiller. "You in trouble with the law, Quinto? Wanted for anything?"

"Nope."

"What else is he gonna say?" Porrock scoffed.

"If he's wanted for anything, we'll have a flyer on him," Braddock said. "Meantime, he's not going anywhere."

Wheeler counted the money in Sixkiller's poke, then whistled. "Two hundred and thirty-four dollars! Whew!"

"No honest prospector makes that kind of money in these parts," Porrock accused.

"I didn't make it in these parts. I panned it out after a couple months on Bitter Creek," Sixkiller said.

"If that's true, it'll go toward paying your fine and costs, like with Bull here," Braddock said. "Fix it up the same way, Chet."

Wheeler put the money in an envelope with

Sixkiller's name and the total amount written on the outside.

Braddock put both envelopes in the cast-iron safe in the corner and locked it closed. "Nobody can say Dick Braddock doesn't run an honest jail."

He tossed a key ring to Porrock and picked up the shotgun, leveling it at the prisoners. "Lock 'em up."

Sixkiller and Bull were herded along a center aisle into the cell area and locked into separate side-by-side cells. Iron-barred doors clanged shut, the key turning in the locks, bolts thudding home.

"When do we get out of here?" Sixkiller asked.

"You'll go before the justice of the peace tomorrow morning at nine when court is in session," Braddock said. "Charges will be read and you'll say how you plead. As for getting out of here, that's up to the Justice Applewhite. But I'll give you a little tip. He's got no use for troublemakers, either."

The lawmen went up front into the office.

"Lucky for you they showed up when they did. I was just getting ready to lower the boom on you," Bull said.

Sixkiller's laughter was loud and insulting.

Chapter Ten

Sixkiller had been locked up before, mostly in the line of duty when his undercover roles required him to assume the guise of a lawbreaker—as he was doing in Ringgold. His strategy was called dynamiting.

There were two ways to fish. One was the usual, everyday way where you take a rod and line, bait your hook, and drop it where you think the fish will be biting. That's for someone with plenty of time on his hands.

The other way, well known to poachers and transgressors of fish and game laws, was to light a stick of dynamite, toss it in the pond, and let 'er rip. The blast killed or stunned all the fish and sent them floating to the surface for netting and collecting.

Both ways were good, but Sixkiller was in a hurry. He'd been away from his home grounds for some time and knew that in his absence the countless malefactors, owlhoots, and bad hats in the Nations would run wild, making his job that much harder on his return.

A certain type of investigator blends in with the crowd and goes about his business without anybody giving him so much as a second glance. Not Sixkiller. He wasn't built that way. His plan in Ringgold was to make a big splash and see what washed up from the bottom of the pool. He wanted to get under the town's skin and make his presence known. Westerners respected a fighting man. Tackling a tough hombre like Bull Raymond got him noticed fast and put him closer to the center of things, the heart of the action.

He hoped the powers in town would take notice. It could make him a target, but that was useful, too. He'd catch hold of whoever was trying to kill him and squeeze them to give up the next one in line. He'd climb the ladder till he found the top man.

Of course, he had to keep from getting killed along the way, but Sixkiller had confidence in his abilities to stay alive and win through all obstacles.

He'd wanted to question at least one of the ambushers at Powder Basin, but it hadn't worked out that way. That's how things went sometimes.

A night in jail could only further his plans, serving as a character recommendation to members of the lawless element. Unimpressed with the quality of law enforcement in Ringgold, he didn't intend to spend much time in the hoosegow. If worse came to worst, he'd break out.

Behind bars in an iron cage, the accommodations were minimal. A crude, wooden-framework bed with a straw mattress inside cloth ticking. A wooden bucket in a corner of the cell for sanitary purposes. A small rectangular window set high up in the stone wall, looking west.

Just for the hell of it he took hold of the vertical iron bars in the window, gripping one in each big hand. He tested their strength quietly, without making a fuss. He pulled on the bars, veins and tendons standing out on his massive forearms like snakes entwined around them. Muscles bunched up under his shirt, shifting and flexing. His face reddened, pencil-thin veins standing out at the sides of his forehead.

The bars were sunk deep in stone casement, top and bottom. He quivered with effort, the bars unmoving. Powdery stone dust sifted down from the top where the bars were implanted.

Sixkiller eased up, abandoning the effort. If necessary, he might be able to work the bars loose and climb out the window.

He looked out at Ringgold. The sun was low in the west, hidden behind a row of buildings. Beyond, lay a distant mountain range. Purple shadows were spreading east. The evening star twinkled.

He sat down on the edge of the bed. The

mattress was alive with insect pests, giving him something to watch to make the time pass.

Sixkiller was stoic with the patience of a hunter and an Indian. He'd kept long vigils in uncomfortable places to nab human or animal prey. He was good at waiting. He neither liked it nor despised it. Worrying at it didn't make the time go any faster so he made sure he had no feelings at all about it.

Bull, less patient, was the first to break the ice. "That was a pretty good fight, huh?"

Sixkiller grunted acknowledgment. "Not so bad at that."

"Maybe later we can pick up where we left off. See who's the better man."

"First, I want to see how much this one'll cost me."

"They're a bunch of soreheads," Bull said. "I didn't think Rourke would take it so hard. I thought he was bigger than that."

"Maybe he'll cool off after he's had time to think about it."

"Sure." After a pause, Bull said, "You think so?"

Sixkiller barked a single mirthless laugh. "I don't know. It's your town. You tell me."

"He's a sporting man, a gambler," Bull said, sounding unsure, as if trying to convince himself. "Hell, he likes a good fight."

"Maybe not in his place quite so much," Sixkiller pointed out.

"I'll tell you this. He didn't sic the law on

us. That ain't Rourke's style. He takes care of his own problems. Braddock probably came a-running to horn in and impress the town council with what a good job he's doing."

"Could be."

There was a silence, then Bull chuckled. "Braddock didn't want to mix it up with us."

"Those shotguns were mighty convincing," Sixkiller said.

"Easier to pull a shotgun on two unarmed men than go chasing some outlaws who'll shoot back at him."

"That's right."

"Ain't like horse stealing or robbing a stage-coach. Just a good clean fight, that's all."

"Reckon the judge'll see it like that?" Six-killer asked.

"We don't go before a judge. We'll get tried by Justice of the Peace Applewhite," Bull said, returning to reality. "There's a circuit judge comes to town 'bout every six weeks or so, but they use him for serious business—killings, holdups, and such. Justice of the peace handles the small stuff."

"What's he like?" Sixkiller asked.

"Applewhite? Prissy, whey-faced son of a gun. He's for the businessmen and the big ranchers, not the cowboy."

"That doesn't look so good for us."

"Oh, he's a fair man. He only fines you for every cent you got. We probably won't get no jail time. The town don't want to pay for our room and board and we ain't done nothing bad enough to get sent to the territorial prison."

"I need my money to kit up for prospecting. I had to leave my gear in Bitter Creek when I was running from some Arapahos. I need provisions—pans for panning gold, a pick and shovel, an ax, hammer and nails for making sluice boxes—and a pack horse to carry it all," Sixkiller said.

"Applewhite will empty your pockets of everything, but the lint in them," Bull said sourly. Then, confiding low-voiced, he went on. "You look like a wide-awake fellow, Quinto. A man can always get along on the Glint if he knows how to use a running iron and ain't too particular about whose strays he rounds up. I know plenty buyers who ain't too particular about where they get their beef from. Throw in with me and you can do all right for yourself. Build up a stake pretty quick."

"I'm a prospector not a cow puncher, but I'll keep it in mind, thanks. I'll tell you this. I'm not leaving the valley broke and with my tail tucked between my legs just because we had a little dustup."

"Now you're talking," Bull enthused.

"Much lawbreaking in Ringgold?" Sixkiller asked, taking a new tack.

"Are you kidding? The whole blamed valley's busting loose. A killing a day and more."

"I don't mind throwing a wide loop or working a running iron, but I ain't much for killing unless somebody's got it coming."

"I feel the same way," Bull said righteously.

"Ever think of taking up prospecting, Bull?"

"I ain't much for digging in the dirt, Quinto."

"Big money in it if you hit pay dirt," Sixkiller pointed out.

"*If*," Bull repeated. "You got to find the gold first, and that's a full-time job. You don't have to look too hard for cattle. They're all over the Glint, just begging to be rounded up, branded, and sold."

"Other people's cattle."

"Not after you steal them."

"You've got something there," Sixkiller allowed.

"Besides, there ain't no gold up in the hills," Bull said, pressing his advantage. "Braddock had the straight of that."

"What about that party of gold seekers that disappeared this summer? The Englishman? Sounds like he was on to something."

"Aw, that was just a wild goose chase. He was a loco foreigner cracked in the head."

"Crazy like a fox. A rich man like that don't just pack up and quit his castle and all the creature comforts of home to cross the sea and the Mississippi and the Rockies to come scratch dirt in Wyoming Territory on a hunch. He must've had some damned good information."

"Pshaw! Shows what you know about it," Bull said. "He was out here on a business trip looking to buy into some cattle ranching. Then somebody put a bee in his bonnet about the Lost Gold Mine and he went clear off his head with gold fever."

"You talk like somebody who knows."

"I seen him! I met him. Lord Dennis. That's how he was called."

"You don't tell me!"

"Swear to die," Bull solemnly declared. "It happened when I was working for Donovan at the B Square B. Lord Dennis came out to the ranch at Colonel Tim's invite, him and his whole crowd. They stayed overnight in the ranch house. Donovan threw 'em a big barbecue and party.

"There's some good hunting in the Black Mesa country at the edge of the B Square range. The colonel took Lord Dennis hunting for elk, bighorn sheep, and even mountain lions. The Englishman was crazy for hunting too, I'll give him that. I went along. I was Donovan's top man on the B Square.

"As for them creature comforts you was talking about, the Englishman did all right by himself, believe you me. You should've seen the outfit he was traveling with—a dozen people or more. He had his own cook with him and a couple flunky menservants and more trunks and bags than you ever did see."

Bull's voice went all raspy and husky. "Why, he even brought a couple fancy gals with him."

"Aw go on," Sixkiller said as if in disbelief, hoping to encourage the other to continue.

"It's the gospel truth," Bull declared. "His main woman was named Val something or something Val and man was she *something*! Another foreigner, only she was from Italy. She could speak good English, though. She was tricked out like a circus queen and built like a brick you-know-what, with a figure that'd make a fire-and-brimstone preacher put aside the Good Book and do bad."

"That's what I call traveling in style," Sixkiller said.

"He brought a couple other girls along for his pals in the party. They was only regular American whores, but damned good-looking. But that Val gal was something special, his own personal, private stock.

"Hell he had to have been loco to go scrabbling around in the hills looking for a lost mine when he could have been laying up in a feather bed with that beauty. I tell you, Quinto, you never seed the like!

"And where did it all get Lord Dennis?" Bull asked, sighing, shaking his shaggy head sadly. "Robbed and kilt along with all the rest of his party, and brother, that was a crying shame. A wasteful loss of a purty woman."

"Maybe he found the lost mine and that's

why he and the others were killed . . . to protect the secret," Sixkiller said.

"Man, you don't let go of that lost gold mine, do you?"

"You don't let go of a dream so easily, Bull."

"That's all it is, Quinto, a dream. Nope, if he or anybody else found the mine some of that gold would have turned up by now, almost two months later. You know how gold seekers are. You're one yourself. Could you find that yellow gold and sit on it and keep it a secret all this time without spending some of it? Could anyone?"

"They could if they wanted to keep from hanging," Sixkiller said.

"Don't need no lost gold mine for that, hombre. Lord Dennis and his party was a big fat target. There's rannies on the Glint who'd cut your throat for a pair of boots or just for the fun of it. The Englishman had plenty of money and stuff worth stealing. Plenty of owl-hoots would have jumped them just to get their hands on the women. They'd get their necks stretched by a rope for a rape, so they might as well kill them all off, anyhow. Dead men tell no tales, and dead gals neither.

"The only gold out of Lonesome Hills is whatever Lord Dennis was carrying on him, which could have been a tidy sum. He always had plenty of ready cash for living high and he paid in gold," Bull said, finishing up.

"Wonder who got it?" Sixkiller asked.

Chapter Eleven

Dinner was served—a stew that was mostly fat, gristle, and greasy gravy, along with a big slab of stale bread laid across it like a roofing tile. A tin cup filled with rusty-tasting water also sat on the metal tray.

Sixkiller was unsure which was more dangerous, the stew or the water. He sat on the edge of his bunk, feet on the floor, picking and pecking at the meal.

He was not usually an overly fastidious feeder. Quite the reverse, considering some of the scraps and slops he'd eaten as a kid growing up in the Nations, the questionable rations when he was a soldier fighting in the War, and the more recent privations on the manhunt trail.

Bull reached into his stew with thumb and index finger, plucking out a cockroach whose body was the size of a .45 cartridge. He held it up for Sixkiller to see. "Looky what I found," he said, with a certain grim cheerfulness in hardship.

"At least you got some meat in yours," Six-killer said.

"It's dead. I think the stew killed it."

"Stew? Is that what this is?"

Bull squashed the roach between his fingers, wiping them clean on the underside of the bunk.

Later, Porrock came to collect the trays. "How'd you boys like your chow?" He grinned, needling them.

"The bug in my stew liked it better than I did and he's dead. The food was lousy and such small portions, too."

"You should have thought of that before you started fighting," Porrock said. "Ringgold ain't rolling in money, you know. The town pays us a certain stipend per day to feed the prisoners and you got to make do with what we got."

"How about letting us use our own money to get some food sent in from the café?" Sixkiller asked.

"And some drink," Bull chimed in.

"What money?" Porrock asked.

"The money you took from us when we were locked up," Sixkiller said.

"That ain't your money. Not till the court says so. It's being held against your fines and damages."

"So you're saying my money ain't my money."

"That's right. You got it. That is, you don't

got it." Porrock stacked the trays the prisoners
had slid through the rectangular slot at the
base of the cell door, readying to leave.

"When Wheeler comes to relieve me for
dinner break, I'm gonna go over to the Bon Ton
café and have me a thick, juicy steak, some of
them fried potatoes, and a quart of ale. Mmm!"
Porrock exited, juicily smacking his lips.

"I'd like to tie that scrawny pencil neck of his
into knots," Bull said feelingly.

Time passed, the window in the wall of Sixkiller's cell becoming a rectangle of blackness
dully lit by the glow of unseen lamps and
lanterns.

Porrock went off duty, replaced by Chet
Wheeler who stuck his head into the holding
area. "Still with us, are you boys? Don't go away."

The night hours dragged on. Sometimes the
prisoners talked, others times passages of silence hung between them. The talk grew less
and the silences longer.

The bunk was too small for Sixkiller, of
course. He lay on his side, back to the wall, legs
folded, listening to the insect life all a-stir inside
the straw mattress. He drifted in and out of an
uncomfortable half sleep.

Bull slept deep, snoring, his breathing
sounding like a dull crosscut saw biting into a
hard log. It was counterpointed by a full spec-
trum of gasps, groans, gurgles, throat clearings,
chokings, hackings, buzzings, and such.

A light sleeper, Sixkiller came fully awake during a late night hour. Moonlight shone through the window, the shadows of the bars inky black, clear cut and solid in the luminous silvery glow of moonbeams.

He thought about the facts of the case, having memorized the material as Vandaman had relayed it to him.

He grunted. Where was Vandaman now? Sleeping the night away in a comfortable bed somewhere in Laramie, most likely, waiting for him to send word to bring a posse into Ringgold . . . with guns blazing.

Shaking his head, Sixkiller sat up and reviewed the names of the members of the Bletchley party, starting with Lord Dennis Bletchley, whose Grand Tour of the West was curtailed by an obsessive quest for a lost gold mine in the Lonesome Hills.

Sir Montague "Monty" Dawlish. Bletchley's lifelong friend, drinking and whoring companion.

Russell. Bletchley's adult nephew and ostensible heir.

Pelton. Bletchley's valet who had been with him for twenty years and more.

Osbert and Beryl Hodder. A married couple, he was a cook and she a maidservant.

They were all English.

In America, Lord Dennis's road show had

picked up W. T. Claiborne. Business agent and tour organizer hired by a U.S. branch of Blethley's British bank.

Gage Noland. Westerner and trail guide. Terry Bails, Noland's partner, an ace packer and wrangler. Yellow Snake, their Shoshoni Indian handyman.

Madge Elliott and Rima Janes. Two fresh and juicy young whores the party had acquired in St. Louis.

Nicola Valletta, La Valletta as she was called. Bletchley's beautiful, exotic mistress, born and raised on the island of Malta in the Mediterranean Sea.

That was the permanent party. Quite a group! They would have created a stir wherever they went.

All dead, with the possible exception of La Valletta according to Dean Richmond.

As happened, Sixkiller believed him, but more than two months had passed since Dean had last seen La Valletta as Bart Skillern's captive plaything.

A lot could have happened since then. Most likely, the Utah Kid had tired of his beautiful toy and broken it.

Chapter Twelve

Ringgold must be on the rise, Sixkiller thought. It had its own town hall building. Most frontier towns held their civil proceedings in the likeliest local structure, usually a saloon. The advantage was that after official business was concluded the politicians could buy the voters a drink.

Ringgold's town hall was a wooden-framed, two-story building. The courtroom was on the ground floor. At one end, a wooden platform had been raised eighteen inches above the floor and placed at right angles to the room's long axis. Centered on it was a table and a high-backed chair, the high throne from which judge or justice of the peace conducted the proceedings.

To one side of the dais at floor level was a small writing table and armless chair. Opposite the dais was a central square of a half-dozen, wooden benches arranged in rows. They were narrow, backless, and uncomfortable.

In the front row, facing the platform, Sixkiller and Bull sat side by side, bracketed by Braddock and Wheeler. Porrock had stayed back at the jail to handle any marshalling business that might arise while they were in court.

A handful of spectators buzzed around the courtroom. Some looked like they worked in other offices in the building, town hall insiders come to kill time before going to work. A couple stood near the open double doors, chatting and joking with each other.

Others were idlers and loafers, old men and drunks mostly, waiting for the saloons to open so they could start cadging spare coins to buy that first morning eye-opener.

Reeve Westbrook entered. He was spiffily dressed with a breezy manner, despite a pronounced paleness.

Hangover, thought Sixkiller.

Westbrook paused to hobnob with some of the insiders standing near the entrance. They greeted him with familiarity and signs of welcome. He caught Sixkiller's eye and gave him a jaunty little wave. Sixkiller nodded.

Westbrook pulled his silver flask from a hip pocket and drank from it, spots of color showing on his cheeks. He passed the flask around to his compadres.

Bull watched enviously, unconsciously smacking his lips several times.

A door in the wall behind the writing desk opened and a man entered the courtroom. He was middle-aged, pasty-faced. Under one arm, he carried a ledger and a seat cushion. He set the ledger down on the writing desk. He was the court clerk.

He stepped up on the dais, went behind the table, pulled out the high-backed chair, and set the cushion down on the seat, arranging it rather fussily until it was positioned just so.

He went to the writing desk and sat down behind it, pulling on a pair of ink-proof, sleeve-protector cuffs. He opened up the ledger, dipped a steel-quill pen into the inkwell and wrote an entry at the top of a new page.

The rear door opened and a man entered. The clerk stood up like a shot, announcing, "Mr. Justice of the Peace Virgil Applewhite. *All rise!*"

The laughing and joking of the town hall insiders ended as the courtroom was silenced. Boot heels and shoe leather scuffled against the uncarpeted wooden plank floor, reminding Sixkiller of the clattering hooves of livestock in a stable barn. Those seated, stood.

Braddock cut a side glare at the prisoners,

but he needn't have bothered. Sixkiller and Bull rose to their feet unprompted.

Applewhite wore no judicial robes, but rather a black broadcloth suit that suggested a parson or undertaker. His gavel was an over-sized wooden mallet as big as a bungstarter.

He went behind the chair at the long table and sat down, placing the mallet within easy reach on the tabletop.

The clerk cried, *"Be seated!"*

Participants and spectators sat.

Applewhite opened a folder, ruffling through some papers until he found the one he wanted and placed it on top of the pile. He studied the top sheet, frowning, whether because of the seriousness of the charges or nearsightedness, Sixkiller was unable to tell.

Applewhite's balding head featured a high shiny rounded dome speckled with faded freckles. Bloodshot eyes were too closely set together on either side of a turnip nose. He was chinless and pear-shaped.

"Funny-looking, ain't he?" Bull said in a hoarse whisper behind his hand to Sixkiller.

"Like a freckled mud puppy," Sixkiller whispered back.

Braddock glared at them. "No talking!"

Bull clamped massive jaws shut, cutting a withering side glance at the marshal.

If looks could kill, thought Sixkiller.

Applewhite faced the clerk. "Call the first case."

The clerk rose. "The People of Ringgold, Territory of Wyoming versus one Quinto. Quinto is charged with disturbing the peace, criminal mischief, brawling, public drunkenness, wanton destruction of private property, and resisting arrest." He turned to Sixkiller. "The accused will rise while addressing the court."

Sixkiller stood up and stepped forward.

"How do you plead to the charges? Guilty or not guilty?" Applewhite demanded.

"Not guilty to resisting arrest, Your Honor," Sixkiller said. "Guilty to all the rest. I had too much to drink and got into a fight. Things happened, though I didn't set out to deliberately break the law.

"I started the fight with Mr. Raymond. All he did was defend himself, Your Honor."

"The question of intent as regards the fight will be taken into consideration when this court passes sentence," Applewhite said. "Let the clerk note that said Quinto pleads guilty to all other charges. We'll return to them later, but attend to the matter of resisting arrest, now."

Braddock rose. "Me and my deputies will testify to resisting arrest, Mr. Justice Applewhite."

Sixkiller noted the marshal's use of that "Mr. Justice Applewhite" title. It was a nice touch. Just the kind of crap a pompous little pettifogger like Applewhite like to hear.

"Does the accused have any witnesses or evidence to present on his behalf?" Applewhite asked.

Sixkiller intended to call Westbrook to the stand to back him, but before he could reply the proceedings were interrupted.

Applewhite glared at the untimely intruder. The newcomer went up a side aisle to face the justice, who made no effort to hide his irritation.

He was all puffed up like a bullfrog getting ready to vent a throaty croak, thought Sixkiller as he sat back down.

"Permission to approach the bench, Your Honor," the man said in flat businesslike tones, clearly unawed by the majesty of the court.

"Apparently your request is unnecessary because you have already approached the bench," Applewhite said.

The man looked bored, impatient. He pressed thin lips together and pressed them out, then flattened them, a motion he repeated several times.

"In any case, the court is pleased to recognize Mr. Milton Dash, special assistant to the Honorable Dawes Ivey, Mayor of Ringgold," Applewhite said, not sounding at all pleased.

Dash had wavy black hair, a thin mustache, and a profile akin to that of an Airedale hound. "Begging the indulgence of the court, but I have some information that will materially affect the proceedings."

"The court is always ready to recognize Mr. Dash, the special assistant to Mayor Ivey."

"Thanks," Dash said, stepping up on to the dais and crossing to Applewhite. He leaned forward to talk to him, speaking so only Applewhite could hear him.

The clerk frowned, looking puzzled. Braddock, too.

Whatever this new development boded, Applewhite didn't look too happy about it. Dash didn't talk long while making his pitch, whatever it was. He clinched his argument by handing Applewhite a piece of paper that looked like some kind of document.

Applewhite cleared his throat. "This is, ah, all highly irregular. . . ."

Dash leaned in for another private word then straightened up, stepping to one side. Apparently he was done saying his piece.

Applewhite fastened a beady-eyed stare on Sixkiller.

Sixkiller lowered his gaze, avoiding any direct eye contact which might be taken as a challenge. He tried to look humble and unassuming, nonthreatening. Not so easy when you're a formidable slab of muscle and bone. The fist graffiti marking his face from yesterday's brawl with Bull included a purple shiner, a gashed cheekbone scabbed over with dried blood, and assorted bruises and scrapes.

Bull Raymond sported an equally marked-up face.

Dash stepped down from the platform to talk to the clerk.

"The accused will rise." Applewhite swallowed hard as if reconciled to eating something he didn't like.

Sixkiller rose.

"The court finds you guilty on all charges. However, sentence is suspended due to special circumstances."

The pronouncement produced no small hubbub in court. Nobody was more surprised than Sixkiller.

Dash tried to keep a poker face, but a self-satisfied smirk kept creeping in around the edges.

"Sentence is suspended on condition that said Quinto submit to the temporary custodianship of Mr. Dash, acting in his official capacity as special assistant to Mayor Ivey," Applewhite continued.

Dash winked at Sixkiller.

Braddock had had all he could take. He leaped to his feet like he'd been goosed. "Now hold on a danged minute! You can't throw the charges out!"

"The court can and the court did, Marshal Braddock," Applewhite said in an ominously quiet voice.

Braddock plowed on, oblivious. "This man's committed some serious offenses, not to mention expensive property damage!"

"This court is not unsympathetic with your feelings, Marshal, but legally our hands are tied. There's nothing we can do. After the morning's session has completed all the business on the docket, I will be glad to enlighten you in a private conference in my chambers as to the legal precedent involved. The case of People of Ringgold versus Quinto is now officially *closed*!" Applewhite picked up the gavel, slamming it down hard on a small square wooden block apparently placed there for that purpose.

It sounded as loud as if he were hammering a railroad spike into place.

Braddock was startled, taken aback.

Dash crossed to Sixkiller. "What all this legal mumbo-jumbo means is that you come with me, if you want to get out of here. Do you?"

"Hell, yeah!" Sixkiller said.

"Then let's go. You're a free man, apart from a few minor technicalities."

Sixkiller didn't like that bit, but there was a time and a place for everything, and he judged it expedient to put some distance between himself, the court, and especially the seething Marshal Braddock . . . at least until he got his gun back. He could sort out the technicalities later with Dash. Still, he hung back.

"Is there a problem?" Dash asked with a

touch of sharpness upon noticing Sixkiller's hesitancy.

"Bull Raymond's a good old boy," Sixkiller said. "Can you get him off the hook?"

Bull leaned forward in his seat, trying to keep a poker face, but unable to hide the eagerness to be away that showed in his eyes.

"Sorry, but my special instructions concerned only you, Mr. Quinto." Dash held out open arms in a gesture that said, *What can I do? This is beyond my control.* "It's quite possible that arrangements can be made later, but there's nothing I can do now."

"Sorry, Bull," Sixkiller said.

Bull sagged, downcast. "You did what you could. Thanks."

"I'll keep working on it. Hang on to that bucking bronc and don't let it throw you, Texas."

"Okay, Quinto," Bull said, flashing a quick toothy grin.

Dash gestured for Sixkiller to follow him and crossed to the side door. Sixkiller fell into step behind him, his long strides eating up the pace between him and the exit.

Dash stepped through the doorway into a corridor, Sixkiller at his heels.

"Would you mind telling me what this is all about?" Sixkiller demanded.

"I don't mind a bit, Mr. Quinto. Mayor Ivey wants to meet you. Something about a job offer."

Chapter Thirteen

Sixkiller did not have to travel far after exiting the courtroom. He and Dash climbed a flight of stairs to the second floor. On the landing lay a door on the right with the words *Mayor's Office* inscribed on the door panel in gilt letters. Dash knocked on the door.

A voice on the other side said, "Come in."

They went in.

The old saw about politics being conducted in smoke-filled rooms was true of Ringgold. The room was filled with blue smoke. Stale tobacco smoke. Most men of the era smoked or chawed. The air was a bit close, but Sixkiller didn't mind. After a night in Ringgold's jail-house, the mayor's office was positively fragrant by comparison.

The door opened on a reception room. It was a big space with a row of windows fronting the street. The shades were pulled down and the curtains were closed. Some of the windows were open, breezes ruffling the curtains. High-backed chairs lined a wall. A waist-high wooden rail balustrade fenced off the waiting room from the rest of the office.

A hinged gate, serving as a door, accessed the inner space.

A man sat with his feet up on a dark brown wooden desk, smoking a cigar. He didn't lower them to the floor when Sixkiller and Dash entered from the landing.

He was short, stocky, balding with a hard square face. The tips of a brown walrus mustache ran downward along the sides of his mouth, which was turned down at the corners, giving him a sour expression.

He looked tough. A long-barreled, big-caliber revolver lay on the desk, along with a whiskey bottle and a half-filled glass . . . and the fellow's booted feet.

Dash opened the hinged gate in the wooden partition fence. "Hi, Sam."

The man behind the desk flipped Dash a casual two-fingered salute. Sam's level-eyed gaze fell on Sixkiller, appraising him. "Yep, he's big enough to tangle with Bull Raymond. And does his face show it!"

"Want to make something out of it?" Sixkiller wasn't in the mood for any guff. He'd had to stand for plenty when he was in jail and in court.

Sam's hard face got stonier. He took his feet

off the desktop and placed them on the floor and started to get up.

"No nonsense, boys," Dash said, moving to get between the two men. "We're all on the same side, remember?"

"Are we?" Sixkiller asked.

"The mayor didn't get the charges dropped to give you a hard time."

Sixkiller wondered if that was true. Dash had spoken of a job offer. There were jobs and then there were jobs. Working undercover to get Bart Skillern was a job of work. Sixkiller wasn't so eager to take on another. On the other hand, if it would move him closer to accomplishing his mission, he'd take it. It wouldn't hurt to listen.

Sam sat with his fists on the desktop. He stared at Sixkiller, the muscles in his jaws working.

"You're not here to pick fights with the mayor's visitors, Sam. Relax and go back to your drinking."

The tip of the cigar clamped between Sam's teeth glowed bright orange. He vented a cloud of blue-gray smoke. His fists unclenched. "Okay."

Dash entered a narrow passage beyond the desk, indicating by a tilt of the head that Sixkiller should follow.

As Sixkiller drew abreast of Sam, he leaned over the desk, thrusting his face close. "I look like this from scrapping with Bull Raymond. What's your excuse?"

"Okay, okay," Sam said again, taking no outward offense now that Dash had reminded him of his duties. "The mayor's waiting for you. Go on in."

The tip of Sam's cigar glowed bright orange again, and Sixkiller hurried past to avoid another cloud of blue-gray smoke.

Room doors lined both sides of the passage. The one with the word *Mayor* painted on it in gold paint was partly ajar. Dash pushed it open and escorted Sixkiller inside.

The room was large. Again, the windows were shaded and curtained, the air close.

A big man, presumably the mayor, sat behind a massive pale-gold, wooden desk, its edges marred with scorch marks where lit cigarettes and cigars had been left, burning and forgotten. A green baize blotter covered most of the desktop. Numerous round circles—watermarks from drinking glasses—were visible on both.

Two of the four big, overstuffed armchairs grouped in a half circle facing the desk were occupied.

In the center of the carpet between desk and armchairs stood a four-wheeled serving cart, its top covered with a variety of bottles, most containing brown and clear liquors. Only one contained water. There were plenty of glasses, too.

A writing table and chair were tucked off to one side in a corner. The floor was mostly covered by a maroon oriental rug decorated with yellow and orange curlicues and bordered on the edge by gold-covered fringe.

It was the most gold he had seen since coming to town, and probably the most he was likely to see during his sojourn in Ringgold, Sixkiller noted.

From chatter he'd overheard before court was in session, Sixkiller knew that Mayor Dawes Ivey was generally regarded as a "man of the people" and "the people's mayor." Sixkiller didn't know if that was complimentary or a good thing. From what he had seen of the people of Ringgold, their ideal representative would be a hard-fisted, avaricious taker out to grab what he could. That wasn't necessarily a bad thing. At least you'd always know where you stood with the administration.

Dawes Ivey was burly, with a craggy potato face, a meatball nose with a red bulbous tip, and hooded reptilian eyes. He wore a loud green and black checked jacket and light colored orange and yellow plaid pants. His garments were rumpled, his cravat was undone, and flecks of cigar ash left gray smears on his wide lapels. A couple buttons on his vest were missing. A thick gold watch chain with an elk's tooth ornament hung out of his watch pocket.

Milt Dash quickly handled the introductions.

"Mr. Mayor, Mr. Quinto. Mr. Quinto, Mayor Ivey." He went to the serving cart to fix himself a drink. He seemed mighty thirsty.

Ivey proved he was a politician, all right. He jumped up from his chair and came around the desk. A lit cigar was stuck in his kisser. "Glad to meet you, Quinto." He gestured toward the men in the armchairs. "Meet my associates Jared Raffin and Milo Tapper. Jared's the town tax collector and Milo's his assistant."

Raffin was long and lean, with wavy black hair, dark eyes and a Mephisto-style goatee. He reminded Sixkiller of pictures he had seen of Texas bad man Bill Longley, although he was sure there was no relation. Longley had died on the gallows years ago, but nobody could say that he hadn't died game.

Tax collector. That's a good one, thought Sixkiller.

Raffin wore a natty sharp-edged suit and white ruffled shirt front. An ivory-handled .44 pistol hung low on his hip in a black leather rig. He looked the very image of what he almost certainly was, a professional gunman. A good choice for tax collector. He could back up his play when citizens kicked about the tax rate.

Tapper was a short, stocky, balding, square-faced man with a whiskery brown handlebar mustache. He looked like a more easygoing version of Sam at the front desk. Maybe because the tips of his mustache were upturned, giving the illusion of a smile, while the tips of Sam's mustache were downturned, giving him a more sullen aspect.

A gun slick and a tough as official tax collector and assistant. Quite a combination, Sixkiller thought.

The mayor and the tax collectors were all drinking. Ivey and Tapper puffed big fat cigars while Ralfin favored a variety of long, skinny, gnarly, brown cheroot that looked like a twig of a tree branch, similar to the kind of smoke Vandaman favored.

Ivey held a whiskey glass in his right hand. He transferred it to his left hand and extended his right for a handshake. "Put 'er there Mr. Quinto, put 'er there."

Sixkiller generally wasn't a big one for shaking hands. It put his dominant gun hand out of action however temporarily, but temporary could easily become permanent on the violent frontier.

He figured he could risk it in the mayor's office. If the mayor wanted to get rid of him for some unknown reason there were likelier places to do it than in his office. He didn't want to offend Ivey by not shaking his hand. After all, the man had gotten him out from under Applewhite's thumb and away.

Sixkiller shook the mayor's hand.

Ivey's palm was moist from the condensation that had beaded up on the whiskey glass. His grip was firm, energetic, yet not overbearing. "Dawes Ivey. Glad to know you, Mr. Quinto, very glad indeed! Hmmm, good strong grip— I like that. I'd expect nothing less from the man who whupped Bull Raymond. By heaven, that must have been some scrap. I'm sorry I missed it. I would like to have seen it. Maybe you'll favor us with a return bout soon!"

"I'm still trying to get over this one." Sixkiller thought of Bull being stuck under the sway of Applewhite's domination and felt bad. It was basically Sixkiller's fault. He had picked the fight with Bull, not the other way around.

Ivey stepped back, appraising the Oklahoman. "You don't look too bad, not bad at all. I'm impressed! Bull is a mighty tough customer, mighty tough!"

"You don't have to tell me that Mr. Mayor. I've got the aches and pains to prove it."

"You don't look any the worse for wear after spending a night in Marshal Braddock's jail, either," Ivey said.

From the distaste with which he said Braddock's name, Sixkiller got the idea that the mayor was not overly fond of the marshal. That could be useful, very useful. Sixkiller didn't like Braddock, either.

Ivey turned toward the men in the armchairs. "Gentlemen, say howdy to Mr. Quinto."

"Howdy," Raffin said, smiling with his lips. He raised his glass in an amiable kind of salute, showing no signs of eagerness to shake Sixkiller's hand. The gun slick would not be one for shaking hands. Those hands were his stock in trade. They were smooth and soft, pampered, looking like he had never used them to do a day's worth of manual labor in his life.

In which case, he hadn't missed much, thought Sixkiller, who had worked hard for most of his life. Federal deputy marshalling was the softest job he had ever had and he was determined to hold on to it with a death grip. He acknowledged Raffin with a nod.

Milo Tapper bounced out of his chair and crossed to shake Sixkiller's hand. He seemed a friendly, decent enough chap, even though he was a taxman.

Assistant taxman, Sixkiller mentally corrected as he realized Milo was horny-handed from toil. Shaking his hand was like shaking hands with a brick. "By any chance, are you related to the fellow sitting outside at the desk?" That had been bothering Sixkiller since he'd entered the room.

"That's my brother, Sam," Milo said, grinning. "So you met Sam, huh? I'm surprised you didn't throw him out the window. He has that effect on people, including me."

"What're you drinking, Mr. Quinto?" Ivey asked with an expansive gesture, indicating the serving cart.

Sixkiller eyed the bottles and chose Old Scout whiskey, a brand he liked.

The mayor poured and rather quickly Sixkiller was sitting in one of the armchairs with a full glass of whiskey in his hand and a couple of the mayor's good cigars in his breast pocket. Ivey had all but forced them on him. Sixkiller decided to hold off on the smoking until later. He didn't want it to interfere with his whiskey drinking.

"Thanks for getting the charges against me dropped, Mr. Mayor," Sixkiller began.

"It was my pleasure, Mr. Quinto, my very great pleasure." Ivey beamed.

"I appreciate it. I owe you."

"You certainly do!" Ivey said, still beaming. "It wasn't easy to get Mase Rourke to refuse to press charges. He was considerably irked with you and Mr. Raymond for the damage you did to the Jackpot. Why to replace the front window alone will cost a great deal of money. I had to call in some favors with Mase to get him to go along. But in the end, he saw the wisdom of it and agreed. Because we're friends, Mase and I. And that's what friends do. They help each other out.

"The theme of my administration is friendship. I want the good people of Ringgold not to think of me only as their mayor, but as their friend. They don't just have a mayor at town hall here, they have a *friend*."

"That was a mighty friendly thing you did for me, Mr. Mayor. Now what can I do for you?" Sixkiller asked, grabbing the hot iron and asking the big question.

Ivey's smile became even wider and more brilliant, more expressive of goodwill, if that were possible.

"Mr. Quinto, I like you. I think we're going to get along fine. I think we're going to be friends. Because we understand each other. You cut right to the heart of the matter. To get along we've got to go along, all of us. Friends helping each other out is the very basis of good government and good citizenship."

Raffin, sitting in the far chair where Ivey could not easily see his face without doing a lot of leaning over his desk, caught Sixkiller's eye. He sardonically raised his eyes to heaven as if seeking divine relief from the mayor's speech about friendship, which he had doubtless heard too many times before.

Milo Tapper sat in his chair as if entranced by Ivey's words.

Dash was deep into his second glass of whiskey and from the way he was going at it with single-minded concentration, he'd soon be working on his third.

Ivey leaned forward in his chair, sitting with hands folded in front of him on his desk. He was looking at Sixkiller as if expecting some kind of response. His eyes were slate-gray, his orbs moist in their baggy pouches.

He really did have a reptilian eye, thought Sixkiller, like an alligator or maybe even a Gila monster.

The mayor's pause lengthened, the seconds ticking past. He was looking solely at Sixkiller.

Sixkiller felt it was incumbent of him to say something, anything. "Please, Mr. Mayor, call me Quinto. Just plain Quinto. No mistering involved." Getting into the spirit of things, he added, "It's the uh, *friendlier* thing to do."

"All right, Quinto." Ivey didn't tell Sixkiller to call him by his first name. He was happy being addressed as "Mr. Mayor." That he liked.

Reminded of Applewhite with his childish pompous pleasure at being called "Mr. Justice Applewhite," Sixkiller thought politicians were all the same. They worked and schemed so damned hard to win their titles that they could never let them go.

"You're a newcomer to our town, Quinto, so let me give you some background first," Ivey went on. "The Glint is on the boom. Between our friends at the Western Territories Mining Company and the big cattle ranchers in the valley, we in Ringgold stand to make a great deal of money. The prospects are astonishing, the potential profits breathtaking. Some of the best grazing land in the territory is located here in the valley. There should be enough for everyone."

"What's the problem then?" Sixkiller asked.

"Some folks want more than their fair share, Quinto. They want to hog it all. Now what do you think of that?"

"Why I'd say that's mighty *un*friendly of them, Mr. Mayor."

"Precisely. That brings us to the subject of our talk, the reason I extended myself to ensure that you'd be free of the reach of men like Marshal Braddock and Justice Applewhite, of Hickory Ned Hampton and even as great a power in the land as Harl Endicott of the High-line Ranch. They are creatures of destruction, all of them. I call them creatures because that is what they are. Their free will is not their own. All of them, Endicott included, bend the knee to a single master.

"And who is he? I do not fear to name him outright, this nemesis who falls on the Glint like a biblical plague. He is the robber bandit chief—Bart Skillern, the Utah Kid."

The effect on Sixkiller was electrifying. He felt like a cardsharp who suddenly discovers that someone else in the game has sneaked an extra ace into his marked deck. Not that any-thing of his sudden unease could be seen on his face. The heavens might fall, yet he'd never outwardly crack to a twinge of anxiety.

Had Sixkiller underestimated Mr. Mayor

Dawes Ivey? How much—if anything—did Ivey know of his true identity and mission in Ringgold?

"I see I have your full attention now, Quinto," Ivey said, smirking slightly.

"I've heard of the Kid, sure," Sixkiller said. "Who hasn't? But to hear you tell it, he's not just another robber and killer. He runs the whole valley from behind the scenes."

"Not yet," Ivey said, shaking his head. "He doesn't have that much power now, as we speak. But I assure you, he seeks total control of the Glint, and that goal is almost within his reach. The time to stop him is growing short.

"Bart Skillern is the most dangerous outlaw in the territory. He is, as you said, a robber and killer. He's also pure hell with a gun—fast!

"But I have reason to believe he is more than that. His is more than the animal cunning of the outlaw breed. He is gifted with intelligence, an intellect free of any considerations of morality, pity, and human decency. He's the leader of a gang of killers almost as bad as he is. Is there any crime they're not wanted for? Believe me, Quinto, when I tell you that because of the Utah Kid, the mining companies have been unable to make one payroll date since last spring. Impossible, you say. And yet it's true. The miners on Sagebrush Flats, several hundred men and the families who depend on them, have not been paid since the month of May. And it's not for lack of trying.

"The company has engaged in every stratagem to ship enough hard cash money through the valley to the mining camps on the flats . . . all with zero success. Every payroll run, express mail, and freight wagon attempt has failed."

Ivey's voice quavered with indignation—or was it fear? "The Kid is a cunning devil. If the payroll funds are guarded by a small army of gunmen, Skillern waits until delivery has been made and they've left. Then he raids the mining company safes and steals the gold before it can be paid out to the workmen.

"He has a thousand eyes. Every harlot, tinhorn, sharper, and barkeep in the valley is a potential source of information to him. His reach extends to high places and low. I've even come to suspect that he has agents planted right here in town hall—but enough of that.

"Perhaps you think I exaggerate. Have his depredations caused me to lose my reason, to become hysterical? No, Quinto. These are facts. Recall if you will the outrages of the James and Younger Brothers in the border states and see how a relatively small band of ruthless and determined outlaws can set the heartland of a great nation into the chaos and confusion of an overturned ant nest.

"That's the condition we're fast approaching on the Glint. Skillern's reach goes far beyond the outlaw gangs. A number of seemingly respectable citizens have allied with him in his attempt to take over the valley. They hide behind the mask of innocence while secretly aiding him in corrupting and subverting the community. I've mentioned some of their names. Marshal Braddock, Justice Applewhite, Hickory Ned, and Harl Endicott are the most prominent.

"Let's make no bones about it. I'm a politician. I try to get along with everyone. I just want to be friends. Why? Because that's where the votes are. But with some folks there's no getting along. That's the Skillern outfit.— The Kid, his gang, and their allies and agents of influence. If I do nothing, they'll eat me up in time, and time is running out," Ivey said. He took a long drink of whiskey, nearly gulping down a whole glassful. It put some color back in his face.

"I've talked long enough, Quinto. Now it's your turn. What are your thoughts on the Bart Skillern problem?"

"The Utah Kid's a bad hombre, Mr. Mayor, but that's all he is—an hombre. A bullet, a knife, or a length of rope will put paid to his career," Sixkiller said.

"Excellent, Quinto," Ivey said, smiling thinly. "Again you cut to the heart of the matter. I shall be equally concise. I want you to join my little war on Bart Skillern."

Chapter Fourteen

"I'm flattered by your confidence in me, Mr. Mayor. But I'm just a prospector who fought Bull Raymond to a draw. What makes you think I'd be any use to you in fighting an outlaw gang?" Sixkiller asked.

"The answer to that question might be indiscreet, Quinto. For that reason, I must request my associates to leave us in privacy for a few moments," Ivey said.

Raffin didn't need to be told twice. He finished his drink in a few gulps, set down his empty glass, and stood up. "Let's go, Milo. Time for you to go collect some taxes."

The assistant rose, and he and Raffin started for the door.

"I'll be in the outer office when you need me, boss," Raffin said over his shoulder.

"This shouldn't take long," Ivey said.

"I won't be far away."

"I appreciate that."

Raffin and Milo went out.

Dash stood at the serving table, filling a glass almost to the brim with whiskey. "I'll be in my office catching up on the paperwork."

"Thank you, Milt," Ivey said.

Sixkiller watched Dash. His hand was steady, his movements sure. Not a drop of whiskey sloshed over the rim of his glass as he crossed to the door and exited the room.

"Now that we are in private, I think it best to put aside all pretense, Quinto."

"I'm an open book, Mr. Mayor," Sixkiller said blandly.

"Anything but," Ivey said, chuckling. "Quinto. That's an interesting name you picked for your alias in Ringgold."

"It's my name."

"Perhaps it would expedite things if I tell you that I know what Quinto is. It's a town in the Indian Nations of Oklahoma. After the Civil War, Quinto was the first big haunt of the border ruffians, an outlaw town."

"I grew up in those parts," Sixkiller said, shrugging. "The name stuck to me and it fit. That's all there is to it."

"Why don't we put our cards on the table?" Ivey suggested.

"Seems to me that you're holding all the cards, Mr. Mayor."

"I wonder. You may better understand my

position when I tell you that I am not only a friend and ally of Western Territories Mining Company, I hold a fair amount of stock in the company. I could not have been elected to this office without the company's support. So you see, I have personal, political, and pecuniary reasons for wanting a quick resolution to the Utah Kid problem, Quinto."

"I see that much."

"The WTMC has branches throughout the Rocky Mountain States, including a Salt Lake division. Naturally the company representatives took a great interest in the recent death of Dean Richmond, a close friend and partner of the Kid's since boyhood days."

"Naturally," Sixkiller agreed.

"The description of one of the posse men who got Richmond fits you to a tee," Ivey said.

"There's a lot of fellows in the West who look like me."

"Apparently. Not long ago, another fellow who fits your description—a big Indian-looking fellow—cleaned up on a gang of killer bandits."

"Small world, ain't it Mr. Mayor?"

"The WTMC has extensive mining interests in New Mexico. One of their sources reported the fellow who cleaned up on the bandits, your lookalike, Quinto, was rumored to be a federal marshal," Ivey said.

"Excuse me for one little minute," Sixkiller said, rising.

Ivey watched in bemusement as the Oklahoman went to the door, opened it, and stuck his head outside. He closed the door, returned to his chair, and sat down.

"For an instant there I thought you were running out on me, Quinto."

"Just making sure nobody was listening at the keyhole," Sixkiller said. "You got to be more careful, Mr. Mayor. You go making statements like the one you just made and they get heard by the wrong set of ears, you could maybe get somebody seriously killed. Me."

"My apologies," Ivey said. "I wasn't thinking."

"Like you said Mr. Mayor, Bart Skillern is a very crafty fellow. He could have spies in your outfit, maybe even on your staff."

"An unpleasant possibility, but one I'll admit to contemplating. That's why I've kept this matter closely held. So close, only you and I know of it."

"I'm not going to ask you what you think you know, Mr. Mayor. My question is, where do we go from here?"

"I think we could do each other a deal of good. Ringgold needs help. I need help. I'm in a position to help you. In fact, I already have. Those charges could have worked you a mischief, Quinto. Whatever your objective is here, you won't get much done from inside a jail cell or on a convict work crew. I'd say I've already made a substantial demonstration of my good faith."

"You have at that, sir."

"I can do more. Through me, you can put the considerable assets of the WTMC to work on your behalf."

"They've gotten nowhere catching Skillern so far," Sixkiller pointed out.

"True. But they can make all kinds of men and materiel available to you," Ivey said. "And I can give you some immunity from interference by the likes of Braddock and Applewhite. Already have given you some."

"It's possible we can come to some kind of working arrangement. Something loose and flexible. I don't work well under a tight rein. I've got to have the freedom to come and go as I please and crack down on troublemakers when I think they've got it coming."

Ivey smiled politely. "My last interest would be in reining you in, Quinto. Raffin doesn't really collect taxes, Tapper does. Raffin's my bodyguard and I keep him close. His official title gives him a reason for being here on the scene to protect me."

"A sensible precaution."

"Raffin's a good gun, but he can only do so much. I'll sleep better once Skillern's dead and buried."

"So will a lot of other folks," Sixkiller said.

"Some of them right here in this very building," said Ivey.

"Taking the Kid is no easy proposition. He's been getting away with it for years. We'll both have to walk soft if we want to get out of this with a whole skin. The most important thing is that our arrangement remains a secret between you and me. Don't tell Raffin or your mining company buddies or anybody else. Don't put anything in writing."

"Give me credit for a little common sense, Quinto. No smart politician ever puts anything important in writing."

"By now, it's common knowledge that you got me off the hook to sic me on Skillern and your political enemies, so let's stick with that."

"I'll do for you what I did for Raffin— appoint you to some official post to give you some cover for your activities."

"Good idea. Only let's try to find something a little more high-toned for me than tax collector. Even for Ringgold, that's kind of raw. How about fire inspector? That'll give me a reason for sticking my nose into other people's business."

"Done," Ivey said. "I'll have Milt Dash work up some kind of certificate of authority with a lot of important looking stamps and ribbons to impress the weak-minded."

"Don't go overboard. A simple certificate will

do. What'll really back it up are my fists and a gun."

"That reminds me. I have something that belongs to you." Ivey opened a drawer in his desk and took out a holstered gun, handing it to Sixkiller. "Reeve Westbrook gave it to me to give to you. He said he thought you might need it."

"Mighty friendly of him," Sixkiller dead panned. "This sure is a friendly town."

He drew the gun from the holster, checking the cylinder to make sure it was still loaded. Bullets filled all the chambers save one that he kept empty for placement under the hammer as a safety precaution against the gun's going off accidentally should it be dropped in a fight or fall out of the holster as he got thrown from a horse.

He eased the gun back into the holster and buckled on the gun belt. "That's better. I felt naked without it."

Sixkiller was still not fully dressed though. "Did Westbrook leave my hat?"

"Sorry, no. No hat here," Ivey said.

"I've got to get it. Can't go around without a hat. Folks'll think I'm a no-account."

"Try the saloons. Westbrook's sure to be in one of them."

"One thing more, Mr. Mayor. How about getting Bull out of jail?"

"Bull Raymond! What do you want him for? He's a rowdy, a troublemaker, a loose cannon.

Let him stay in the jailhouse as Braddock's headache."

"Bull's my buddy."

"He tried to knock your brains out!"

"I admit the getting acquainted part was a little rough, but he's a decent fellow at heart, I do believe. At the showdown, I'd rather have him with us than agin' us. Have him paroled into my custody. I'll be responsible for him."

"Who's going to pay for the damage he does? You?" Ivey asked.

"If he gets out of line, I'll just have to whup him again."

"All right. If that's what you want. I hope you know what you're doing." Ivey sighed. "When do you want him out?"

"After lunch should do it. I've got a few things to attend to before then. I want to be there when Bull gets sprung. I want him to know who he has to thank," Sixkiller said. "Braddock has my money, and I'm gonna get it back from him. It'll be good to have Bull there for backup."

"I'll get Mitch Evert on it. He's the town prosecutor. Applewhite should have known something was coming when Mitch wasn't in court this morning to prosecute you."

"Much obliged, Mr. Mayor, much obliged," Sixkiller said. "Things are going to start popping in Ringgold pretty soon, so be ready. Keep Raffin close and warn your people to beware of bushwhackers and shotgunners in dark alleys. But don't get excited if you hear some shooting in a couple minutes. That'll just be me taking some target practice to work the rust off my trigger finger."

"This is exciting," Ivey confided. "The other side's had the way of it up till now. It'll be a pleasure to start hitting back."

"Why, Mr. Mayor, what an *unfriendly* thing to say!" Sixkiller went out of the office and out of the building.

Walking east, he was looking for a place to try out his gun without setting off a ruckus. He didn't have to walk far to run out of Ringgold town, only a couple of blocks before coming to a stretch of vacant fields used as a town dump.

The gun had been out of his possession. He didn't know who besides Westbrook and Ivey might have handled it during the interval. He had to be sure that it hadn't been tampered with, the firing pin filed down or broken, bad cartridges substituted for good. "Only a damned fool takes a weapon on trust."

The iron checked out okay on inspection, but the proof was in the shooting. He picked up an empty tin can and tossed it in the air with his left hand. He drew and fired, hitting the can in mid-air, sending it soaring off at a tangent. He threw a few more slugs into it on the fly, the can dancing and bobbing aloft.

He left the last bullet unfired so as to not leave himself unarmed.

Sixkiller looked around. He was alone. He broke the gun, opened the cylinder gate, shucked out the spent cartridges, and dropped the brass into a pocket of his vest. Thrifty, he saved the brass for future hand loading. He liked to make up his own special rounds so they'd have extra man-stopping power.

Also, as a veteran trail man, he disliked like leaving evidence of his presence—a good habit to cultivate if he wanted to stay alive.

He reloaded his gun, holstered it, and went back into town, intercepting Westbrook as he crossed the intersection a couple blocks south of Liberty Street.

"I've been looking for you," Westbrook said.

"Here I am," Sixkiller said. "Thanks for looking after my gun. Where's my hat?"

"At the *Banner* office. I left it there for safekeeping."

"Let's go get it."

"All right."

They walked north toward Liberty Street.

"How do you like working for Mayor Ivey?" Westbrook asked.

Sixkiller cut him a sharp side glance. He reckoned the mayor was too sharp to crack to the reporter the nature of their real working relationship, so he must have fed Westbrook the cover story about using Quinto to crack down on his political foes. "You get around."

"I'm a reporter, remember? Who do you think was the flea who first put the word in the mayor's ear that you could be more useful to him outside jail rather than in?"

"That was you? Thanks."

"Don't mention it."

"What do you get out of it?"

"A good story, apart from any feelings of civic betterment engendered from trying to make Ringgold a decent place to live—one where you can stick your head out the door without someone trying to shoot it off."

"Ringgold's a long way off from there."

"And likely to be farther still before you're done?" Westbrook suggested slyly.

"Could be. I'm going to do a few things for the mayor," Sixkiller allowed, "but don't print that."

"I won't print a word about your activities until you give me the okay. Just make sure you give me the story first."

"Who else would I give it to?" Sixkiller asked rhetorically.

"Oh boy! I can't wait for the fireworks," Westbrook said.

Chapter Fifteen

Sixkiller and Westbrook turned left on Liberty, walking west toward the *Banner* office. The sky was hazy with high, thin, whippy clouds. Gusts of north wind blew a bit brisk for a late summer day. It would have been chilly in Oklahoma, but maybe considered a balmy morning in Wyoming, Sixkiller thought. He was beginning to appreciate the truth of the old saw that "There's only two seasons in Wyoming, winter and the Fourth of July."

Noise flared up, the clamor coming from a side street that opened on Liberty. Near a row of small stores on the south side of the street, loud voices racketed. Whooping and hollering were mixed with bursts of raucous laughter, rude and rowdy.

Although it was the middle of the morning, five drunken cowboys came stumbling into view. Loudmouthed, unkempt hardcases, they were a rough bunch outfitted like ranch hands, but armed like gun hands. They wore range hats and sombreros, vests, and leather chaps. Drunk and disorderly, they swayed, staggered, and reeled.

Westbrook halted, placing a restraining hand on Sixkiller's left. "Uh-oh. Trouble! Those are Highline hands. Real bad 'uns. Stay back."

"Endicott's bunch, eh?"

"You catch on fast, Quinto."

"I get around," Sixkiller said, frowning at the Highline quintet. "Kind of early to get a load on, and I say that as a drinking man who likes his drink."

"They're probably coming off an all-nighter at French Marie's. She runs a bordello a couple streets down," Westbrook said.

The mid-morning eruption took by surprise those citizens of the law-abiding element unlucky enough to be on Liberty Street. The quick-thinking ones got off the street fast.

As the rowdies came out of the side street, a young woman came out of a tiny dry goods store unawares. Slim and sweet-faced with blue eyes and straight yellow hair, she wore a light blue-and-white gingham dress and carried a wicker sewing basket under one arm. She stopped in her tracks, dismayed.

The cowboys set up a howling like dogs scenting fresh red meat.

The girl had the right idea. She turned on a dime, ducking her head and hurrying back into the dry goods store.

The cowhands shouted words at her, most of them not very nice.

The shopkeeper, a sensible older woman, shut the front door and locked it tight, pulling down the shade.

One of the cowboys rushed to the door, a gangly, mean-faced youth with lank blond hair so pale it was almost white. He strutted around like the cock of the walk in too-tight jeans and fancy boots with high built-up heels.

"That's Romeo, one of Port's crowd," Westbrook said. "Very tough boys."

The cowboy rattled the door handle till it shook the frame. He banged on the glass of the door like to break it.

A dignified-looking old man rounded the corner, preoccupied with his own thoughts. He carried under an arm several brown paper-wrapped parcels tied with twine.

A cowboy dashed up, knocking the packages out from under the man's arm and sending them scattering along the boardwalk.

"Foley," Westbrook said, naming the cowboy.

The citizen stiffened, his reddening face contrasting with a white mustache. He knew better than to make a fuss. He stooped stiffly, laboriously picking the packages up.

A third bad man moved behind the oldster, cueing his fellows in with a high sign that something was coming.

"Lew," Westbrook mumbled.

The cowhand planted a hard kick on the seat of the oldster's pants, sending him uncurling up into the air.

"Like a jumping frog," Lew crowed. "Haw, haw, haw!"

The kick hurt. The oldster sat down in the street and didn't get up, his face flaming red.

A couple schoolboys raced past. A fourth rowdy stuck out a leg and tripped one of them, sending the kid tumbling.

"Virgil," Westbrook identified.

The other schoolboys stopped, a couple of them helping their pal up.

"Why don't you pick on somebody your own size?" one demanded.

"'Cause there ain't nobody big enough to tackle Virgil Akins, sonny boy," the rowdy said. "Now git on home and cry to your momma."

"Tell her to come look up Romeo. I'll make her cry . . . for more," Romeo chimed in.

"Cry from laughing, you mean," Foley said.

The fifth and final member of the group— a big bearish hombre whose unshaven face bristled like a hog's back—came swaggering to the fore. Left-handed, he wore his gun on the left hip.

He had little, piggy, red eyes just like a hog, Sixkiller thought.

"And that's Port, the leader of the bunch," Westbrook said.

The street was clear, free of any more citizens to torment, the civilians having gone to cover. Portand and his crowd stood with their backs to Sixkiller and Westbrook, not seeing them.

"Fun's over boys. We done chased 'em all away," Port said.

"I'm thirsty," Foley complained.

The others all agreed. They, too, were thirsty. Laughing and scratching, they lurched across the street and went into the Paradise Club.

"No action?" Westbrook asked, arching an eyebrow. "I thought you'd go after them like you did Bull."

"It's early yet," Sixkiller said.

They crossed to the *Banner* office.

Cass stood outside the door, having just witnessed some of the cowboys' "fun." She was indignant. Being a redhead, her color was up. "Too bad you don't feel like fighting when it would do some good," she said to Sixkiller.

"Sorry, ma'am, but I just spent a night in jail for fighting and I'm in no hurry to go back. Besides, cracking down on troublemakers is the marshal's job."

"Humph!"

"Say, where is Marshal Braddock, anyhow?

Or his deputies? Seems like this is a job for them, protecting the citizens and all."

"I'm quite sure I couldn't say."

"Or is it that Braddock's heart just ain't in it when it comes to laying down the law to Endicott and the Highline riders?" Sixkiller asked slyly.

"I'm quite sure Marshal Braddock's inner workings are a mystery to me," Cass said.

"Might be a story in it, a big one. Might make for some interesting reading."

That drew Cass up short, piquing her interest. She studied Sixkiller, her eyes thoughtful. "By the way, what are you doing out of jail and on the loose?"

"You might say I've reformed. I'm working for the city now. Reeve'll tell you all about it." Sixkiller indicated Westbrook with a jerk of his thumb. "Much as I'd like to stay and pass the time of day, I've got business needs tending to, so if it's all right with you, I'll get my hat and be on my way."

"I'll get it." Westbrook went inside, returning a moment later with Sixkiller's hat.

"Thanks for taking care of it. I'd hate to lose it," Sixkiller said. "Hard to find another like it."

"Who would want to?" Cass said.

"You might not think it to look at me, but I'm really a very sentimental fellow."

"That is hard to swallow."

"That's what all the girls say, but never mind about that. . . ."

"Well!" Cass's face reddened as she got it.

Sixkiller put a fist inside the tall crown with the rounded top, knuckling out some of the dents, working it into shape. He fit it on his head, tilting the brim at a rakish angle. "See you in the papers, ma'am." He turned and went on his way.

Chapter Sixteen

Town Prosecutor Mitch Evert's office was on the second floor of the courthouse. Evert had handled Bull's freeing, it being agreed by the prosecutor and Mayor Ivey that events might proceed more smoothly if Sixkiller was away from Braddock's jailhouse at that time.

Medium-sized, sandy-haired, and compactly built, with dark eyes, long sideburns, and a mustache, Evert was in the office with Bull when Sixkiller entered after lunch.

Bull rushed Sixkiller, clasping his big meaty paws on the other's upper arms in a gesture of enthusiastic fraternal feeling and concord. "My pal! I had you all wrong, Quinto. I thought you was throwing me to the wolves at Braddock's jail!"

Sixkiller's arms went temporarily numb. "Wolves is stepping up in class for them, Bull. Call it a snake den."

"Maybe you don't think Braddock wasn't mighty sore when Prosecutor Mitch came around with a court order to get me out of jail. Man! He was fit to be tied."

"Just remember, Bull, you're working for me now. They released you into my custody," Sixkiller said.

"That's because you're the only mug with guts enough to mix it up with me."

"You're too tough for me, Bull," Sixkiller said, shaking his head. "Next time I'll just shoot you." Sixkiller grinned to show he was joking . . . wasn't he?

"You're the boss, Quinto," Bull said. "Who do we kill?"

Mitch Evert looked pained. "Please, not when I'm listening!"

Sixkiller tsk-tsked. "You've got to rid yourself of such notions, Bull. You're a peace officer now . . . of a sort. We're going to see that the laws are enforced. We're kind of unofficial roving agents for Mr. Evert here."

"So unofficial I don't even know you. Unofficially speaking," Evert said.

"Got that, Bull?" Sixkiller asked.

"No."

"Prosecutor Mitch can't convict without evidence and can't trust Braddock and company to get him the evidence he needs to bring before a jury. So we're going to help him out— unofficially, of course," Sixkiller explained.

This was a new wrinkle he had worked out with Ivey and Evert to sow mischief among the ungodly, in addition to his fire inspector dodge.

Sixkiller went on. "Let's say we catch us a rustler and the others get away and our man won't talk. Well, it's our job to make him talk. Have I got that about right so far, Mr. Prosecutor?"

"Call me Mitch. That's right. That's about the size of it."

"I'll make that rustler talk," Bull said, his expression so fierce that the others grew mildly alarmed.

"He's got to be able to testify in court, Bull," Sixkiller said.

"What about Braddock?" Bull asked.

"What about him?"

"You know how he is. What if he tries to interfere?"

"That'll be just too bad," Sixkiller said, "for him."

"I'm gonna like this job," Bull said, grinning hugely.

"Remember you're working for Quinto, not me," Evert said. "You take orders from him. He seems to know enough law to keep you both out of trouble."

"I do the thinking for both of us, Bull."

"Sure, Quinto, sure. I got it."

"By the way, Mitch, what do you know about an hombre named Port?" Sixkiller asked.

"Too much," Evert said. "You can thank Port for making Braddock marshal."

"How's that?"

"Port killed Braddock's predecessor stone dead. Braddock was deputy and took over the marshal's job. It was coldblooded murder. Port gunned the marshal down without warning. We couldn't get a conviction, though. The witnesses were too scared of Port to testify. He's one of Endicott's top guns.

"How'd you get on to Port, Quinto?"

"Oh, I saw him and his pards cutting up earlier today on Liberty Street."

"Nobody was killed or I'd have heard of it. Lucky," Evert said.

"Reckon we'll mosey along then and make the rounds," Sixkiller said.

"What have you got in mind or is it something I shouldn't know about?" Evert asked.

"Whatever it is, it'll be perfectly legal," Sixkiller assured him. "Keep any weapons here?"

"What do you have in mind?" Evert said, repressing a slight start.

"Oh, nothing fancy. A shotgun, double-barreled twelve-gauge. For deterrence purposes . . . to stop trouble before it gets started," Sixkiller said.

"You seem to know a good deal about the workings of the law, Quinto."

"When you've been around as many jails and

sheriffs as I have, Mitch, you can't help but pick up something."

Evert went to a desk in a corner of the room and pushed up the rolltop. Stretched lengthwise on the desktop was a sawed-off, double-barreled shotgun. He picked it up, hefting it, showing it to the others.

Sixkiller looked at the prosecutor with new eyes. "You're a man of many ways, Mr. Prosecutor," he said respectfully.

"In Ringgold, a prosecutor has to be able to defend himself," Evert said. "I never know when some hothead will come busting in here looking for trouble. This is a most convincing persuader."

"I don't want to leave you without protection," Sixkiller said.

"You won't." Evert flipped back his baggy suit jacket to reveal a gun holstered in a shoulder rig harnessed under his left arm, the piece worn butt-out.

Sixkiller had thought the prosecutor had been looking a little bulky under that suit.

Evert opened a side drawer in the rolltop desk and took out a leather pouch. It was closed at the top by drawstrings. He opened it. Inside were several dozen shotgun shells. "I assume that'll be enough for your purposes," he said dryly.

"For a start," Sixkiller said. "Figure you can handle this, Bull?"

"Can I? Just watch the fur fly!" Bull enthused.

"Reckon we'll be on our way," Sixkiller said to Evert. "See you."

Chapter Seventeen

The Jackpot saloon looked somewhat bedraggled, like an attractive blonde with a black eye. The disreputable condition was due to the condition of the left front window, the one Sixkiller and Bull had gone crashing through during their previous day's tussle. It was boarded over, a patch-up job.

"We're not looking for trouble now, Bull, so be nice. Let me do the talking," Sixkiller said.

"Hey, you started the fight, not me!"

"Hmm, so I did. Best hold that sawed-off pointing down. We don't want to be misunderstood."

Bull looked formidable walking around with the shotgun. The pouch of buckshot shells was tied to his belt at the hip.

The duo went into the saloon. It was slack time after lunch—only a few handfuls of patrons were scattered around the big space. A quiet hour. Good food smells wafted from the free lunch table.

It got a lot quieter. Only the spinning of a Wheel of Fortune could be heard.

Stunned saloon girls froze while leaning over the serving tables to afford the customers a better look at the décolletage of their low-cut dresses. The customers were so shaken up they forgot to look. They were too busy staring at the newcomers.

A white-aproned chef at the carving table glared daggers at them, putting extra effort into sharpening the carving knife, which already had a keen edge on it.

"As you were, folks," Sixkiller said breezily to the assembled. It didn't seem to ease the tension much, if at all.

Mason Rourke came out of his office, impeccable in a dove-gray suit with gray satin ribbon trim on the lapels. A gray leather gun belt was wrapped around his waist.

Sixkiller glanced at Rourke's boots where they showed below the cuffs of his pants and was mildly disappointed to see that they were not gray, but tan. He made a mental note to ask Rourke when he was in a better humor if it was so hard to find gray boots.

Not that Rourke seemed in a bad humor. He was his usual unflappable self. He was a gambler and a successful one so he knew how to keep a poker face. No warmth showed in his pouchy, heavy-lidded eyes, but was there ever?

"You again!" Rourke said.

Sixkiller began by country-boying it. "Howdy, Mr. Rourke. We're not looking for trouble—"

"No? Too bad, because I've got plenty if that's what you're looking for. More than enough," Rourke said, glancing pointedly at Bull's shotgun.

"Oh, that sawed-off's got nothing to do with you. This is strictly a social visit," Sixkiller said.

"That's nice. Steve and Roy aren't looking for trouble either. They're sociable, too." Not taking his eyes off Sixkiller and Bull, Rourke indicated Steve and Roy with a tilt of his head.

Those so indicated were Jackpot staffers posted on the right-hand second floor balcony, each armed with shouldered rifles pointing straight down at Sixkiller and Bull.

"Howdy boys," Sixkiller said, waving at Steve and Roy, who failed to return or even acknowledge his salute. They kept their rifles pointed at their human targets.

"You're a busy man, Mr. Rourke, so we won't take up any more of your time. We just dropped in to apologize. We're real sorry we busted up your window—"

"And some tables and chairs," Rourke said quickly. "Don't forget them."

"I know you've been paid to cover the damages." Sixkiller knew Mayor Ivey had arranged the payment to sweeten the gambler. Sixkiller wanted Rourke to know that he knew. "We're sorry for what we did and trust that you'll accept the apology in the spirit it's offered. We've said our piece now, so we'll be on our way."

Rourke was a bit nonplussed. Whatever he'd been expecting, an apology wasn't it. He was thrown for an instant, a rarity for the smooth gambler. "Well sure, okay. Apology accepted."

"No hard feelings?" Sixkiller asked.

"No hard feelings," Rourke said. "Only next time you feel like busting loose, do it in somebody else's saloon."

Sixkiller smiled in an odd way. "Funny you should mention that . . . but you'll hear about it soon enough. See you."

He and Bull went out.

Rourke called up to Steve and Roy. "Hold your places in case it's a trick or they change their minds." Hand on the butt of his holstered gun, Rourke went to the entrance, looking out above the tops of the swinging doors. He watched Sixkiller and Bull walk away, their forms dwindling down the long street.

At Sixkiller's prompting, he and Bull went into Tobey's hardware store.

Sixkiller selected an ax handle, the biggest he could find.

Shopkeeper Tobey was beefy with wavy,

ginger-colored hair and muttonchop side-whiskers. "Good choice! That's a real lumber-jack's model. Now let me show you some A-One double-headed ax blades—"

"No thanks. Just the handle will do this time out," Sixkiller said. "But we need some kind of leather strap, something we can rig to that sawed-off so Bull can carry it over his shoulder and keep his hands free."

He turned to Bull. "Folks'll breathe easier that way, Bull. Seeing that sawed-off in your hand ready for action tends to have a powerful disturbing effect."

"But that's what we want, ain't it, Quinto?"

"Not all the time, no. We want to scare our enemies, not our friends or folks who might be inclined to be our friends. Besides, you need to keep your hands free for riding a horse or taking a drink or whatever."

"Okay."

"Make it a nice long strap," Sixkiller told Tobey. "Bull's got big shoulders."

Sixkiller paid for his purchases, then rigged the strap around the shotgun. The stock had been shaped into a kind of pistol grip. He tied the strap to the narrow waist of the grip and the other down near the twin muzzles.

Bull slung it over his right shoulder. "Not bad," he judged, adjusting it a bit.

When Sixkiller was satisfied Bull could wear

the piece comfortably, he thanked the shopkeeper and they left the store.

Standing on the boardwalk, Sixkiller looked
Bull over. "You know who wears a rig like that?
Doc Holiday."

"You don't tell me!"

"That's the honest truth. Doc's a big one
for working a sawed-off and that's how he
totes his around. I've seen him."

"If it's good enough for Doc, it's good
enough for me! Where to now?"

"I've some unfinished business to attend to,"
Sixkiller said.

They headed to the Paradise Club.

Sixkiller and Bull could smell the place long
before setting foot in it—raw whiskey fumes, a
haze of smoke, sweat, stale beer, and cheap
perfume.

They climbed three stairs to the porch of
Hickory Ned's saloon and went in. Even by day
it had a cavelike appearance, milky daylight fil-
tering in through dirty windows.

Sixkiller glanced down. Sawdust covered the
floor, all the better to soak up blood, of which
plenty was spilled, according to rumor.

He looked around, his eyes lighting up.
Smack-dab in the center of the place, like a cow
pie ringed by swarms of flies, were the Highline
riders he had seen earlier on the street—Port's
crowd. They had a table to themselves and

plenty of empty tables around it, others not wanting to sit too close for fear of attracting their attention and becoming the butt of their roughhousing.

There they were—Port, Virgil, Romeo, Foley, and Lew—seated in the center of things, facing the door.

Lew had taken on too much of the whizz. His arm was on the table, the side of his head lay on his arm, his hat covered his head. Dead drunk, apparently.

Romeo had a saloon girl on his lap. No mystery there. The girls at Hickory Ned's did more than sell drinks. They sold themselves, pure and simple . . . or maybe impure and not so simple.

He had his hands full, and was whispering sweet nothings in her ear or maybe sticking a tongue in there because she really started squirming on his lap. Not hard enough to get away though. She was too savvy for that.

Virgil slipped an arm around a saloon girl with curly blond hair, a plain face, and a sensational figure. She kept easing out of his grasp, but that snakelike arm of his kept returning to encircle her.

Foley was a mean drunk, not that he was much easier to get along with sober. He sat there scowling, eyes muddy, muttering a stream of obscenities.

Behind the bar stood a demented caricature of a white-bearded oldster as seen in a fun-house mirror in Hell. He was a scrawny old goat in a crooked top hat, white-haired with the beady red eyes of a drunken white mouse, blue drinker's veins webbing his long sharp face with its tufted, white billy goat beard.

He saw Sixkiller and Bull, and looked worried. The place was a bucket of blood saloon with an outlaw clientele, a murderous clientele he had to ride herd on with six-gun and shotgun. But Bull Raymond was more trouble than any saloon keeper should have to deal with, a one-man wrecking crew when his fighting blood was up, and it didn't take much to rouse his ire.

As for the stranger, he was an unknown quantity. The only known thing was that he had fought Bull to a draw, if not a victory. Now they were together, yoked in tandem and ready for . . . what?

"Mind your manners, Bull," Sixkiller said in a low-voiced aside, "but mostly keep your eye on that white-haired bird behind the bar. He looks shifty."

"That's Hickory Ned hisself."

"Well!"

Port was first to take notice, but it wasn't Sixkiller he focused on. It was Bull. The sawed-off slung over Bull's shoulder intimidated him not at all. Port was fast.

"Hey boys!" he roared. "Take a look at who just come slinking in. Bull Raymond!"

The others of his crowd—all but Lew—listened and looked up. He stayed head down, inert, oblivious.

Foley's mean face got meaner, eyes shining with anticipation of fresh sport in the offing. He was unworried because he figured . . . actually, he knew . . . that speedy Port could draw and shoot Bull through the heart before Bull could unlimber the sawed-off.

The rest of the crowd figured the same way, all but Lew, who was too drunk to do any figuring at all.

Sixkiller knew the type, the outlaw kind. He had had them sized up from the start when he saw them earlier on the street.

Cowboys? No, they were not working cowboys, men who worked damned hard for low wages and played hard. Honest cowboys could run mighty rough indeed, especially when in their cups. A cowboy had to know how to use a gun. It was a tool of the trade like a lariat or branding iron. They'd shoot if they had to, mostly rattlesnakes, but sometime rustlers. They weren't killers.

The crew at the center table was a different story. Port and his crew were not cowhands but gun hands. These rannies didn't give a good damn that Bull was a terror with his fists. They weren't fist fighters. Come at them with fists clenched and they'd put a bullet in him without thinking twice.

The only reason a rancher would hire them was because he meant to make war on his neighbors, to take all he could grab at gunpoint.

So—no mercy, from them or for them.

The inevitable taunts came quickly, foreplay to explosive violence.

"Hey Bull, who laid that mouse under your eye?"

"That ain't no mouse. It's a rat!"

"Looks like he was dragged down forty miles of bad road, facedown!"

"Naw, he always looks like that!"

"Bull, what's up, buddy? You come sucking around looking for a job on the Highline? Might be an opening. The cook's looking for a pot boy."

"Pot boy? You mean *prat boy*, don'cha? Haw!"

The two saloon gals, Polly and Flo, were cackling, laughing so hard the white face powder caked on their faces started coming off in flakes. Their laughter went a bit hollow when Sixkiller loomed over the table, ax handle held dangling down at his side.

Port sat with his chair pushed back from the table to give him room to draw. He wore his gun reversed, butt-forward, possibly a quicker reach if seated than the standard style for a gun grab.

"Vamoose, Chief. They don't serve redskins in this establishment," Romeo said.

Polly and Flo convulsed into mirth like it was the funniest thing they'd ever heard. When Flo laughed, her bountiful bosom heaved, threatening to spill free of the tight confines of her outfit, which was frayed at the edges and straining at the seams.

Lew stirred restlessly in a drunken stupor, arms flapping like a land-bound walrus using its flippers to drag itself along the beach.

"Say . . . wasn't it a redskin that whupped Bull?" Virgil asked, eyes narrowing.

"Sure was! Now Bull's carrying his water," Romeo said.

"Bull's already got hisself a job as prat boy for the big chief," Foley spat out.

Sixkiller was smiling, if you could call that jack-o'-lantern grimace of his a smile. It might be mistaken for a smile if one didn't look too closely . . . or if he were drunk enough.

Port wasn't that drunk. He was suspicious and ready for action.

Foley was geared for trouble, too. Virgil and Romeo not so much, but they'd follow their leader.

"Gee, he's a big one, ain't he?" Polly said, looking Sixkiller up and down.

"I'll give you a big one," Romeo growled.

"What do you think you're gonna do with that ax handle, boy?" Foley demanded.

"You know the Bible Psalm that goes 'Thy rod and Thy staff, they comfort me'? Well, this here's my rod." Sixkiller paused a moment, then added, "Not the kind of rod you gals take your comfort from." He was playing up to the women because he knew that would burn the Highline riders even more.

Flo was taking a drink when Sixkiller cracked wise. She choked on her laughter, whiskey spewing out of her nostrils. It burned, making her cough and choke.

Polly screamed with laughter at her.

Port's crowd didn't like Sixkiller taking the play.

"What're you, one of them Mission Injins that got the white man's religion? You're preaching to the wrong choir," Romeo said.

"You gone git yourself a pair of wings sooner than you expect, boy," Virgil said.

"You in an all-fired hurry to get into that white man's Heaven?" Romeo asked.

"He cain't get in. No redskins allowed," Virgil said.

Port wasn't joking. He'd had enough cat-and-mouse. Trouble was, he was a mite confused about who was the cat and who was the mouse. "Mister, you're going straight to the Devil." He clawed for his gun.

Sixkiller held the ax handle like a baton, gripping it in the middle. He reached across the table, lunging like a fencer, thrusting the wide, blunt end into the hollow at the base of Port's throat. The vicious strike stopped the gunman cold.

Not as vicious as it could have been, though. With more force it would have been lethal—a killing stroke.

Port choked, gasping for breath, face purpling. Both hands reached up to clutch his throat, as he wheezed and sucked for air.

As long as the ax handle was in the neighborhood, Sixkiller meant to keep it working. He swung it sideways, a slashing circular strike that whammed Virgil on the side of the head below the hat brim so there was nothing to cushion the blow. It struck with a snap like the crack of a whip.

Virgil followed the direction of the blow, toppling over sideways out of the chair and taking the gal with him down to the floor.

Flo started screaming from the floor in the sawdust, her limbs all tangled up with Virgil's.

Foley grabbed for his gun.

Sixkiller's free hand grabbed the table edge and heaved, uplifting and overturning the table.

Polly jumped out of Romeo's lap, slipping off to the sidelines as the table toppled, knocking Lew, Foley, and Port to the floor. Clear of the overturned table and free of Polly on his lap, Romeo was free to go for his gun.

Too bad for him.

Sixkiller had a two-handed grip on the ax handle and jabbed it to the point of Romeo's chin, snapping his head back. He followed through with a couple more jabs, liking the popping sound it made when it connected with Romeo's chin and liking the way his head kept snapping back.

Romeo's eyes rolled up in his head so only the whites showed. He was *out. O-U-T Out!* He fell backward to the floor, gun undrawn. He'd never had a chance to clear the holster.

Lew somehow woke up amid all the turmoil. Deprived of the resting place for his heavy drunken head he flopped around on the sawdust.

Between Sixkiller and Foley and Port, the table balanced upright on the rounded rim, two legs on the floor, two in the air. Sixkiller circled around it, bringing him to Foley, who had his gun up and swinging it toward Sixkiller.

The Oklahoman sliced with an upward thrust that caught Foley on the underside of the wrist, driving his gun hand up. Ax handle impacted flesh and bone with a cracking sound that was drowned out by a blast of gunfire as Foley reflexively jerked the trigger.

The shot went harmlessly into the ceiling.

Sixkiller slashed again, knocking the gun from Foley's hand. Foley screamed.

A booming blast sounded a warning shot as Bull cut loose with one of the barrels of the sawed-off shotgun.

Sixkiller spared a glance to see what was going on.

Bull had fired in the direction of Hickory Ned, not at him, for if he had it would have been Hickory Ned who had the big hole in him rather than the wall beside him.

Ned had been reaching under the bar for a weapon. Covered by Bull's shotgun, he froze.

"Ah-ah." Bull grinned, wagging a finger at Ned.

No one else in the saloon was minded to catch the buckshot in the other barrel.

All of which Sixkiller took in an eye blink. He still had work to do.

In the prone position, Virgil stirred on the floor, trying to rouse himself. He was out of the picture, merely something in the way, and Sixkiller stepped on him, stomping him flat. Virgil stopped trying to get up, and Sixkiller moved on to Port.

With his right hand clutching his throat, Port pulled his gun with the left.

Sixkiller stepped down hard, pinning the gunman's wrist to the floor.

Port worked the trigger, slugs burning a few inches above the floor, tearing into the base of the bar across the room. Patrons at the bar previously stupefied by Bull's shotgun blast had to step lively as bullets blazed around their feet.

Standing over Port, Sixkiller thrust straight down with the ax handle, using it like a spear, hammering Port's chin. Port became unconscious.

Sixkiller looked around the saloon. Port was knocked out stone cold. Foley, ditto. Virgil lay with arms and legs feebly flailing. Romeo sat huddled in a heap on the floor, holding his head in his hands, moaning. Lew had come out of it the lightest, mainly because he had never really been in the fight. He was on hands and knees, head bowed, dazed, and covered with sawdust like all the others who'd hit the floor.

Sixkiller bent down, prying the gun from Port's unresisting fingers. He kicked it across the floor. Raising the ax handle high overhead in both hands, he brought it down sizzling hard on Port's gun hand. It was like crushing the head of a poisonous serpent. There was a crackling sound of breaking bones.

Somebody screamed. But it wasn't Port. He was knocked out, stirring not at all.

Assorted gasps and groans came from the spectators as Bull held the shotgun leveled, covering them.

"Port's out of the gunslinging business—permanently," Sixkiller announced in a voice of doom. "I'm feeling charitable today so I didn't gun him out. I won't be so easygoing next time. Any rannies who try to hoorah the town will get the same or worse."

Lew had kicked the oldster in the seat of the pants earlier. Sixkiller snaked Lew's gun out of the holster. Lew flinched, shouting out loud and cowering.

"Bellowing like a yearling roped for the branding," Sixkiller said in disgust. "Quit your squalling. You ain't hurt yet." He gripped Lew's upper arm, hauling him up on his feet.

Lew shivered, nearly hysterical. "What— what're you gonna do?!"

"This is for that old gentleman you booted in the tail," Sixkiller said. "You thought that was so damned funny, maybe you'll get a kick out of this!"

Sixkiller planted a tremendous kick to Lew's tailbone, lifting him straight up into the air with both feet leaving the floor. Lew was pro- pelled a goodly distance across the floor to land belly down, skittering through the sawdust, leaving skid marks to mark his trail.

"One last word," Sixkiller said to Hickory Ned. "I'm Quinto. Tell Bart Skillern I've got a message for him from Dean Richmond. I'll tell it to him when I meet him face-to-face."

"I'll just do that little thing, mister," Hickory Ned said.

"See that you do or I'll be back for you and I

won't be so gentle next time," Sixkiller said. "We're done here, Bull."

"Right!"

Sixkiller went to the saloon doors, hand on his gun. He looked outside to see if anybody was laying for them. "All clear, Bull. Let's go."

"Be polite, gents," Bull said, backing out of the entrance, still covering the customers with the sawed-off.

They went outside, where knots of curious onlookers had gathered at a safe distance, staring at the saloon and wondering what was happening inside. Some scattered when they saw Sixkiller and Bull emerge.

The duo hustled east on Liberty Street, not exactly running, but not taking a leisurely stroll either. No habitués of the Paradise Club followed to pursue the matter further.

They nearly collided with Reeve Westbrook coming the other way. Westbrook had a notepad in hand and his face was shiny.

Bull said, "Look who it is. Johnny-on-the-spot!"

"What happened? I heard shooting! Anybody killed?" Westbrook craned to see past them to the saloon.

"Nothing to get excited about," Sixkiller said. "Some Highline hands fell down and knocked themselves out. It's a shame when grown men can't hold their liquor."

"What're you doing with that ax handle?"

"I need it for prospecting."

"But there's no blade on it."

"Damn! Knew I forgot something. No wonder Tobey let me have it so cheap."

Sixkiller and Bull absented themselves from the scene, while Westbrook rushed into the Paradise Club.

Chapter Eighteen

The law in Ringgold, such as it was, waited until dinnertime to make its move against Sixkiller.

At the Bon Ton Café, he and Bull sat at a corner table with both seats turned so they could see the front door. It was a popular eatery and most of the tables were full. There was a lively buzz of conversation and the clatter of knives and forks on plates.

Sixkiller added to the conversation, filling Bull in on his afternoon. He had finally enjoyed the luxury of a hot bath, washing the jail-house stink out of his skin. A loaded gun had sat on the stand beside the tub throughout, but nothing had interrupted his steaming soak.

Bull didn't believe in baths, a topic he held forth on during dinner. "I don't hold with it. Too much bathing can weaken you," he insisted.

"Where'd you hear that?" Sixkiller asked.

"From an old buffalo hunter."

"It might be good advice if you want to sneak up on an old buffalo, but there ain't too many of them left around no more."

"Ain't it the truth?" Bull lamented. "The herds are just about gone from Wyoming. Come next spring there won't be none left."

"Funny—everywhere you go in the West there's always a Bon Ton café," Sixkiller said. "Why is that? I don't know why. It just is. I don't even know what *Bon Ton* means."

"Who cares? Just so long as the chow's good," Bull said.

It was good, with thick juicy steaks big enough to cover the plates, and the plates were big. The steak was done the way Sixkiller liked, blackened on the outside, red on the inside. He had a side of fried potatoes, some sliced tomatoes, and bread, washed down with mugs of sharp tangy ale. Bull had pretty much the same, only more.

The café owner, Alex, was short and squat with slicked down curly black hair and a mustache. He manned the register by the door as diners finished and cleared out. Soon, only a few tables were occupied. A handful of miners who'd come down from the camps sat at a side table working their forks and spoons like shovels as they excavated their plates clean. A few solitary eaters sat at small tables scattered around the room.

"You know the food's good here because the waitress ain't nothing to look at," Bull said, loud enough for Cora to overhear.

She was big with a mammoth bosom, thick middle, horse buttocks, and a visage like a shaved dish-faced bear. She called Bull a dirty name.

"I don't think Cora likes us too well," Sixkiller said.

"Hell, she don't like nobody too well," Bull opined.

Sixkiller and Bull cleaned their plates. Cora sullenly stacked them to take them away.

"We ain't done yet," Bull said. "Bring me a quart of coffee." No need to specify black coffee. That's how men in the West took their coffee. "A meal ain't a meal without coffee."

"Agreed," Sixkiller said. He told Cora, "I'll have a pot of coffee too, a separate pot. I ain't much for sharing. Bring me half an apple pie. Not a slice. I want a whole half a pie."

"I'll take the other half," Bull said.

Dessert and coffee arrived at the table quickly.

"Got any whiskey to go with that coffee?" Sixkiller asked.

"No hard liquor served here, mister," Cora said.

"Come on. Don't tell me you don't have a bottle or two set aside for special customers or cooking purposes?" Sixkiller pressed, suggestively rattling some gold coins in his hand.

"I'll take a look." Cora went into the kitchen, returning with a pitcher. She set it down on the table.

"You call that service? We want whiskey, not cream," Bull said in an aggrieved tone.

"Look inside, grumpy," Cora all but spat.

Sixkiller lifted the shiny metal lid. Brown whiskey filled the pitcher, its aromatic fumes wafting out. "Better have a look, Bull."

Bull held the pitcher under his face, which lit up. He inhaled deeply. "Ahh . . ."

"If I brought out a bottle of whiskey everybody would want one," Cora said snippily.

"Why don't you? What's wrong with whiskey anyhow."

Cora paused before lowering the boom. "It brings in undesirable customers." She went away, waddling into the kitchen.

"I guess she put me in my place," Bull said, grinning.

"That's us—undesirable customers." Sixkiller poured a generous splash of whiskey into his cup, filling the rest with coffee. Bull did the same only with a bigger splash and less coffee.

Sixkiller held the cup under his nose, savoring the heady aroma of rich fresh-brewed coffee laced with whiskey. He took a long pull. "That cools down hot coffee better than cream."

A small lithe form floated up on the other side of the café's front window. It was Eli, the boy Sixkiller had met when he first rode into town, the kid who'd steered him to Noble's livery stable. A street kid, frontier town version.

Boys are useful lookouts. Adults pay no attention to them except to chase them away to loiter somewhere else. Boys of a certain age are small and sneaky and as the saying goes, "Little pitchers have big ears."

And bigger eyes, seeing plenty more than adults think they do, a fact well known to Sixkiller, who found them useful aides in the sleuthing game. Earlier that day he had located Eli and pitched him a business proposition, one given careful consideration by the youngster now that Sixkiller had the prestige of being the man who fought Bull Raymond to a draw.

Sixkiller put Eli on the payroll and fed him some spare coins with the promise of more to come. "Watch the marshal and his deputies and keep me posted on their comings and goings. Be on the lookout for any hardcases riding into town, especially if they come in force. It's a big job and it'll take a passel of kids so rope your friends in on this. I'll pay you and you pay them. When you get them lined up ready to work, let me know because there's some town hall characters I want watched, too."

Sixkiller gave Eli the high sign, motioning him to come inside.

Alex scowled at Eli's entrance. No paying customer. Kids were a nuisance.

Eli dodged him, rushing to Sixkiller's table. He was a bright-eyed youngster with excited high color in his cheeks.

Sixkiller paused with a piece of pie impaled on a fork halfway to his mouth. "What's up?"

"The marshal and his deputies are standing around the corner keeping an eye on this place. I seen them. They got shotguns. Looks like they mean business, mister," Eli said.

"I'll be mindful of it, thanks. You got your buddies following those fellows I pointed out to you this afternoon at the courthouse?"

"Sure do!"

"Keep watching." Sixkiller passed Eli some dollar coins under the table. "Thanks, partner. Best go through the kitchen out the back door so the law don't see you."

"That's what else I wanted to tell you," Eli said excitedly. "One of the deputies went around the back way. I saw him sneaking around the back before—Wheeler, the one who's always smiling all the time."

"Much obliged. Better go out the front way and make yourself scarce," Sixkiller said. "Keep your eyes open and don't forget to duck."

Eli bobbed his head, nodding yes. He scooted up the aisle and went out the front door, vanishing into the darkling dusk.

"That idea of yours of hiring them kids as lookouts is starting to pay off big," Bull said.

"It'll pay off even better if my hunch about

the courthouse crowd pans out," Sixkiller said. "Right now we've got a more immediate problem. Looks like Braddock's crowding for a showdown."

"He's the one who's got the problem." Bull pushed back his chair and stood up. "I'll cover the back door." He reached for the sawed-off shotgun hanging by its strap on the back of an empty chair at the table. "I'll take care of Wheeler."

"Don't kill him if you don't have to," Sixkiller cautioned.

Bull looked disappointed. "You ain't gonna turn into one of them reformers, are you?"

"Not hardly."

"Good." Bull hefted the sawed-off and lumbered toward the rear of the café, into the kitchen.

At the register in front, Alex started to protest, thought better of it, and kept quiet. He looked worried, fretting.

Sixkiller rose to speak to his fellow diners. Luckily they were few, the dinner crowd having peaked earlier. "There's liable to be some trouble, folks, so if you're nervous about gunplay, better clear out now." Sixkiller said.

"Why the hell don't you get out instead," Cora demanded angrily. "Why do you have to make trouble?"

"I'm still working on that pie, ma'am."

Cora told him what he could do with the pie.

"I haven't finished my coffee, either."

She told him what he could do with the coffee . . . and the coffeepot, too.

"I'm sorry you feel like that," Sixkiller said.

Cora muttered something so deep under her breath that he couldn't hear it. She breathed hard, her massive bosom heaving with indignation.

Alex was anxious about the threat of upcoming action, but not so much that he failed to get between the front exit and some diners who tried to clear out without first paying their bill.

A lone diner threw some dollar coins on the table, leaving most of his meal uneaten. "That'll cover it," he said, hurrying out.

Alex must have agreed because he let the man slip out the front door without a further accounting.

Two other diners paid up and went out fast, not looking back.

Not the miners at the big side table. They kept on stolidly eating, while showing some interest in the coming clash.

Sixkiller picked at his pie, working his fork with his left hand. His right held his drawn gun in his lap, under a white cloth napkin. The piece was covering the front door.

Sure enough in they came, Braddock and Porrock, full-length shotguns in hand, held pointed downward. They entered one at a time, Braddock first, then the deputy.

"That's close enough," Sixkiller said. "Keep those shotguns pointed straight down at the floor, boys. Else there's gonna be two vacancies opening up in the jailhouse department."

"Mighty big talk," Braddock said, but he stopped advancing and kept the shotgun lowered. Porrock followed his lead, doing the same.

"How you figure on backing your play?" Braddock demanded.

"With this here Colt I'm holding under the table aimed at your belly," Sixkiller said.

"Aw hell, you ain't gonna fall for that line of horse pucky? He's bluffing." Porrock sneered.

"I'd say that too, if I was standing behind Braddock, you yellowbelly."

Braddock didn't like that so well. He wanted to glance back to see what Porrock was doing and if he was really using his boss as a shield, but he didn't dare take his focus off Sixkiller.

Sixkiller raised the barrel of the Colt, causing a fold of the napkin to fall back, baring the gun muzzle so Braddock could get a look at that big black hole death came out of.

"He's got that gun drawn," Braddock said tightly. "What kind of game you playing, Quinto?"

"I was eating pie before you came horning in," Sixkiller said. "You got the drop on me the last time we tangled. I was kind of distracted at the time, trying to keep Bull Raymond from beating my brains out. And I wasn't wearing my gun. I couldn't have made it easier for you, if I'd tried. Things shape up different now, huh?"

"You can't be that drunk, Quinto, and you ain't loco, so drop that gun and raise your hands," Braddock said.

"Now who's loco?" Sixkiller said, smiling nastily.

"You're under arrest."

"Prove it."

The issue hung fire for a long pause, the tension mounting. Even the miners had stopped eating, their eyes big in their heads as they watched the confrontation.

Sixkiller reckoned that Braddock was stalling for time, waiting for Wheeler to come in through the back door. Then they'd have lined up in a squeeze play, caught in a shotgun crossfire.

It didn't work out that way.

The Ringgold lawmen had forgotten about Bull.

Wheeler's shriek from the kitchen rang with the mortal terror of instant death. "*No, don't!*—"

It was cut short, silenced by the booming blast of a shotgun exploding in the tight confines of the kitchen. The concussion had a physical presence, like a thunderclap or a bomb going off. It had different effects on the players.

Braddock froze. Porrock jerked the shotgun up toward Sixkiller.

Porrock made a fatal miscalculation, forgetting that while Braddock's body shielded him from Sixkiller's bullets, Sixkiller was screened by Braddock from Porrock's shotgun.

Braddock was the man in the middle, the one caught in a crossfire.

Sixkiller's gun barked twice, putting two slugs into Braddock's middle. He had to drop Braddock to get Porrock. Braddock wouldn't shoot under Sixkiller's gun. Porrock was sure to make a play.

Sixkiller threw himself to the right-hand side the instant he squeezed off the two shots, diving for a clear line of fire on Porrock.

Braddock was already folding at the knees when Porrock panicked, loosing a shotgun blast before his weapon was clear of the marshal's falling form. Braddock took most the blast in the back.

Sixkiller fired from the floor, twin lances of light that were muzzle flares licking out at an upward angle to spear Porrock in the middle.

Already off-balance when he was tagged, Porrock vented an inarticulate, strangled cry of fear and rage that was chopped off by Sixkiller's slugs. His feet got all tangled up, tripping him on twisted legs. He backpedaled, falling through the café's front window. A musical clangor sounded as the glass pane exploded outward into the street.

Porrock lay bent backward, his upper body

hanging out the window sill and his lower body inside the café.

The silence of stilled guns was a physical presence, an oppressive weight. Glass shards jangled as they worked loose from the window frame, falling to the floor.

The walls and ceiling looked like a blood bomb had gone off, largely the result of Brad dock catching Porrock's shotgun blast in the back. Upper walls were peppered with buckshot pellets.

The place stank of blood, gunpowder, and death.

Braddock lay facedown on the floor. He was shredded and raggedy, the back of his clothes smoking and burning from stopping a shotgun blast at point blank range.

Sixkiller lay on his side on the floor, raised on his elbows, gun arm extended. A wispy line of gun smoke curled from the muzzle of his gun.

The miners at the side table began cautiously raising themselves from the floor where they had flung themselves once the gunplay opened.

Alex's head raised from behind the counter where the register was kept.

The hushed silence was suddenly interrupted by a rustling in the kitchen. Sixkiller swung his gun to cover it.

He eased off the trigger when he saw Bull stick his head into the dining area. Bull was tough, but he couldn't help wincing when he saw the carnage in the café.

Sixkiller got to his feet, brushing himself off.

Bull looked like he had showered in blood. He had—but none of it was his.

"Wheeler," Bull said in answer to Sixkiller's questioning glance. "He tried to make a play." He paused a moment, then added, "What else could I do?"

"I ain't kicking," Sixkiller said.

"Oh. Good," Bull said toothily.

"Cora?" Sixkiller asked.

"Out the back door," Bull said. "She was so scared she didn't bother to open it first. She hit that door running, knocked it flat off its hinges, and kept on going. Last I saw of her, she was still running."

"Too bad. She was a good cook," Sixkiller said, sighing. "I reckon she was right, though."

"Eh? How's that?"

"We are undesirable customers."

Chapter Nineteen

The Hour of Death had come and was raging.

Not where Sixkiller was to be found, however. Not yet, but soon.

The night after he and Bull retired with bullets Braddock and his deputies, gunfire blazed across the Glint. Colonel Donovan led his riders on a smashing raid against Endicott's Highline Ranch. The Highline crowd was seriously, perhaps mortally wounded by the double loss of Port and his crew and the elimination of Marshal Braddock and the protection he provided to the bad men.

The furious gun battle raged on the Highline as long-suffering Donovan and his men tore in righteous fury at the vitals of Endïcott's outfit.

Sixkiller was far from the scene of the action, honchoing an eerie midnight ride of an armored pay wagon. He held the reins as coachman for the midnight pay run to the mining camp at Sagebrush Flats.

In their wisdom, the directors of the Western Territories Mining Company had decided there would never be a better time for a payroll run than while all Ringgold and the valley were distracted by the final chapter of the Donovan-Endicott war.

Were the WTMC division bosses right in their calculations?

The answer would not be long in coming.

The payroll delivery wagon was no ordinary stagecoach, not a passenger vehicle at all. It looked uncomfortably like to a hearse. It was long, narrow, and high-sided, with no windows and double doors in the rear, drawn by a team of ten black horses yoked in tandem, two by two.

The midnight pay run made up in stealth, speed, and surprise what it seemingly lacked in firepower.

Sixkiller wore a long, dark duster. Beside him, riding shotgun was Bull Raymond. Several big-caliber rifles lay in the boot at the foot of the seat. No cashbox rode on top of the coach. The money chest was locked inside the wagon out of sight.

At the foot of the hill, Sixkiller lit up a fat cigar, took up the driver's whip, a wicked blacksnake whip he handled with authority, and cracked it expertly over the heads of the horses. Thus began the last leg of the journey—the

climb up the slope of the rise to Sagebrush
Flats. The landscape of the valley flattened and
spread out below. Atop the summit awaited a
quick mad dash across open flat ground to the
mining camp where supervisors and armed
guards were gathered.

It was something of a wild night—clouds at
the remote heights of the dome sky scudding
along under brisk, chilly winds blowing not
from the prevailing north, but rather from the
west. The moon at the zenith alternated floods
of silver light with great curtains of blackness
depending on whether it was covered by clouds.

The summit drew near.

This is the hinge, thought Sixkiller. *This is where
Bart Skillern would make his play.* The team of
horses would be at their slowest and most tired
when they reached the crest, less able to pour
on the extra speed needed to outdistance
charging outlaws.

The coach crested the summit, topping
Sagebrush Flats. Rock spurs and outcroppings
ahead upthrust out of the soil to display weird
wind-eroded rock forms, twisted gnarly pillars
of stone.

Suddenly, a brassy metal bee—a bullet—
whined past Sixkiller's head. Dark riders emerged
from behind the rocks ahead to fan out, blocking the road. They whooped, hollered, and
hoorahed, firing into the air.

Sixkiller set aside the whip and hauled in on

the reins, throwing the hand brake. Horses were drawn up short, halting the coach. He puffed on his cigar, unconcerned. He was holding something up his sleeve, hidden by the cuff of his duster coat.

Shots came from behind, too. Sixkiller glanced over his shoulder. Another half-dozen riders came up from behind the coach, charging from the rear. The bandits had the coach boxed in, front and back.

"The gang's all here" Sixkiller said. Bart Skillern, Lonnie Brett, Josh "Haywire" Haworth, Denver Ralls, Beany Evans, Carlton T. Olin and a couple new hands unknown to Sixkiller, hands the gang had added along the way.

Bart Skillern rode ahead, taking the fore of the group of riders blocking the road ahead. He closed on the coach, halting less than a stone's throw away. "Quinto?" he called.

"That's right," Sixkiller said. One name's as good as another when you're on the hunt, closing in for the kill.

"I'm Bart Skillern—the Utah Kid. I heard you were looking for me."

"Shoot him and be done with it," one of his men advised. But Bart Skillern was not one to take advice, good, bad, or indifferent.

"Quinto interests me. He got closer than any of the others," Skillern said. "Who are you, Quinto? I don't know you. You with Pinkerton?

You a Pink? Continental Detective Agency, maybe?"

"No," Sixkiller said.

"That's good. Makes it more interesting. Bounty killer, maybe? You sure come on like one, leaving a trail of corpses from Nibiru to here. Impressive!

"You were looking for me, and you found me. I should say, I found you. Others tried to find me. They're all dead. Now you're gonna join them."

Sixkiller puffed away at his cigar, the orange disk glowing brightly, lighting his face with a webwork of orange-red lines. Reaching to take it from between his jaws, he flicked off a half-inch of dead ash at the tip.

"You did better than the rest, if it's any consolation," Skillern went on. "You busted up Port and his boys pretty good, but he wasn't much. Took out Braddock, too. He was faster. Was that you who did for Freedy and Hooper?"

"Those the clowns at Powder Basin?" Sixkiller asked.

"Yup. So it was you who got them," Skillern said, laughing. "In the end, though, what did it get you?"

"You."

"You know the old saying, 'Be careful what you wish for, you just might get it'? You got that backwards, son. You ain't got me. I got you."

"Depends on your point of view," Sixkiller said.

Bull Raymond stirred restlessly on the seat beside him, longing to get into action. But he knew not to jump the gun on Sixkiller's plan.

"I heard you had a message for me from Dean Richmond," Skillern said. "That for true?"

"True."

"What is it? What's the message?"

"They were his last words. His very last words. He said, 'Tell Bart I'll see him in Hell.' And since we don't want to keep him waiting—"

Sixkiller brought his hand up to his face, lighting the short-fused stick of dynamite hidden up his sleeve. It hissed, sputtered, then burst into crackling flame, a line of fire stabbing into the stick. He tossed it at Skillern and dove off the left side of the coach, while Bull threw himself off the right.

Short fuse? A *very* short fuse. Skillern's gun cleared leather and swung toward Sixkiller even as the dynamite exploded.

It struck like a thunderbolt crashing to earth. It was the signal for mayhem, a blinding blast of heat, light, and smoke spoiling the aim of Skillern's riders.

It also signaled Vandaman and the federal agent's gunmen hidden in the wagon. The armored sides were hinged and fell down, opening the upper halves of the long walls of the vehicle.

Its back doors flung open. Riflemen inside

opened fire, cutting down the bandits to the rear of the coach.

The harnessed team wanted to bolt, but couldn't move forward with the handbrake locked and set the way Sixkiller had left it.

As he rolled clear of the coach, Sixkiller started slinging lead into the bandits in front of the coach. On the other side of the vehicle, Bull was shooting too, his shotgun blasting.

The riflemen in the carriage weren't the only shooters in the area. Other posse men hidden in the hills behind the rocks opened fire. Skillern's gang was caught in the crossfire, shot to pieces.

But not the Utah Kid. He did not share their fate.

He had been blown to pieces, scattered to the four winds by the stick of dynamite Sixkiller had tossed at him.

Chapter Twenty

Once again, it was a case of, "the gang's all here."

Different gang, though, thought Sixkiller.

They were assembled in the courthouse . . . without Mr. Justice Applewhite presiding. Applewhite had shrunk mighty small as a prisoner of the law.

Collected on hard wooden benches in the courtroom were Sixkiller, Bull, Vandaman, Cass Horgan, Reeve Westbrook, Edmund Bigelow, Mayor Dawes Ivey, Prosecutor Mitch Evert, Mason Rourke, Colonel Tim Donovan, his foreman Pete Pecos, and Jackpot saloon girl Brenda.

Conspicuous by his absence was Milt Dash.

The get-together was part victory celebration and part inquest.

"Man, you missed a real brawl," B Square B foreman Pete Pecos told Bull. "Endicott and his boys rode into a buzz saw! With us on one side and Rourke and his men on the other, we shot the buttons off them rannies."

"What about Endicott?" Bull asked.

"He broke off running, him and what was left of his men. At the rate he was going, he won't stop till he hits Montana!"

"If he comes back here, there'll be a rope waiting for him," Evert vowed grimly.

"Better save more than one rope," Sixkiller cautioned. "There's still a rascal or two left unhung. Or even unknown. A secret plotter, a hidden hand not entirely unknown, not to me and not to one other party here tonight."

No small uproar followed Sixkiller's words. When the clamor had quieted, he went on. "Bart Skillern wasn't alone in this scheme. Endicott neither. There was a third man, an inside man tipping them off on our every move and more.

"That's why I put young Eli and his friends to watching everybody who knew about the so-called secret payroll shipment to the mines last night. Or thought they knew. There never was a payroll shipment. It was a scheme worked out by Vandaman and me to flush out Skillern and bring him out in the open.

"The secret was told to a handful of people here and I had Eli and the kids spying on each and every one of them, morning, noon, and night. Watching to see who—if anybody—

would ride out to tip off Skillern about a fat midnight payroll run to the mines.

"The skunk in the garden patch turned out to be Milt Dash, the mayor's special assistant. When Eli tipped me that Dash was acting suspiciously, I saddled up and followed him out of town. He led me not to Endicott, but to the Utah Kid and his hideout. A good one, most forgotten by the town—the old flooded Mine Shaft Number Seven.

"Nobody goes there anymore. Why would they? That's what made it a good hideout. Still some old buildings up there to live in. Underground diggings and aboveground tailings for the gang to hide their horses and lights at night.

"But there was more up there. A woman. She was one the reasons Skillern's longtime pard Dean Richmond split with him. What woman? Lord Dennis's lady, La Valletta, a famous beauty who could turn most any man's head. You all thought she was killed with the rest of the Bletchley party, but with no bodies to be found no one could be sure.

"But it didn't work out that way. Bart Skillern had found the one thing money can't buy—the one woman in the world he most wanted and had to have, no matter what. Since he was a thief and killer, he did what comes naturally and took what he wanted. He took her and made her his prisoner—slave—call it what you will.

"The only one of his gang he trusted to keep an eye on her was old Nestor Fox. Figured he was too old to be swayed by her charms into letting her go free or falling for her charms enough to let down his guard to give her a chance to escape. When the rest of the gang went out on jobs, Fox stayed behind at the hideout to watch over her, make sure she didn't escape, and that none of the gang ever got close enough to her to fall under her spell.

"I followed Dash to the hideout. When Skillern and the others rode out to set up the midnight ambush at Sagebrush Flats, old Fox stayed behind guarding the girl. Dean Richmond had told of Valletta before he died so I knew who to look for. I put down Fox and freed the girl, taking her to a safe place before going to the showdown with Skillern.

"Valletta's got one final key to the puzzle. Who put the idea of the Lost Gold Mine into Bletchley's head, luring him and his party to ambush and death by Skillern's gang? Lord Dennis was an Englishman and a foreigner but he wasn't a complete damned fool. It took a mighty slick talker to convince him to go take a look.

"Who was he? Who was this silent partner, the third man in the combine with Skillern and

Endicott? I'll let Val tell you herself. Folks, meet La Valletta," Sixkiller finished up.

The door opened and in she came, escorted by Brenda and Rourke. Valletta had had a chance to wash and clean up after her long ordeal. She was a beauty with a wild mane of golden hair, dark almond-shaped eyes, and a mouth of ripe passion. The bitterness and hardship of her experience couldn't erase her stunning beauty.

Valletta set eyes on the silent partner the moment she entered the room. If she'd had a knife in her hand she'd surely have used it on him. He jumped up and started running for the door even before she stabbed an accusing finger at him to point him out to the others.

Reeve Westbrook, ace reporter for the *Banner*.

Sixkiller was ready for him, his gun drawn. He shot him in the leg, blowing off a kneecap to bring him down. He wanted Westbrook alive.

"They'll have to prop him up when he goes to hang, but they can always sit him on a horse when he swings, so that's no problem," Sixkiller said. "Why did Westbrook do it? Maybe he got tired of writing news and wanted to make some of his own, behind the scenes. Maybe it tickled him to pose as a drunk newsie when he was laughing up his sleeve at the rest of the town—but who knows?"

"Why'd he help you out, Quinto?" Bull asked.

"To start thinning out his partners in the Skillern and Endicott camps. With those two gone, he was poised to lay title to the Highline spread with some documents he forged on the newspaper's printing press.

"Funny, ain't it? The biggest news story to come out of these parts ever and he'll never get to write it a word of it—or maybe he will, a real exclusive for the *Banner*.

"As for Lord Dennis and the others, their remains are weighted down and sunk to the bottom of flooded Mine Shaft Number Seven." Sixkiller was eager to get back to Oklahoma to start cracking down on the bad men there. He had one last detail to attend to. "This town needs a marshal. I saved Braddock's badge, figuring it would come in handy. It's tarnished, but a little polish and the right man to wear it will make it shine again."

He pinned the badge on the breast pocket of the dumbfounded Bull Raymond, the new marshal of Ringgold. "You'll do fine, Bull."

Nobody had any objections. Mayor Ivey was huddled close, already trying to convince Bull to run as part of his administration.

With the business part of the session completed, the party went into full swing, finally breaking up around dawn.

Sixkiller saddled up the roan. Town folks gathered to watch him go.

He rode east into the rising sun. At the edge of town, he spurred his horse, causing it to uprear and stand on its hind legs. Sixkiller took off his big hat and waved it in the air—good-bye. The horse touched down and he rode south toward Rock Spring and the Union Pacific train line.

Then he was gone.

J. A. Johnstone on William W. Johnstone
"When the Truth Becomes Legend"

William W. Johnstone was born in southern Missouri, the youngest of four children. He was raised with strong moral and family values by his minister father, and tutored by his schoolteacher mother. Despite this, he quit school at age fifteen.

"I have the highest respect for education," he says, "but such is the folly of youth, and wanting to see the world beyond the four walls and the blackboard."

True to this vow, Bill attempted to enlist in the French Foreign Legion ("I saw Gary Cooper in *Beau Geste* when I was a kid and I thought the French Foreign Legion would be fun") but was rejected, thankfully, for being underage. Instead, he joined a traveling carnival and did all kinds of odd jobs. It was listening to the veteran carny folk, some of whom had been on the circuit since the late 1800s, telling amazing tales about their experiences, which planted the storytelling seed in Bill's imagination.

"They were mostly honest people, despite

the bad reputation traveling carny shows had back then," Bill remembers. "Of course, there were exceptions. There was one guy named Picky, who got that name because he was a master pickpocket. He could steal a man's socks right off his feet without him knowing. Believe me, Picky got us chased out of more than a few towns."

After a few months of this grueling existence, Bill returned home and finished high school. Next came stints as a deputy sheriff in the Tallulah, Louisiana, Sheriff's Department, followed by a hitch in the U.S. Army. Then he began a career in radio broadcasting at KTLD in Tallulah, Louisiana, which would last sixteen years. It was there that he fine-tuned his storytelling skills. He turned to writing in 1970, but it wouldn't be until 1979 that his first novel, *The Devil's Kiss,* was published. Thus began the full-time writing career of William W. Johnstone. He wrote horror (*The Uninvited*), thrillers (*The Last of the Dog Team*), even a romance novel or two. Then, in February 1983, *Out of the Ashes* was published. Searching for his missing family in the aftermath of a post-apocalyptic America, rebel mercenary and patriot Ben Raines is united with the civilians of the Resistance forces and moves to the forefront of a revolution for the nation's future.

Out of the Ashes was a smash. The series would continue for the next twenty years, winning

Bill three generations of fans all over the world. The series was often imitated but never duplicated. "We all tried to copy *The Ashes* series," said one publishing executive, "but Bill's uncanny ability, both then and now, to predict in which direction the political winds were blowing brought a certain immediacy to the table no one else could capture." The Ashes series would end its run with more than thirty-four books and twenty million copies in print, making it one of the most successful men's action series in American book publishing. (The Ashes series also, Bill notes with a touch of pride, got him on the FBI's Watch List for its less than flattering portrayal of spineless politicians and the growing power of big government over our lives, among other things. "In that respect," says collaborator J. A. Johnstone, "Bill was years ahead of his time.")

Always steps ahead of the political curve, Bill's recent thrillers, written with J. A. Johnstone, include *Vengeance Is Mine, Invasion USA, Border War, Jackknife, Remember the Alamo, Home Invasion, Phoenix Rising, The Blood of Patriots, The Bleeding Edge,* and the upcoming *Suicide Mission.*

It is with the western, though, that Bill found his greatest success and propelled him onto both the *USA Today* and the *New York Times* bestseller lists.

Bill's western series, co-authored by J. A. Johnstone, include *The Mountain Man, Matt Jensen the*

Last Mountain Man, Preacher, The Family Jensen, Luke Jensen Bounty Hunter, Eagles, MacCallister (an Eagles spin-off), *Sidewinders, The Brothers O'Brien, Sixkiller, Blood Bond, The Last Gunfighter,* and the upcoming new series *Flintlock* and *The Trail West.* Coming in May 2013 is the hardcover western *Butch Cassidy, The Lost Years.*

"The Western," Bill says, "is one of the few true art forms that is one hundred percent American. I liken the Western as America's version of England's Arthurian legends, like the Knights of the Round Table, or Robin Hood and his Merry Men. Starting with the 1902 publication of *The Virginian* by Owen Wister, and followed by the greats like Zane Grey, Max Brand, Ernest Haycox, and of course Louis L'Amour, the Western has helped to shape the cultural landscape of America.

"I'm no goggle-eyed college academic, so when my fans ask me why the Western is as popular now as it was a century ago, I don't offer a 200-page thesis. Instead, I can only offer this: The Western is honest. In this great country, which is suffering under the yoke of political correctness, the Western harks back to an era when justice was sure and swift. Steal a man's horse, rustle his cattle, rob a bank, a stagecoach, or a train, you were hunted down and fitted with a hangman's noose. One size fit all.

"Sure, we westerners are prone to a little embellishment and exaggeration and, I admit it, occasionally play a little fast and loose with the facts. But we do so for a very good reason—to enhance the enjoyment of readers.

"It was Owen Wister, in *The Virginian* who first coined the phrase *'When you call me that, smile.'* Legend has it that Wister actually heard those words spoken by a deputy sheriff in Medicine Bow, Wyoming, when another poker player called him a son-of-a-bitch.

"Did it really happen, or is it one of those myths that have passed down from one generation to the next? I honestly don't know. But there's a line in one of my favorite Westerns of all time, *The Man Who Shot Liberty Valance,* where the newspaper editor tells the young reporter, 'When the truth becomes legend, print the legend.'

"These are the words I live by."

**Keep reading for a preview of an
All New Jensen Series!**

**THE JENSEN BRAND
From bestselling authors
William W. Johnstone and J. A. Johnstone**

Bestselling authors William W. Johnstone and
J. A. Johnstone have thrilled readers with the
epic struggles and hard-fought triumphs of the
pioneering Jensen family. Now this great
American saga continues—with the
next generation of Jensens . . .

JENSEN PROUD. JENSEN TOUGH.
It's the dawn of a new century. But on the vast
Sugarloaf Ranch not much has changed since
legendary gunfighter Smoke Jensen and his wife,
Sally, tamed the land two decades ago. Raising cattle
is still a dangerous business—and just as deadly as
ever. When Smoke is injured swapping bullets with
some cow thieves, Sally puts out a call for help to
Matt, Ace, and the rest of the Jensen clan.
But time is running out. The bloodthirsty rustlers
are ready to strike again—and there are
lots more of them. And the Sugarloaf's
last defense is Smoke and Sally's next of kin . . .

Enter the Jensen twins. Denise and her brother
Louis have just returned home from their schooling
in Europe. Louis is studying to be a lawyer and is
too sickly to defend the ranch. But Denise is to the
manor born—she can ride like a man, shoot like
her daddy, and face down the deadliest outlaws like
nobody's business. And there'll be plenty of
opportunity to prove she's got Jensen blood in her
veins—cold, deadly, and playing for keeps . . .

Available now wherever Pinnacle Books are sold.

Live Free. Read Hard. www.williamjohnstone.net

The Jensen Family
First Family of the American Frontier

Smoke Jensen—*The Mountain Man*
The youngest of three children and orphaned as a young boy, Smoke Jensen is considered one of the fastest draws in the West. His quest to tame the lawless West has become the stuff of legend. Smoke owns the Sugarloaf Ranch in Colorado. Married to Sally Jensen, father to Denise ("Denny") and Louis.

Preacher—*The First Mountain Man*
Though not a blood relative, grizzled frontiersman Preacher became a father figure to the young Smoke Jensen, teaching him how to survive in the brutal, often deadly Rocky Mountains. Fought the battles that forged his destiny. Armed with a long gun, Preacher is as fierce as the land itself.

Matt Jensen—*The Last Mountain Man*
Orphaned but taken in by Smoke Jensen, Matt Jensen has become like a younger brother to Smoke and even took the Jensen name. And like Smoke, Matt has carved out his destiny on the American frontier. He lives by the gun and surrenders to no man.

Luke Jensen—*Bounty Hunter*

Mountain Man Smoke Jensen's long-lost brother Luke Jensen is scarred by war and a dead shot—the right qualities to be a bounty hunter. And he's cunning, and fierce enough, to bring down the deadliest outlaws of his day.

Ace Jensen and Chance Jensen—*Those Jensen Boys!*

Smoke Jensen's long-lost nephews, Ace and Chance, are a pair of young-gun twins as reckless and wild as the frontier itself . . . Their father is Luke Jensen, thought killed in the Civil War. Their uncle Smoke Jensen is one of the fiercest gunfighters the West has ever known. It's no surprise that the inseparable Ace and Chance Jensen have a knack for taking risks—even if they have to blast their way out of them.

Chapter One

The Sugarloaf Ranch, Colorado, 1901

A thin sliver of moon hung over the mountains bordering the valley, casting such a feeble amount of light that it did little to relieve the pitch blackness cloaking much of the landscape.

A rustlers' moon, Smoke Jensen thought.

"Are they there?" Calvin Woods whispered next to Smoke. "I can't see a blasted thing!"

"They're there," Smoke told his foreman. He raised the Winchester he held in both hands but didn't bring it to his shoulder just yet. A shot would spook the men who had been stealing his cattle, and he didn't want them to take off for the tall and uncut before he had a chance to nab them. "Hold your fire . . ."

Hidden in the trees along with Smoke and Cal were half a dozen more Sugarloaf hands, all of them young and eager for action, like frisky colts ready to stretch their legs. One reason cowboys signed on to ride for the Sugarloaf was the prospect of working for Smoke Jensen, quite possibly the most famous gunfighter the West had ever known. They figured just being around Smoke upped the chances for excitement.

That was true. Even though Smoke had put his powder-burning days behind him more than two decades earlier and settled down to be a peace-loving rancher, things hadn't quite worked out that way. Trouble still seemed to find him on a fairly regular basis, despite his intentions.

That was the way it was with Jensens. None of them had ever been plagued with an abundance of peace and quiet.

In recent weeks, for example, Sugarloaf cattle had begun disappearing on a regular basis. Only a few at first, then more and more as the thieves grew bolder. Smoke was in his fifties, and it only made sense to believe that he might have slowed down some. Some might have figured he wasn't the same sort of pure hell on wheels he had been when he was younger.

Those rustlers were about to find out how wrong they were to assume that.

"There to the right," Smoke whispered as he looked out across the broad pasture where a couple hundred cattle were settled down for the night. "Coming out of that stand of trees."

"I see 'em," Cal replied, equally quiet. He had started out as a young cowboy, too, twenty years earlier. Back then, the reformed outlaw known as Pearlie was the Sugarloaf's ramrod, and he and Cal had become fast friends. Pearlie was also a mentor to Cal, who'd learned everything there was to know about running a ranch. When it came time for Pearlie to retire, it was only natural for Cal to move into the foreman's job.

He still looked a little like a kid, though, despite the mustache he had cultivated in an attempt to make himself seem older. However, no one on the crew failed to hop when he gave an order.

On the other side of the pasture, several riders moved out of the trees and rode slowly toward the cattle. It was too dark to make out any details about them or even to be sure of how many there were. But they didn't belong and there was only one reason for them to be there.

Calling out softly, slapping coiled lassos against their thighs, they started moving a jag of about a hundred head along the valley, toward the north end.

"I've seen all I need to see," Cal said. "Let's blast 'em outta their saddles."

"I'd rather round up a few of them if we can," Smoke said. "I'd like to know if they started this wide-looping on their own or if they're working for somebody."

"You got suspicions?"

"No . . . but if there's a head to this snake, I'd just as soon know about it so I can cut it off." Smoke leaned his head to indicate they should pull back, although it was doubtful Cal saw the gesture in the thick shadows. "Let's drift on back to the horses."

"If we go chargin' out there, we'll scatter those cows all over kingdom come," Cal warned.

Smoke chuckled. "They can be rounded up again."

Silently, the men moved through the trees until they reached the spot where they had left their horses and swung up into the saddles. Over the years of his adventurous life, Smoke had learned to trust his gut. He'd had a hunch the rustlers might strike again that night, so he, Cal, and some of the hands had gone out to a likely spot for more villainy where they could stand watch and maybe catch the cattle thieves in the act.

"Are you gonna give those varmints a chance to surrender, Smoke?" Cal sounded like he hoped the answer would be no.

"Yes . . . but not much of one. They'd better throw down their guns and get their hands in the air in a hurry. Otherwise . . ." Smoke didn't have to elaborate.

All the cowboys would be checking their guns before they rode out into the pasture.

He gave instructions. "We'll swing around and come up behind them. I'll hail them. If they start the ball, you fellas do what you have to. Like I said, it would be nice to take some of them alive, but I'd much rather all of you boys come through this with whole hides. Now let's go."

With Smoke and Cal in the lead, the men rode slowly through the trees until they reached the edge of the growth. The dark mass of the cattle was to the left, moving away as the rustlers pushed the reluctant animals along. Smoke and his companions moved out into the open and started after them, still not hurrying but moving fast enough to catch up to the plodding cattle.

The sounds made by the cattle and the hooves of the rustlers' horses were enough to muffle the advance of Smoke and his men. At least Smoke hoped that was the case. The rustlers hadn't panicked yet, at least.

The group from the Sugarloaf closed in.

Smoke had his Winchester in his right hand and the reins in his left. He looped the reins around the saddle horn, knowing he could control the rangy gray gelding with his knees. With both hands gripping the rifle, he shouted, "You're caught! Throw down your guns!"

Instead of surrendering, the rustlers yanked

their horses around. Spurts of gun flame bloomed in the darkness like crimson flowers as they opened fire.

In one smooth motion, Smoke brought the rifle to his shoulder, aimed at one of the spurts of orange, and squeezed the trigger. The Winchester cracked. He barely felt the weapon's recoil. Working the lever to throw another round in the chamber, he shifted his aim, and swiftly fired a second shot then kneed his horse into motion and charged toward the rustlers.

Around him, Cal and the other Sugarloaf hands galloped forward, yelling and shooting.

The thieves scattered in all directions, abandoning the cows they were trying to steal.

Although it was difficult to see much, Smoke and his allies continued aiming at the muzzle flashes of their enemies. Of course, the rustlers were doing the same thing. The air was filled with flying lead.

Smoke always hoped his men would come through such encounters unscathed, but knew better than to expect it.

He made out one of the fleeing rustlers and closed in on the man, who twisted in the saddle and flung a shot back at him. Smoke felt as much as heard the slug rip through the air not far from his ear. That was good shooting from the back of a running horse. He leaned forward to make himself a smaller target and urged his mount to greater speed.

As he drew close to his quarry, the rustler turned to try another shot, but Smoke lashed out with the barrel of the Winchester. It thudded against the rustler's head and swept him out of the saddle. Both horses galloped on for a few strides before Smoke was able to swing his mount around. Elsewhere in the big pasture, gunfire still crackled.

He swung down from the saddle and let the reins drop, knowing the horse was trained not to go anywhere. Keeping his rifle pointed at the dim figure on the ground, Smoke approached him. The fallen rustler didn't move.

Smoke ordered, "Put your hands in the air!" but there was no response. Wary of a trick, he lowered the rifle and drew the Colt on his right hip. The revolver was better for close work. Almost supernaturally fast with it, he was confident he could put a bullet in the varmint before he had a chance to try anything.

"On your feet if you can, and keep your hands where I can see 'em!"

The rustler remained motionless. He appeared to be lying facedown. Smoke hooked a boot toe under his shoulder and rolled him onto his back.

The loose-limbed way the man flopped over spoke volumes. The fall from the running horse had either busted the rustler's head open or broken his neck, more likely the latter. Either way, he sure looked dead.

Or he was mighty good at playing possum.

Smoke backed off and holstered the Colt. He'd return later and check on the rustler. At the moment, his men needed his help elsewhere.

He mounted up quickly and rode toward the sound of the guns, which had become intermittent. The shots died out completely as Smoke approached several dark shapes that turned into men on horseback as he got closer.

He had his rifle ready, but he recognized the voice that called, "Smoke? Is that you?"

"Yeah, Cal, it's me. Are you all right?"

"Fine as frog hair. How about you?"

"A few of those bullets came close enough for me to hear, but that's all. How about the other fellas?"

"Don't know. Randy and Josh are with me and they're all right, but I can't say about the rest."

"And the rustlers?"

"We downed a couple. Don't know about the rest of *them*, either."

Smoke said, "The fight seems to be over. Let's see if we can round up the rest of our bunch."

"Then we can round up those cows," Cal

said. "They scattered hell-west and crosswise, just like I figured they would."

"But they're still on Sugarloaf range," Smoke pointed out. "Those rustlers didn't succeed in driving them off."

"They sure didn't!"

Smoke drew his Colt and fired three shots into the air, the signal for his riders to regroup. Over the next few minutes they came in. One man had a bullet burn on his arm, but the others were unhurt . . . until the last two horses plodded up. One man rode in front, leading the other horse.

Smoke could make out a shape draped over the second horse's saddle, and the sight made his jaw tighten in anger. "Who's that?" he snapped.

"I'm Jimmy Holt, Mr. Jensen." With a catch in his voice, the young cowboy said, "That's Sid MacDowell behind me. He . . . he cashed in his chips. One of those damn rustlers drilled him right through the brisket. I ain't sure Sid had time to know what happened."

"Might be better that way," Smoke muttered. "What about the rustlers? Did any of them get away?"

"I think one of them did," another cowboy reported. "I'm pretty sure he was hit, but he managed to stay on his horse. Do you want us to see if we can trail him, Mr. Jensen?"

"The best tracker in the world couldn't

follow a trail on a night like this, and I've known a few who could lay claim to that title." Smoke shook his head. "No, we might see if we can find any tracks in the morning, but right now, some of you boys start gathering those cows and the rest of you come with me and Cal. I want to see if any of the rustlers are still alive."

For the next half hour, Smoke, Cal, and a couple other men rode around the pasture, hunting for the bodies of the rustlers. Smoke hoped to find at least one of them only wounded and still able to talk, but as thief after thief turned up dead, that hope began to fade.

Finally they rode over to the man Smoke had knocked out of his saddle. Smoke knelt beside him, struck a lucifer, and saw by its flaring light that the rustler's wide, staring eyes were sightless. The unnatural twist of his head told that his neck was broken. Smoke had tried to take him alive, but fate had had other ideas.

Smoke straightened and told Cal, "You can bring a wagon out here in the morning and collect the bodies . . . if the wolves haven't dragged them off by then. Haul 'em into Big Rock to the undertaker. I'll pay to have them put in the ground if they don't have enough money on them to cover the cost."

Cal nodded. "Should I get Sheriff Carson to take a look at them?"

"Wouldn't hurt. Chances are some of them

are wanted. You fellas might have some reward money coming to you."

Cal rubbed his chin. "I'm not sure I'd want to take blood money. On the other hand, the world's probably better off without these varmints, and that's worth something, I guess."

"Up to you." Smoke wouldn't be taking any reward money. Between the Sugarloaf's success and the lucrative gold claim he had found many years earlier, he was one of the wealthiest men in Colorado, although no one would ever know it to look at him. He still dressed like a common cowhand.

"We'll make sure none of those cattle ran too far when they spooked, then head back to the bunkhouse," Cal said. "How about you?"

Smoke had already turned his horse. He said over his shoulder, "I'm headed home."

Chapter Two

The small ranch house that Smoke had built when he and Sally first settled on the Sugarloaf had been added onto many times over the years, until it was a big, sprawling, two-story structure surrounded by cottonwoods and oaks. He always felt good when he rode up to it. He couldn't help but think about all the fine times he and his wife and their children had had. More often than not, the house had rung with laughter.

As he approached the house, he saw that a lamp still burned in the parlor despite the late hour. The glow in the window was dim enough he knew the flame was turned low. More than likely, Sally had waited up for him. That came as no surprise.

Movement on the porch caught his eye. Out of habit—one that had saved his life on occasion—his hand was close to the butt of his revolver. He relaxed, though, as he recognized Pearlie's tall, lanky figure.

"Thought I heard shots up yonderways a while back," the retired foreman said as he came down the steps from the porch. "You must've had a run-in with those wide-loopers."

"We did." Smoke dismounted. "They figured on chasing off a hundred head. We changed their minds."

Pearlie reached for the reins of Smoke's horse. "I'll take care of that for you. I ain't forgot how to wrangle a cayuse. How's the kid?"

Even though Cal wasn't that far from being middle-aged, he would always be a kid to Pearlie. The two of them had shared many adventures, had been through tragedy and triumph together, and were fast friends.

"Cal's fine," Smoke assured him. "We lost one man. Sid MacDowell."

"Blast it! I didn't really know the younker— Cal hired him, not me—but he deserved better'n a damn rustler's bullet."

"That's the truth. We tried to even the score for him, though. Five carcasses are still out there for Cal to haul into town in the morning."

"Didn't manage to take any of 'em alive?"

Smoke shook his head. "Nope. And one got away, although he might've been wounded. We'll do some tracking in the morning and see if we can turn up another body."

"Even if you don't, killin' five out of six practically wipes out the gang," Pearlie said.

"Only if there were just half a dozen of them to start with," Smoke pointed out.

"No reason to think otherwise, is there?"

"Not really," Smoke admitted. "If the rustling stops now, I reckon we can assume that was all. But if they were just part of a bigger gang—"

"We'll probably know that soon enough, too," Pearlie said in a gloomy voice. He started toward the barn, leading Smoke's horse, and added over his shoulder, "Miss Sally's waitin' up in the parlor."

Even though Smoke was tired and the smell of gun smoke clung to him, he was smiling as he stepped into the house.

Wearing a soft robe, Sally was sitting in one of the rocking chairs beside the table where the lamp burned. She was reading a book, but she set it aside on the table and looked up with a smile as he stepped into the parlor.

She was on her feet by the time he reached her. Her arms went around his neck and his arms encircled her trim waist. Their mouths met in a passionate kiss that had lost none of its urgency despite the time they had been together.

He lifted his lips from hers and said, "You ought to be in bed getting your beauty sleep . . . not that you need it."

That was certainly true. There might be a

few more small lines on Sally's face, and if you looked hard enough you could find a strand of gray here and there in her thick, lustrously dark hair, but to Smoke she was every bit as beautiful as when he had first laid eyes on her in the town of Bury, Idaho, all those years ago.

Smoke knew he hadn't changed much, either. If there was gray in his hair, its natural ash blond color made that sign of age hard to see. Most men on the far side of fifty were past the prime of life, but not Smoke Jensen. He was still as vital as ever, his muscular, broad-shouldered frame near to bursting with strength. He attributed that to fresh air, sunshine, clean living, and being married to the prettiest girl alive.

"I didn't see any bloodstains on your clothes when you came in," Sally said, "so I assume you're all right."

"How do you know there was even any trouble?"

"You went out looking for it, didn't you? If there's one thing Smoke Jensen is good at, it's finding trouble."

He chuckled. "I'd like to think I'm good for more than one thing."

"Well, we might find out about that in a little while, but first, tell me what happened."

Smoke grew serious as he said, "Those rustlers made a try for the stock in the big pasture up north of Granite Creek, just like I had a hunch they might. We killed five out of the six of them and probably wounded the one who got away. No telling how bad." He paused a moment. "But Sid MacDowell was killed in the fight."

Sally took a step back and put a hand to her mouth. "Oh, no. Sid was a fine young man. I'll have to write to his mother and sister down in Amarillo."

Smoke hadn't known that the young cowboy had a mother and sister in Amarillo, but he wasn't surprised Sally was aware of it. She made it a point to be a good friend to every member of the ranch crew.

"We'll send them the wages he had coming, and more besides," Smoke said. "Of course, that won't make up for losing him."

"No, but it's all we can do, I suppose."

He changed the subject by gesturing toward the book on the table. "What are you reading?"

"Charles Dickens's *A Tale of Two Cities*. It's very good."

"Maybe I'll read it one of these days," Smoke said.

She reached for the book. "There's something else in here you'll want to see right away." She opened the volume's front cover and took out a small, square sheet of yellow paper. "Late this afternoon, right after you and Cal and the others rode out, a boy from town brought me this telegram that had just come in."

"Telegrams are usually bad news," Smoke said with a slight frown.

"Not this one, I'm happy to say. Denise Nicole and Louis Arthur are coming home!"

Smoke's frown disappeared. He reached for the flimsy and scanned the words printed in block letters by the telegrapher in Big Rock.

ARRIVING BIG ROCK 27TH STOP
COMING HOME FOR GOOD STOP
LOVE TO YOU BOTH STOP
LAJ AND DNJ

Smoke's heart beat faster as the news soaked in on him. His kids were coming back to the Sugarloaf, and according to the telegram Louis had sent, they would be staying. That was enough to quicken the pulse of any man who loved his children and missed them when they were away.

For most of their lives, Louis and Denise had indeed been away from the Sugarloaf. Twins, they had been inseparable as youngsters, and when sickness had threatened Louis's life and forced Smoke and Sally to seek treatment for him in Europe, Denise had gone along. Sally had taken the children back east to her parents' home, and then John and Abigail Reynolds had sailed across the Atlantic and delivered Louis to top specialists in France. Through their efforts, the boy had been saved, but his health had remained precarious enough that he had remained in Europe to be closer to the medical help he might need.

That wasn't the only reason the twins had stayed in Europe, living on an estate in England owned by Sally's parents. They had traveled all over the continent and soaked up all the education and culture available to them. Smoke's mentor, the old mountain man called Preacher, thought such behavior was plumb foolishness, and to be honest, at times Smoke felt sort of the same way, but it seemed important to Sally and her folks, so he had gone along with the idea. He missed his kids, but he wanted what was best for them.

They had come back to Colorado for frequent visits to the Sugarloaf, and each time Smoke had harbored the hope in the back of his mind that they might decide to stay. Judging by the telegram in his hand, it looked like that might finally come to pass.

"It'll sure be good to have the kids around again," he said as he placed the telegram on top of Mr. Dickens's novel.

"I'm not sure we can think of them as children anymore," Sally said. "They're twenty years old. They're grown, Smoke."

"Twenty's not grown."

"Think of all the things *you* had done by the time you were twenty years old."

Smoke scowled. He had killed more than two

dozen men and been forced to battle for his life countless times. He had married a woman, fathered a child, lost them both to vicious murderers, and avenged their deaths by tracking down those killers and blasting them to hell. He had been a wanted outlaw and worn a lawman's badge.

Yes, it was safe to say that Smoke Jensen had grown up fast. Too fast.

But his children hadn't lived that sort of life, thank God. Instead of dodging the law and shooting it out with gunmen, they had spent their time in clinics and universities and concert halls. They had learned mathematics and natural science and literature instead of how to track an enemy and reload a gun in the heat of battle and stay calm with bullets whipping around their heads.

Smoke was glad they hadn't had to endure such hardships. To his way of thinking, that easy life meant they were still kids. Nothing wrong with that.

Instead of arguing with Sally about whether or not the twins could be considered grown, he said, "The twenty-seventh is only a couple days away. Can we be ready for them by then?"

"There's no getting ready to do," Sally said. "I keep their rooms just like they've always been. They can move right in."

"It's been a while since we've seen them. I wonder if they've changed much."

"Probably not. Louis Arthur will still be handsome and Denise Nicole will be as beautiful as always."

Smoke smiled. "I don't doubt it." They had always been beautiful to him, even as red-faced, squalling babies.

Louis Arthur was named for two of Smoke's oldest friends, the gambler and gunman Louis Longmont and Preacher, whose real name was Arthur. The name was also a way of honoring Smoke's first son, the one who had been murdered, who was named Arthur as well. Along with the old Reynolds family name Denise, Nicole, Smoke's first wife, had inspired the middle name given to his daughter.

Smoke would never forget his first family, the one that had been ripped brutally from him. That tragedy had forged his steel-hard determination to see evildoers brought to justice, and he was more than willing to deliver that justice from the barrel of a gun whenever and wherever necessary.

He wasn't one to dwell on the violence of the past, though. It was more his nature to look ahead to the future with optimism and a friendly smile.

Sally put a hand on his arm. "Would you like a cup of coffee before we go upstairs?"

Smoke slid his other arm around his wife's waist again, feeling the supple warmth of her body under the robe, and smiled "No, I reckon not. If I'm going to be kept awake for a while, I'd rather it was by something else besides coffee."

She laughed and linked her arm with his as they turned toward the parlor entrance. They had gone up only a few steps when she said, "Do you think the rustling is over?"

"I hope so. There's no reason to think otherwise, but we'll just have to wait and see. I can trust Cal and the others to keep a close eye on the stock and let me know if any more turn up missing."

"I hope that's the way it turns out. I'd hate to have a bunch of trouble going on just as Louis Arthur and Denise Nicole finally come home to stay."

"Yeah," Smoke agreed. "Jensens and trouble just don't mix."

She laughed and swatted him lightly on the shoulder, and they continued on their way upstairs to their bedroom.

Chapter Three

Louis Arthur Jensen reached out and caught hold of his sister's arm as she started to get up from the bench seat in the train car. He said in a low, urgent voice, "Blast it, Denny, do you always have to cause trouble?"

"I didn't start it," Denise Nicole Jensen replied through clenched teeth. "That son of a—" She caught herself before the oath could slip out. "That scoundrel in the derby hat started it, and you know it, Louis!"

As she pulled her arm free from her brother's grip and stood up, the train went around a fairly sharp curve and swayed. Denny lost her balance, but her hand shot out and gripped the back of the seat, and she steadied herself before Louis could steady her.

Then she took off up the aisle after the man who had leered at her and made an improper suggestion. "Sir!" she called, although "Hey, you!" would have been more appropriate for such an uncouth hombre.

He had a broad, beefy face and a mustache that curled up at the tips. His attire, as well as his general demeanor, suggested that he was some sort of traveling salesman. The man stopped and turned to look at her. A stub of a cigar protruded from thick lips that curved in a smile. "Well, howdy again, little missy. I didn't expect you to take me up on my offer. At least not so soon. But I'm happy you did. Let's go on up to the club car and have that drink." He put out a hand as if he intended to take her arm.

She caught hold of his little finger, twisted it enough to make him let out a little yelp of pain, and leaned in close. "I can snap this off before you can stop me, mister. And I'm mighty tempted to. So maybe you'll think twice before making inappropriate remarks to young ladies again!"

His eyes bulged as he said, "I-I didn't say anything like that! I just asked you if . . . if you'd like to have a drink with me in the club car."

"And then you said maybe we could find someplace more private and you could show me something you thought I'd like!" She put more pressure on his finger and made him breathe harder.

"I was talking about hats! I-I sell ladies' hats. I've got my sample case in the next car—"

"Hats?" Denny said. "You were talking about hats?"

"Yeah. Honest, lady. I didn't mean anything forward. I mean, sure, you're a pretty girl, and I'd enjoy having a drink with you, but I can tell you've got good taste and might be interested in buying a hat. I wholesale 'em to stores, but I don't mind sellin' to an individual if I think she'd like—"

"Are you married?" Denny cut into his babbling explanation.

"What? Married?" He looked pained again, and by more than his finger. "Yeah . . . I got a wife and four kids back in Kansas City."

"Then you shouldn't be acting forward with young women on trains."

"You're right," he said hastily. "You're absolutely right. I was out of line. I'm sorry. If you could . . . could let go."

"Just remember this," Denny said as she released his finger and moved back a step.

He rubbed the painful digit. "I will, lady. You can count on that. And if your brother was offended, please convey my apologies to him, too."

"How do you know he's my brother?"

"Well, hell. Uh, I mean, the two of you are sort of like peas in a pod, aren't you?"

"Not hardly." Denny turned back toward her seat, well aware that many of the other passengers in the car had been watching the confrontation and were looking at her like she was some sort of crazy woman. She didn't care. Let them think whatever they wanted to, she told herself.

If she worried about what other people thought of her, she'd never have time to do anything else.

Things like that bothered Louis, however. He looked like he wanted to crawl under the seat rather than sitting on it.

Grudgingly, Denny had to admit that she and Louis did look considerably alike. They had the same fair hair, a legacy from their father, and the fine-boned features of their mother. Smoke Jensen was handsome in a rugged way, and Sally was a true beauty, so both Louis and Denny were attractive. Denny was levelheaded enough to acknowledge that.

Her face had a golden tan to it that Louis's lacked. He spent most of his time indoors, poring over books, while Denny preferred to be outside riding horses or practicing her marksmanship. Derringford, the butler at her grandparents' estate in the English countryside, had been appalled at first to see a young woman wearing trousers, riding astride, and carrying a rifle around. He had grown more accustomed to Denny's behavior over the years, but he would never fully accept it.

Old Rosston, the estate's gamekeeper, had been impressed by Denny's ability to shoot from an early age. It came naturally to her. Her father was Smoke Jensen, after all.

She sat down next to Louis again. "See? I didn't make too much of a scene."

"Well, you didn't break the poor man's finger," Louis said. "So I suppose we should be thankful for that. His spirit may be broken beyond repair, though."

Denny snorted, knowing it was an unladylike sound and not caring. "He needed to learn a lesson. He can't just go around flirting with any young woman who takes his fancy. And you know good and well he wasn't just talking about trying to sell me a hat!"

"No, probably not," Louis admitted. "Anyway, it's over, so let's try to maintain some decorum the rest of the way to Big Rock."

"Decorum's overrated," Denny muttered as she looked past her brother and out the window at the plains of eastern Kansas rolling by.

Tomorrow they would be able to see the mountains, she thought, and that would be a most welcome sight indeed.

That would mean they were almost home.

Sheriff Monte Carson was leaning against one of the posts holding up the awning over the boardwalk when he saw the wagon rolling down the street. Calvin Woods was at the reins, and another of the Sugarloaf hands was on the seat beside him.

Monte straightened up from his casual stance as the wagon went right on past the general store. He had expected the Sugarloaf's foreman to stop there and pick up supplies. As the wagon drew closer, though, Monte spotted several blanket-wrapped shapes in the back, and that brought a frown to his weathered face.

Once an outlaw but for the past two decades a dedicated lawman, he was getting on in years. Before too much longer, he knew he was going to have to give some real thought to retiring as Big Rock's peace officer. His draw, never as fast as his friend Smoke Jensen's but pretty darned swift, had slowed down in recent months. Monte knew that age was catching up to him. It happened to everybody and was inevitable.

But that didn't mean he had to like it.

He was still sheriff, and when somebody brought in a load of dead bodies—he was pretty sure that was what Cal had in the wagon—it was still his job to find out what in blazes had happened. He stepped down from the boardwalk and moved out into the street to intercept the wagon.

As Monte raised a hand, Cal hauled back on the reins, brought the vehicle to a halt, and nodded. "Mornin', Sheriff."

"If I'm not mistaken, that's sort of a grim load you got there, Cal."

The Sugarloaf foreman shrugged and turned to jerk his head toward one of the shrouded shapes that was placed a little apart from the others. "That's Sid MacDowell, one of our hands. I don't have names for the others, but they're all no-good rustlers."

Monte let out a low whistle. "Five of 'em, eh?"

"Yeah, and one got away, damn it. But we came close to makin' it a clean sweep."

"I take it they hit the Sugarloaf last night?"

"Tried to," Cal said. "I'm takin' them down to the undertaker's, but if you want to have a look at them, see if you recognize anybody from the reward dodgers you've got, I can uncover them."

Monte shook his head. "No, you go ahead. I'll come down there and have a gander at them before they're planted. In the old days, we would have strapped the carcasses onto planks and stood them up so the whole town could gawk at them, but I reckon Big Rock is too civilized for that now."

Cal grinned. "You sound like you think that's a bad thing."

"You get to be my age, you start missin' the old days, whether they were really all that good or not." Monte stepped back so Cal could drive on.

He would allow some time while the bodies were prepared and laid out in cheap pine coffins, then check them before the lids were nailed on. Simon Rone, who had taken over Big Rock's undertaking business, knew to send a boy to fetch him before burying any outlaws.

Monte was a bit surprised the slain Sugarloaf man wasn't being laid to rest in the little cemetery out at the ranch. Maybe the fellow had kinfolks elsewhere, and Cal was going to have the body sent back to them. Monte put those thoughts out of his head for the moment. It was time for a second cup of coffee. He wondered sometimes how people ever lived before they started drinking coffee.

As he ambled toward the café, he noticed a man walking toward him, and the instincts that had kept him alive through a lot of long, dangerous years warned him that the hombre intended to brace him. Monte's eyes, still keen as ever even though his gun hand was slowing down, took in the man at a glance.

Late twenties, more than likely, which was still young to Monte. Medium-sized, but he moved with a sort of wolflike grace. He wore denim trousers, a soft buckskin shirt with a drawstring neck but no fringe, and a light brown hat with a rounded crown. A fine layer of trail dust covered the outfit.

A gun belt with a single holstered Colt attached to it was buckled around the stranger's lean hips. He had a pleasant smile on his face, but a certain hardness in his eyes.

The lawman recognized that look. He had

seen it in Smoke's eyes many times. The stranger wasn't the sort to call attention to himself.

The truly dangerous ones usually weren't.

The man raised his left hand in an innocuous gesture of greeting as his right hand remained close by the revolver on his hip. "Excuse me. You're Sheriff Carson, aren't you?"

Monte pointed toward the badge pinned to his vest. "That's what this tin star says. What can I do for you?"

"I was hoping I could talk to you for a minute, maybe in your office."

"You have business with the law?"

"You could say that." The stranger lowered his left hand to his waist, slid his fingers behind his belt, and brought out something he concealed in his palm. He turned his hand just enough for Monte to catch a glimpse of a badge.

"You're a lawman?" Monte asked, pitching his voice quietly so that no one else could overhear.

The stranger's attitude made it plain he didn't want his true identity spread around town. His answer was equally quiet. "Deputy U.S. marshal."

"Come on, then," Monte said as he turned toward the sheriff's office. He tried not to sigh. "There'll be a pot of coffee on the stove. I warn you, though, it won't be as good as what we could get at the café."

"As long as it's coffee, that's good enough for me. I started out from Denver early this morning."

The two men walked to the square stone building that housed the sheriff's office and jail. The front office was empty, the two deputies who were on duty at the moment being out walking around town. Monte went over to the potbellied stove in the corner and took down two tin cups from the shelf on the side wall. Using a piece of leather to protect his hand from the heat, he picked up the pot and poured strong black brew into both cups.

"You know who I am." He handed one of the cups to the stranger. "Now, who are you besides somebody who packs a badge for Uncle Sam?"

"My name is Brice Rogers," the young man said. "I'm told you've got a rustling problem around here, and I've come to solve it."

Chapter Four

Monte managed not to laugh in his fellow lawman's face, but it wasn't easy. "You have, have you?"

"That's right. We've had reports that cattlemen around here have been losing stock, and my boss, the chief marshal, wants it stopped."

"Since when is stealing cows a federal crime?"

"When those ranchers have contracts to sell those cows to the army, as most of the ones located in this valley do. Anything that interferes with that puts the case under federal jurisdiction."

Monte blew out a breath. "Sounds like a pretty far reach to me."

"You can take that up with Chief Marshal Horton if you'd like."

Monte waved a hand dismissively. "No, there's probably no need to go to that much trouble. Anyway, there's a good chance Smoke

Jensen has already solved that little rustling problem his ownself."

"Smoke Jensen? The notorious gunman?"

"Smoke's one of those ranchers you were just talking about. That gang of outlaws tried to hit his spread last night, but Smoke and his men were ready for them. Did you see me talking to that fella who brought the wagon into town?"

Rogers nodded. "I noticed that, yes."

"That was Cal Woods, the foreman of Smoke's ranch. The bodies of five dead rustlers were in the back of it."

"Jensen executed them?" Rogers asked with a frown. "Was it a lynching?"

"Not hardly. There was a fight when the rustlers tried to drive off some stock. One of Smoke's men was killed, too, but the Sugarloaf came out on top."

"That's Jensen's ranch? The Sugarloaf?"

"Yep. You see now why I said Smoke may have taken care of your problem for you?"

Rogers didn't look convinced. "How do you know there aren't more rustlers?"

"I don't," Monte admitted with a shrug. "In fact, Cal told me that one of the bunch got away, although it's likely he was wounded . . . no telling how bad."

"So the problem may not be over after all. My boss won't like it if I come back without being sure. It looks like I'll be sticking around here for a while, at least until I'm convinced that's nothing else to interfere with those beef contracts."

"Suit yourself, Marshal. I appreciate you letting me know that you're here, as well as what brings you to Big Rock."

Rogers took a sip of his coffee. He didn't make a face at the taste, but he glanced down into the cup as if he'd never encountered anything quite like it before. "You know, now that I think about it, I seem to recall reading quite a few reports about outbreaks of trouble in these parts. Would that have something to do with Smoke Jensen?"

"Smoke's not the kind to start trouble," Monte said. "But if it comes along, he can damn sure finish it in a hurry."

"He was a wanted man at one time, wasn't he?"

"So was I." Monte's tone was curt. "But that was a long time ago for both of us. I reckon if you care to go back to Denver and dig deeper, you'll find that he's done a lot of good for Colorado, including helping out the governor on occasion."

Rogers lifted his eyebrows. "You're not telling me to get out of town, are you, Sheriff?"

Monte shook his head. "No, just saying you shouldn't jump to any conclusions about Smoke on account of stories that may have been told about him. I've never known a finer, more decent man in all my life. If my word's not good enough for you—"

Rogers raised a hand to stop him. "It's plenty good enough for me. I'm just trying to get a handle on what's going on around here. I'll be around for a while. Marshal Horton didn't put any time limit on this assignment. Actually, I think he'd like to have a man in this part of the state on a semipermanent basis. Times are changing, you know. Civilization has spread all across what used to be the frontier, and it's up to us to make sure that it stays that way. The lawless elements aren't going to go away quietly, though."

"No, I reckon you can count on that," Monte agreed. "From the looks of the way you showed me your badge, I get the idea you don't want it spread around town that you're a lawman."

Rogers nodded. "Yes, I'd rather keep that quiet. I get better results if not everyone in the area knows who I am. I have a little pocket here on the back of my belt where I cache my badge and bona fides."

"Be happy to. If you need a hand with anything, let me know."

"I will, Sheriff." Rogers lifted the cup in his hand. "I'd thank you for the coffee, but—"

"Yeah, I know. Don't worry about—" He stopped when the door opened.

Phil Harrigan, one of his deputies, hurried

in. "Sheriff, looks like trouble at the Brown Dirt Cowboy."

Monte bit back a groan. "Again? Blast it. If this keeps up, I may have to ask the town council to shut that place down. It was always a little wild, but since Emmett Brown died and his nephew took over, it's gettin' to be a damn nuisance!"

"What's the Brown Dirt Cowboy?" Rogers asked. "A saloon?"

"Yeah. The second biggest one in town. And the roughest."

Harrigan nodded toward Rogers. "Who's this?"

"Brice Rogers," Monte said. "He's new in town. Just thought I'd have a word with him, let him know how we do things around here."

"You don't have to worry, Sheriff," Rogers said, playing along with Monte's response. "I'm a peaceable man."

"I wish everybody was. See you around, Rogers." Monte headed for the door with Harrigan following him. He asked over his shoulder, "What's going on down there?"

"The Gunderson brothers are at it again."

"Oh, Lord," Monte said. "I should have known."

Arno and Ingborg—who went by the nickname Haystack—Gunderson were a pair of bachelor Swedish brothers who had a farm east of Big Rock, where the terrain was more suitable for growing crops. They were both big, blond, and heavy with muscles from hard work. Normally they were as peaceful as could be. Even when they lost their tempers, they never bothered anyone else . . . they just tried to beat each other to death.

And it was usually over a woman. Not the same woman every time, just one in a succession of soiled doves who found themselves working at the Brown Dirt Cowboy.

Whenever they started a ruckus, Monte had to arrest them to keep them from wrecking the place. They were so big and hardheaded, they could pound on each other for a long time without doing any real damage, but in the process, they fell over tables and chairs and busted them to pieces. Sometimes bottles flew and broke windows and mirrors. It could turn into a real mess in a hurry.

"Who are they fighting over this time?" Monte asked as he and the deputy strode along the street toward the saloon.

"That soiled dove called Cindy."

"I can't keep up with them, the way Claude Brown runs them through there. Is she the one with the red hair and the big . . . uh—"

"That's her all right, Sheriff," Harrigan said.

"Well, I can see how she could get a man riled up." Monte was happily married, but he wasn't blind. "Especially fellas like those Gundersons, who spend so much time by themselves out on that farm, working so hard. When they do come into town, they like to have themselves a good time."

"Cindy can sure provide that." Harrigan added hastily, "Uh, from what I've heard. I wouldn't really know."

As Monte stepped up onto the boardwalk in front of the saloon, a crash came from inside, followed by a scream. He picked up his pace, slapping the batwings aside as he plunged through the entrance. Two massive figures were lying on the floor amid the wreckage of a table as they kicked and gouged and punched at each other. A lushly built redhead in a short, spangled dress stood not too far away, her hands pressed to her mouth. She was trying to look horrified by the violence, but her eyes watched the battle with avid interest.

The saloon's other patrons had abandoned their tables and drawn back around the walls to give the combatants plenty of room. Some of them were casually fondling the scandalously clad serving girls who stood with them.

Claude Brown, the current owner of the establishment and the nephew of the man who had started it, stood behind the bar. A florid-faced man in a collarless shirt, he had a bungstarter in his hand, as did the bartender in a grimy apron standing next to him. Monte figured that if either of the Gundersons had come close enough, Brown or the bartender would have leaned over the hardwood and walloped him. Neither of the Swedes had strayed into that danger zone, however.

Spotting Monte, Brown said, "Thank God you're here, Sheriff! You've got to put a stop to this!"

"I intend to." Monte drew his gun as the brothers rolled close enough that they were almost under his feet. He leaned over and shouted, "Hey! Arno! Haystack! That's enough!"

They ignored him, got sausagelike fingers around each other's necks and started squeezing. Both faces under disheveled blond hair began to turn red.

Monte thought about clouting them with his Colt, but he knew it might do more damage to the gun than to their heads. He jammed the revolver back into its holster and called to Brown, "Gimme that bungstarter!"

Brown tossed the mallet to Monte, who caught it and then stood there watching for an opening to use it. He told the deputy, "Phil, get the other bungstarter."

Harrigan hurried over to the bar. Arno and Haystack suddenly lurched up from the floor and crashed into the sheriff's legs, knocking Monte down. It was an accident. They hadn't even noticed him standing there, as intent on choking each other to death as they seemed to be. But whether it was deliberate or not, he found himself on the sawdust-littered floor, trapped between what seemed like two wild bulls.

Monte swung the bungstarter at a slablike Swedish jaw but missed. The Gundersons rolled on top of him as they continued to struggle, and upwards of four hundred pounds pinned him to the floor. He couldn't breathe, and he didn't have enough air to shout for help.

A shot blasted. The brothers broke apart and rolled off him. That was a huge relief. He could drag breath into his lungs again, but he hoped Phil Harrigan hadn't shot one of them. They might be a couple crazy Scandihoovians, but they weren't outlaws.

Monte looked up. Brice Rogers stood there, gun in hand. A tendril of smoke curled from the revolver's muzzle.

Yelping in outrage, Claude Brown said, "Sheriff, that stranger just shot a hole in my ceiling!"

"I . . . I almost did the same thing . . . myself," Monte said as he sat up, still gasping for air. "Reckon I . . . should have . . . instead of trying to pound some sense . . . into these two."

"You bane all right, Sheriff?" one of the Gundersons asked. Blood leaked from his swollen nose. The other one's mouth was bloody.

"I'm fine," Monte snapped. "Give me a hand, Phil."

Harrigan helped Monte to his feet. "Sorry,

Sheriff. I was tryin' to figure out what to do when this fella barged in and let off that shot."

"And it's a good thing he did. Those two oxes might've crushed every bone in my body if they'd rolled around on me for a while." Monte looked at Rogers. "I'm obliged to you, mister."

Coolly, Rogers returned his Colt to its holster. "Seemed like somebody needed to break it up. That seemed like the quickest way of doing it."

Claude Brown leaned both hands on the bar. "Damn it, somebody has to pay for fixin' that hole in my ceiling."

"The damage will come out of Arno and Haystack's pockets." Monte glared at Cindy. "Were you the cause of this, young woman?"

"I didn't mean anything, Sheriff. I just sat on Arno's lap . . . or was it Haystack's? . . . and then they started arguing—"

"All right." Monte suspected she had been trying to stir up the Gundersons enough to get both of them to pay for her favors, but it didn't really matter.

A soiled dove was never going to take the blame for anything.

He turned his attention to Arno and Haystack, who had climbed to their feet. "Here's what we're going to do. You pay Brown for the damages, and I won't throw you in jail."

"They ought to be fined for disturbing the peace!" Brown protested.

Monte ignored that. "I won't throw you in jail on the condition . . . that the two of you don't come into town together anymore. One at a time, got it?" He knew that given their generally placid nature, they wouldn't likely start fights with anybody except each other.

"But we are brothers," Arno said.

"We do things together," Haystack said.

"You *work* together," Monte said. "From now on you come into town alone. Or you can be locked up together. Your choice."

Arno looked at his brother. "I do not like being locked up."

"Neither do I," Haystack said. "Should we do what the sheriff says?"

"Yah, I think maybe we should."

Both of them looked at Monte and nodded solemnly.

Arno said, "Thank you, Sheriff. You bane a good man."

Monte grunted. "I just don't want to have to feed you. The two of you could bankrupt the town if I kept you behind bars for very long." He leaned his head toward the bar. "Go settle up with Brown. And Claude, you charge those boys a fair price for what they busted up."

Brown scowled, but he didn't argue.

Monte nodded to Rogers, said, "Thanks again," and started toward the door with Harrigan following him.

Outside on the boardwalk, the deputy started making excuses for not acting quicker to stop the fight. "I really didn't have much of a chance to, Sheriff. That fella who came in, he had his gun out mighty slick and fast. I hardly even saw him draw before he squeezed off that shot."

"Is that so?" Monte said. "That's interesting."

So Brice Rogers was fast on the draw. Some lawmen were and some weren't. Those who weren't generally relied on shotguns or lots of deputies.

"You think he's a gunfighter like Smoke?" Harrigan said.

"No," Monte said. "There aren't any gunfighters like Smoke Jensen."

Connect with Us

Visit us online at
KensingtonBooks.com
to read more from your favorite authors, see books
by series, view reading group guides, and more.

Join us on social media

for sneak peeks, chances to win books and prize packs,
and to share your thoughts with other readers.

facebook.com/kensingtonpublishing
twitter.com/kensingtonbooks

Tell us what you think!

To share your thoughts, submit a review,
or sign up for our eNewsletters, please visit:
KensingtonBooks.com/TellUs.